I0736229

# HONOR AND COMPROMISE

## ANDROS ODYSSEY

**Stavros Boinodiris PhD**

Honor and Compromise by Stavros Boinodiris PhD

ISBN 978-1-952027-90-1 (Paperback)
ISBN 978-1-952027-91-8 (Hardback)



Printed in the United States of America.

New Leaf Media, LLC
175 S. 3rd Street, Suite 200
Columbus, OH 43215
www.thenewleafmedia.com

# Contents

# Table of Figures



---

[1] Licensed by Alamy Inc. Invoice number: IY01106414.

# Prologue

Honor and Compromise is a section of the Andros Odyssey story, which was written earlier by the author. This section highlights a period in Byzantine History in the 9th century. All major characters in this book were real historical figures, described by historians of that period and periods thereafter. This period was chosen because it stands out in both, challenges and accomplishments in the life of this extraordinary Empire. During recent centuries, Byzantium had an undeservingly critical view by western authors. Only lately people realized how important Byzantine culture was in the development of Western civilization.

Byzantium was formed By the Roman Emperor Constantine I on 324 AD and was a continuation of the Roman Empire, with capital the city of Constantinople, lasting until the fall of Constantinople on 1453 AD. During its life of about eleven centuries Byzantium formed a federation of various people with different cultures and backgrounds. Yet, during most of its existence, the empire was the most powerful economic, cultural, and military force in Europe. The terms of "Byzantine Empire" and "Eastern Roman Empire" are terms created after the end of the empire. Its citizens continued to refer to their empire simply as the Roman Empire and its citizens as Romans. Under Theodosius (379-395 AD) Christianity became the Empire's official state religion. Finally, under the reign of Heraclius (610-641 AD) the Empire's military and administration were restructured and adopted the Greek language for official use instead of Latin. So, although the Roman state continued, and its traditions were maintained, modern historians distinguish Byzantium from ancient Rome because it was oriented towards Greek rather than Latin culture.

The 9th century, when the events of this book took place, represents approximately the mid-term of the empire. During this period, the federation of the people of this empire was at its peak of being the most powerful force in Europe. If we look at this federation in 20th century terms, it was like the United States of that era. It consisted of people of various cultures, depended on the collaboration of its allies, and faced challenges internal and external. They could handle most of the external wars using techniques which we know today as "trade war," "proxy war," "police actions" and "fake news." Most of their challenges though were of an internal nature. Their system allowed people of various cultures to become leaders. Some of these people assumed leadership without the right qualifications. Very often these people were "self-indulgent," "arrogant," and "narcissistic "in nature. Some displayed a "know-it-all," "liar" and "corrupt" character; and, upon occasion some acted in a "deviously murderous" way.

The Byzantines had to deal with such challenges in a *"byzantine way,"* or (as the western mind saw it) an excessively complicated way, typically involving a great deal of administrative detail in defining laws that controlled judicial, legislative and executive powers. It was during this period that these powers started to crystalize in the bright minds of educated persons in key positions, mostly of Greek origin and education such as Leo the Philosopher and Patriarch Photius. It was these people that set the foundation of today's legal and governmental structures. They did not work alone. They had plenty of help from institutions that resemble today's universities. A few scholars have gone so far as calling the Magnaura Pandidakterion the first "university" in the world, but this view does not seem to consider that the Byzantine centers of higher learning generally lacked the corporative structure of the medieval universities of Western Europe which were the first to use the Latin term *universitas.* If someone ignored such structural difference, the Magnaura acted as a university in a marvelous manner. It excelled in its task to provide us with substantial benefits that we may take for granted today. Among the most profound benefit was the Cyrillic alphabet, being used today by more than 50 languages, including Russian, Bulgarian, Serbian and Ukrainian. Another benefit, which we may take it for granted today is the organizational structure of government, the division of powers and the structure of a legal system that became the foundation of today's civilized world.

"Honor and Compromise" takes you through the tumultuous time of three Byzantine emperors with all their strengths and weaknesses amid passionate love affairs, assassination plots, wars, family squabbles, conversions to Christianity and the schism between Catholic and Orthodox churches. At the same time, it shows how some gifted, honorable minds did contribute to improving our way of life despite the difficulties of their environment, sometimes having to compromise their honor in order to achieve their goals.

# Escape to Constantinople (October 864 AD)

It was late October and the sea was somewhat choppy in the Sea of Marmara. John Psellus was lying in his cot of the captain's quarters of the galley and was feeling sea sick after the long voyage from the island of Andros. Being fifty years old, the journey took a toll on his stamina. The galley was swaying in the waves, making him drowsy and he had fallen asleep, on, and off. He had left the porthole shutters open, to allow a sea breeze to ventilate the crammed cabin, which smelled, something between wine, vinegar and rotting fish. John was lying there, thinking about the losses he had incurred in his beloved island lately by the raiding Saracens. He was also thanking God that his losses were not as bad as some other islanders.

John was more fortunate than other people of Andros. From his six small galleys that his family managed to build with great pains over many years, he had lost only two with most of the men on them killed or taken into slavery. He had lost some very dear cousins and nephews, because all the crewmembers of his galley were also relatives. The cousins and nephews that worked in the galleys were either from the Psellus, Ducas, Kontos, or Keramidas family. His family and those working in these galleys made a living by transporting people, animals and trade cargo to and from the neighboring islands. Many galleys of the island were either destroyed or taken by the Saracens. He was now hoping to use his four galleys doing business closer to Constantinople, taking advantage of the protection that such proximity offered to him.

It took two deaths, to cause John to abandon his island. One was the death of his uncle, the famous Michael Psellus, director of the Academy of Andros, two years earlier. His death left the Academy in limbo. Many of his notable students had left. Among them, Leo, known as "Leo the Mathematician," or "Leo the Philosopher" was now in Constantinople.

He had left some time ago for Constantinople, where he became a private teacher. Rumor has it that during the Byzantine-Arabic wars, one of his students was captured and taken to the Arabic caliphate. The Caliph al-Mamun was amazed by his mathematical knowledge. Leo had made his name known by many contributions to the study of mathematics including geometry, number theory, mathematical analysis, and applied mathematics used in modern science, engineering, and business. On learning the name of his teacher, the Caliph sent a delegation to Byzantium and invited Leo in his caliphate offering him a rich life. Leo answered, "I refuse to serve the enemies of my faith" and so the Byzantine emperor Theophilos offered him a position of tutorship in a school (ekpaideuterio) of the capital. Soon after, during the period between 840 and 843, Leo was Metropolitan of Thessaloniki. Afterwards he returned to Constantinople where he was appointed to teach philosophy in the newly founded School of Magnaura. It was said that he conceived the machinery that used lights in order to warn Constantinople of Arabic raids from Tarsos of Cilicia and created automata of various kinds. He was also a great astronomer and philosopher. He was a prolific writer of philosophical, philological and literary works.

The other death that had a major impact on John was that of his father in law, Stephen Keramidas. After that, John had enough. Stephen was seventy-nine and was sleeping quietly in his hut at his vineyard when the Saracens attacked. The attackers, with only two ships came and left within one day. These were hit-and-run raiders. The rumors after the raid said that they were part of a fleet of about thirty ships that attacked the Cyclades. They raided a town with amazing speed before the residents could organize a defense. They were after fresh provisions, including vineyards and goat or sheep pens. They found Stephen in his hut and hit him on the head. He died a few days later from his head wounds, in the arms of his daughter Anna.

Ever since that day, Anna turned her sorrow into anger against her husband John. She continued to nag him from morning's breakfast to the bed at night about leaving the island. Finally, after serious planning, he agreed to act and told her the outline of his plan to silence her nagging. He realized that his family was vulnerable and should have left Andros a long time ago. This was not an isolated attack. They were attacked multiple times. About twenty-five years earlier, the Saracens looted the Academy at the monastery of Virgin Mary and destroyed most of the monastery.

     STAVROS BOINODIRIS PHD

The well-known Andros Academy had to become mobile. The treasured Academy manuscripts went into large houses, and teachers held classes at various locations. The remaining icons from Virgin Mary and treasures of the monasteries were hidden into caves. Yet, the most important act that John did was to move many copies of the works of his uncle, Michael Psellus to Constantinople, to the library of the School at Magnaura, now under the care of Leo, one of Michael's students.

"We are here father," said a soft voice.

John opened his eyes and faced his son, Constantine. He got up and the two men went up on the deck. The galley was already anchored at the Port of Theodosius, and the crews were securing it with heavy lines. It took a while for his wife, Anna and his son to gather their belongings with the help of the galley crew and take them on land. There, they hired two horse carts, loaded everything and after telling the cart driver where to go, proceeded towards Magnaura. In front of them lay the busy streets of Constantinople, with the fantastic skyline formed by the Great Palace and Aghia Sophia, surrounded by the city walls. Vendors of all sorts were scurrying around, loudly trying to sell their wares. Different odors of fish, meats, spices, fruits and vegetables blended with smells of dung from animals and formed a unique symphony of odor and sound. Constantinople was said to be the most populous city of Europe with over half a million people living in it. Everyone wanted to be here, because here was most of the action, in all aspects.

As they rode through the street, they could hear the loud bargaining between black clad women with the peddlers. These women must have been in long term mourning due to the loss of a spouse or relative. Black clad priests were also mingling in the crowd, buying various items. In one corner, two Verangian mercenary guards, with their distinct features were surrounded by some scantily dressed women from a local brothel. Monks, in their drab outfits were pulling donkeys, laden with supplies for their monasteries. A fancy carriage passed them by, and the head of a bishop from Italy peeked out. Some escorted women from the West, probably France, or Italy were negotiating in front of a stand with a Syrian merchant that sold fancy silk and damask cloth. Here and there you could see children, running among the crowd, begging or pick-pocketing from absent-minded people. A group of laborers, carrying products with hand carts labored among the cobblestones. One of them saw the mischievous children, stopped his cart, caught one child and started spanking him. The mixture of people and animal noises, together with the smell made Constantinople have a distinct characteristic of odor and sound.

After weaving through the crowded streets, the two carts arrived in a residential area of Magnaura, filled with taverns and one, or two-story houses. They parked in front of one single-story house with a uniquely larger, gated garden. John and Anna were helped off the cart and accompanied by his son proceeded and entered the gate. A bell attached to the gate announced their entry to the occupants of the house. Soon, a young man appeared. He was simply dressed.

"May I help you?"

The young man spoke broken Greek. His dark skin indicated that he may have been an Arab, but his demeanor showed that he was well bred.

"I am John Psellus from Andros," was the reply. "Please inform Master Leo. He is expecting us."

"Please come with me," said the young man leading them inside the house. They entered in a den, full of manuscripts. The young man cleared some chairs. "Please be seated."

All three sat and looked around, as the young man disappeared into another room. A few minutes later he appeared, helping another man, supported by a cane.

"Leo! How nice to see you? How are you?"

"I am well, God Be praised," said Leo with a crackling voice. "I have some problems with my joints, but I cope with them."

Leo was now seventy-four years old and was indeed suffering from aching joints. Constantine pulled a chair for him to sit. As he sat, all the Psellus family rose and greeted him respectfully by bowing and kissing his hand.

"We have our carts waiting outside, loaded," said Anna.

"This young student of mine can help you get situated," said Leo. "His name is Theodore. He is from Antioch. I secured a small residence, not very far from here for you. Unload any material from the Academy here and take the rest there. As I said, your place is small, but that is all I could find. There is a shortage of housing here these days and the prices have gone sky high."

"I am sure we will be fine," said John. Leo asked Theodore for some wine. Theodore brought a clay decanter of red wine and two clay cups. John proceeded to fill them. Then, Theodore, Constantine and Anna went out, to take care of unloading partly the carts and taking the rest of them to their new residence, while Leo and John sat and started exchanging information.

John was eager to get to the Constantinople news, but Leo insisted that John goes first. After John told his adventures in the island of Andros, Leo took over. The hot topics in Constantinople these days were the events generated by a bright personality in the person of Patriarch Photius.

"You see, my son, we had struggled for years to persuade the masses of our people about what icons represent, and to finally stop the bloody iconoclastic wars. Icons are nothing more than wood and paint. What they do is to provide us with a means of thinking about what they represent and projecting ourselves on how that representation affects us spiritually."

"I understand," said John nodding, "but why did we go through all this disunity and bloodshed?"

"We had to finally realize that painting or sculpting was of paramount need for human freedom of expression. Our ancestors in Ancient Greece discovered that need long ago, but our Eastern brethren from Palestine and Syria were told otherwise.

They were told by Moses to fear any such representations because humans are like sheep and literally worship any fancy piece of art that is laid in front of them. It took quite a struggle for us to settle this bloody argument which still haunts us. It took an Empress, like Irene from Athens to inspire some of the wisdom of Ancient Greece into the heads of the leaders of the Church during the Seventh Ecumenical Council of 787. We still do not have the fervor and creativity of ancient Greek theatre. We now must contend with liturgical dramas of the Church. If it was not for the three Athenian educated patriarchs, Gregory, Basil and Chrysostom, we would not even have those."

Leo took a sip of wine and continued.

"I can imagine all sorts of future improvements to our life with innovations made possible by not only allowing but encouraging human freedom of expression. For example, some of my automata that I made were derived from my freedom to study ancient Greek automata makers, like Hero of Alexandria."

He gazed wistfully outside, towards the sky. Then he stopped, looked to the tip of his cane on the floor and continued.

"Yet, there are many among us that still think otherwise. Since Byzantium is a Federation of multiple cultures, it means that we must wait, until the human brains of most of us can catch up with the right, logical approach, which allows for the free expression of ideas, like art, science, or anything else. Even though for some of us it is painful to wait for the maturity of all, we cannot leave our neighbors behind."

"Why not?" said John.

"Because sooner or later, we will have to deal with them, and the farther behind they are, the more difficult it becomes to make them believe otherwise. You see, they will resist more when you ask them for a greater rate of change. It also becomes a matter of political expediency. If one of those with the wrong approach to logical thinking is a person in power, like an Emperor, everything gets reversed. So, instead of being bullishly arrogant on what we consider honorable and is of logical thinking, we compromise. And, in the act of compromise we seek honor in the belief that we did not destroy the peace of our world. Instead we allowed some future generations to achieve what we hoped to achieve, but could not, even if we tried our best. We could not, because our society was not mature enough. Please follow me John in my thinking. Even though Byzantium is the richest area in this world, in wealth, knowledge and opportunities, everyone around us jealously wants a piece of what we have. They come here to attack and loot us, to get educated and learn from us, or to become part of us. If we put a barrier in that, by excluding them as barbarians and become bigots because they are so far behind in their ways, we will be swamped by their numbers and sooner or later we will perish. So, we must swallow our pride and find an honorable compromise of patient tolerance, while we slowly educate them and make them come closer to our thinking."

Leo took another sip of wine.

"Let me give you an example by telling you what is happening here. Up until six years ago, we had Patriarch Ignatius, who with support from the Emperor and the Pope in Rome started a bigoted, non-compromising campaign against those poor souls that fought any images. Moderates, like Gregory, the Archbishop of Syracuse were deposed and excommunicated. Resentment started piling up until he fell out of favor with our young Emperor Michael III. His brave and arrogant policies had no room for compromise or forgiveness, and he made many enemies, including Bardas,

 STAVROS BOINODIRIS PHD

brother of the Regent Theodora mother of the young Emperor. Then, the Emperor was told by none other than his uncle Bardas that his mother was plotting to assassinate him with the blessings of the Patriarch."

"To assassinate her own son…?"

"Yes. After that, the Emperor decided that he had enough of interference and ordered to send off to a monastery his pesky mother and his unmarried sisters. He ordered Ignatius to shave their heads and after Ignatius refused, he was immediately arrested, banished without a trial and sent to his monastery at Terebinthos. Bardas then recommended to the young Emperor a brilliant scholar as a replacement. Even though he was a layman, Photius had chosen a political career and soon became friends with Bardas. So, with Bardas' help, and in five days he became a bishop. Soon after, he was declared as a de facto patriarch, even when Ignatius refused to resign. Then he proceeded to communicate with Pope Nicholas in Rome, to consolidate his position. That is when the political fireworks started."

"What fireworks!"

"The Pope received very polite letters from both, Photius and the Emperor. Then, when the Byzantine legates appeared with presents, he made it clear to them that he was not ready to recognize Photius as Patriarch. In return for such a decision, he wanted certain concessions from the Emperor. These were the bishoprics of Sicily and Calabria, the vicariate of Thessaloniki and various other Balkan dioceses. Before the Emperor could decide what to do with the Papal demands, he and his uncle went on another campaign against the Saracens. While they were in Asia Minor, we get another sudden attack from the Russians, who sailed and raided wealthy monasteries, killing many around the Bosporus beaches and islands, including Terebinthos. Ignatius barely escaped with his life. By the time the Emperor received the news and hurried back, the raiders disappeared."

"So, what happened with the Papal demands?"

"To insist on his demands, the Pope sent two emissaries here, about three years ago. Photius made sure that they were impressed through entertainment and presents. After several sessions in a Council, which included Ignatius, a formal document was signed confirming the deposition of Ignatius and signed by many, including the Papal emissaries. Yet, when they returned to Rome, Pope Nicholas was furious because they exceeded their authority. Worse yet, they did not obtain a single concession of what the

Pope wanted. Then a letter from Photius arrived, describing the minutes of the Council, but addressing the Pope as an equal, asserting the independence of Constantinople from Rome."

"This must have infuriated the Pope," said John, shaking his head.

"Of course," said Leo. "He wrote letters to the Patriarchs of Alexandria, Antioch and Jerusalem, informing them that Ignatius was illegally deposed and usurped by a scoundrel.

This brought no results, since the Saracens had occupied all these places and their intervention was futile. The frustrated Pope then turned to the Emperor, pleading his position. Then, last year he summoned a synod at Lateran, declaring Photius excommunicate unless he immediately denounced all claims as a Patriarch. A similar sentence was passed to all signatories of the Constantinople Council. He also restored Ignatius to his post. This act annoyed the Emperor, or rather Bardas, who was now the heir apparent to the throne, but they had their hands full with the Slavs and Bulgars to deal with the politics of the Church. So, right now our Christian Church is divided, due to stupid, uncompromising pride and self-indulging intolerance."

"What a mess," said John Psellus, staring at the saddened face of Leo." Given all that, what is being done about this by the government?"

"Not much!" replied Leo. "The person that really governs Byzantium now is Bardas, the brother of the Empress Theodora. You see, Theodora, after a failed assassination attempt against her young son is now retired in the Gastria monastery. She and her daughters Thekla, Anna, Anastasia and Pulcheria were tonsured and taken to that monastery by force. Bardas took over as heir apparent to the throne. Bardas is from a noble Armenian family and now governs with the help of his younger brother Patronas. He tries to keep Emperor Michael educated in military arts, fed and happy until he matures enough to become a good Emperor. He even sent him on an expedition against the Abbasids in the East, to harden him up. I heard that young Michael participated in the siege of Samosata, but when we were threatened by another wave of the Rus from up north, he came back to repel them. I don't know what happened back in the East, but after he came back that young man started drinking a lot. He must have seen lots of killing. According to many, he became the Palace drunkard."

 STAVROS BOINODIRIS PHD

"What is wrong with these Armenians? Don't they have any dignity? Why was the mother trying to assassinate her own son?"

"We, humans are jungle creatures John, when it comes to politics. There is no dignity, or honor, like the one stated by Socrates, or as we Greeks say "philotimo". This is especially true when it comes down to governing the richest place in the world. From all this dysfunctional Armenian family, the one that I respect the most is Bardas. Yes, he may be vain and power-hungry, but he is a very capable administrator, better than the rest of them combined. He is the one that helped me found the Magnaura School with seats for philosophy, grammar, astronomy and mathematics. Now, most of our capable administrators, educators and heads of the military are educated there. He is also the one who supported Photius financially on the missionary activities of Cyril and Methodius in Greater Moravia and Bulgaria."

"Why do they call him Caesar?"

"This is nothing more than a Byzantine title John. Its roots are from Julius Caesar, of the Roman times. It means that he is an heir apparent to the Emperor. If something happens to the Emperor, he takes over. Of course, what happens in this case is that the Emperor is too young and immature. So, he governs."

They both sipped some wine, as they stared outside. They noticed some pigeons cooing on a nest on the eves of Leo's house. Then a church bell rang near-by and some of them flew away towards the cathedral of St. Sophia.

# Photius (Constantinople, Aghia Sophia, 864 AD Christmas Eve)

A flock of pigeons flew and landed on top of the cathedral buttresses, as people were milling around the courtyard of St Sophia. The cathedral was splendidly lit by the sunlight that streamed through the windows this afternoon.

Methodius sat in one of the courtyard benches, admiring the view. The splendor of the largest cathedral in Christendom had not diminished, despite earthquakes and the fire that damaged it six years earlier. The brilliantly architected cathedral remained a stalwart symbol of Christianity, even though it was more than three centuries old. Several people, including clergy were scurrying about the cathedral, some preparing for the evening service.

Methodius was waiting for Patriarch Photius to appear. As he waited, he was thinking of the events that transpired recently, that changed his life. He remembered that extraordinary day when his brother Constantine sat and told him the news about what he and Photius had discussed. The whole discussion began with the Moravian king Rotislav, who sent representatives to inform Photius that the Bulgar King Boris struck an alliance with the Frankish King Louis.[2] Rotislav wanted a strong ally against the Bulgars, so he proposed adoption of Orthodox Christianity by his people. Photius saw that as an opportunity, especially since this conversion could induce Boris to announce a mass conversion of his people, most probably under the Roman influence. The Pope was anxious to have his authority over all newly converted people in the Balkans, and this was not acceptable

---

[2]  This is King Louis II, sometimes called the Younger (825 – 12 August 875). He was the King of Italy and Holy Roman Emperor from 844, co-ruling with his father Lothair I until 855, after which he ruled alone.

 

to Photius. So, Photius came with a brilliant idea. He approached his thirty-five-year-old brother Constantine, a monk from Thessaloniki with the proposal to undertake the mass conversion of a nation. His brother was in Constantinople, brought there earlier and pursued his studies under Photius himself. He was a saintly monk, but he had a remarkable flair for languages. Photius was so impressed, that he made him his librarian. By the time he came back from a conversion trip to the Khazars, he managed to get two thousand Christian prisoners released and he acquired the Slavic name of Cyril, which stuck on him since then. Then, as the Bulgarians were ready to attack Moravia, Emperor Michael put his forces against the Bulgars, forcing Boris to give up the alliance with the Franks and accept conversion to Orthodox Christianity. In September of last year, Boris was baptized by Photius himself in this cathedral of Aghia Sophia and given the name Michael.

Methodius was proud of his brother's achievements and showed interest on what was going on. Photius did not miss out on the eagerness of this second brother to join into this enterprise. Then, last summer, Cyril and Methodius were both summoned to be sent by Photius to Moravia. As Photius was giving them instructions, Cyril was skeptical.

"These people are simple, illiterate, naïve peasants believing in simple ways of life. Are you sure that we must go there and corrupt their gullible minds with our ways of life?"

Photius laughed.

"We plan to do no harm, either by me, or by you. It is not a bad thing for the pigeons to have a cat among them from time to time. In this way, they become alert, so that they are not devoured by a more dangerous animal."

Methodius remembered vividly the instructions of Photius. He told him personally that he was chosen because he had been in government service before, but most importantly, his service was in a Slavic region, and he had already learned their language.

As Methodius was thinking all the events that transpired in the past, he noticed that several clergies, some of which he recognized as the assistants to Patriarch Photius were also waiting close by, staring at him and chatting among themselves. They probably were waiting to hear the news that Methodius was bringing, in his first report to Photius. After months of intense work in Moravia, Cyril asked his brother to go to Constantinople to report, seek advice and get supplies.

A few minutes later Photius entered through a side door of the courtyard accompanied by a few clergy. They gathered around Methodius who rose, kneeled and kissed the hand of the Patriarch. Photius asked him to follow him, dismissed most of his entourage and the two men with some select advisors proceeded to a room of an adjacent structure to Aghia Sophia, used as an office by the Patriarch.

"Tell me what happened in Moravia. Is Cyril well?"

"My brother is well Your Eminence. We reached Moravia. We also had contacts with the Slavs from various locations around the Danube and the land of Rus. We are now working on being able to communicate with them. Cyril is working on an alphabet that allows Moravians, Slavs and Bulgarians to write down what they speak. We will need additional assistance from certain scholars of the University of Constantinople to cover all requirements. We will also need some supplies."

"God be praised. Let us go to Magnaura to discuss it with some of the University staff. Brother Elpidios, can you please ask our staff to join us there? Make sure that Leo the Philosopher is available."

The clergy headed towards the University. The University had fallen apart during the reign of iconoclastic Emperors. Photius re-established it and placed it in the capable hands of Leo the Philosopher, who now was the Dean. Leo gave regular lectures in philosophy and mathematics at the church of Forty Martyrs.

It was late that evening when Photius finished his meeting at Magnaura. He took off with a carriage and after dropping Methodius at a home where he slept, he and two of his closest advisors headed to the Palace. There he looked to find Bardas, but instead he found Emperor Michael having a feast with few of his friends. He wanted to see Bardas, to apprise him of the situation in Moravia and to ask for more money, but Bardas was not in the feast. Instead, the Emperor had surrounded himself with a bunch of Armenian peasants, like those that flatter anyone in return for a good time in the Palace. Among them was a hefty peasant with the body of Hercules, called Basil.

"Come and have a seat Patriarch," ordered the Emperor. The Patriarch and his advisors sat on the empty seats.

 STAVROS BOINODIRIS PHD

"I came to see Caesar," said the Patriarch "but they told me he is gone somewhere."

"I cannot say where," said the young Emperor. "What we have today here is a feast of good lamb roast with an excellent barrel of wine from the Pangaion hills. We just got started. We also make bets on who can out-drink me, the current champion."

"Are you telling me that you out-drank these Armenian peasants?"

"Yes, Your Eminence, I did. You are looking at the champion."

At this time, Basil, the huge Armenian spoke laughingly.

"I bet that the Patriarch can out-drink you, Your Highness."

Everyone started laughing.

"You have nothing to bet, other than what I give you," said the Emperor.

"I have myself, Your Highness," said Basil. "I will be your servant for the rest of my life if I lose. But if I win, I want you to raise me to a significant post in the Palace. Then, I can serve you from that post."

Michael laughed. "So, either way, you will be my servant." He turned to Photius. "What do you say, Your Eminence?"

"I don't see what I get from all this," said Photius.

"Hmm," pondered Michael. "What is your pleasure?"

Photius pondered for a while. Then he turned with a smile to the Emperor.

"If I win, you shall not break your vows of your current marriage. It would create a great deal of trouble for me by the Ignatians if you did. If I lose, you can do as you please."

"My accursed current marriage is nothing but a prison sentence," Michael said with hate in his face. "You are driving a hard bargain priest. Yet I am not going to back out of this bet for you and for this illiterate peasant that wants to become a Palace member."

So, silver cups were filled with wine and each drank one after the other. Both Michael and Photius were enjoying their wine until they hit thirty cups each. There was a slight difference on their drinking though. Michael reached the thirty cups first, drinking only. Photius on the other hand drank slowly, and between each cup he ate a very small piece of lamb. The Patriarch also seemed to have had something under his sleeve. He was very familiar with the Pangaion wine. Constantine, or Cyril, being from Thessaloniki regularly brought him this wine. In fact, he had two barrels in his cellar and he regularly consumed it during each of his meals.

The contest continued. By the time Michael raised his fiftieth cup, his feet buckled from under him. He rolled under the table unconscious. Photius continued beyond that, and for a good measure he drank his sixtieth cup. Then, he looked at his advisors and mumbled:

"Pl...please.... Take me home."

The two advisors supported the Patriarch from under his arms and proceeded to the stagecoach.

The rest of the group looked at each other, and then they started clapping their hands. Basil smiled and instead of clapping he turned to his friend, named Symbatius and slapped him on his shoulder.

"We are in business," he said in a whisper.

          STAVROS BOINODIRIS PHD

# Emperor Michael (The Great Palace, October 865 AD)

Emperor Michael was involved in a different sort of business that morning. He was now barely twenty-five and he loved passionately this woman since he was fifteen. As he laid in bed, in Ingerina's quarters making love to this gorgeous, blond, half Greek and half Swedish girl, he could not imagine life without her. The two enjoyed each other for many hours this day. After they were both pleasantly exhausted, he turned to the side table and poured some of the red wine of a decanter on two silver cups. He gave one to his partner and after clanking it he smiled.

"Let us drink to us my love." He drank and then kissed her.

Ingerina drank a sip. She looked at him silently with a depressed look.

"What is wrong?" Michael blurted.

"I am very worried about us," she responded. "Unless you can divorce your wife and marry me in church, we have no future."

"You worry too much," he replied laughingly. She responded by grabbing his genitals.

"Get serious, otherwise bid me farewell."

She was right. Michael winced from pain as she let him go. Michael sat back in bed and pondered his situation. They made him an Emperor, since he was two, with his mother as a Regent but he also realized lately that he never had enough training for the responsibilities attached to the job. Did they deprive him of his training on purpose? Who was behind it? It must have been his mother's doing.

His mother, Theodora was a strong willed, decisive Armenian woman from Paphlagonia who kept him always in the background. She initially ruled with the help of her brother Bardas, but very soon the two were in combat with each other. As Michael was growing up, his mother made him look weak and easily led. His uncle Bardas then introduced him to

Eudokia Ingerina at the age of fifteen in the court, and he immediately fell in love. Eudokia Ingerina was the daughter of one named Inger Martinakios, a product of a Swede Verangian officer and an iconoclastic Byzantine noble family of Martinos. She had taken the Swedish looks and was blond and blue-eyed. Looking back, he now knew that his uncle had brought Ingerina to his life to needle his sister. Naturally, Empress Theodora and the then powerful minister strongly disapproved of any attachments to the Martinos iconoclasts. They both ganged up against the hapless fifteen-year-old Michael and forced him to marry another Eudokia, named Eudokia Dekapolitissa. Unable to do otherwise, Michael went through the marriage ritual, but in secret, he tried to visit Ingerina. Yet, every time he visited Ingerina, he found his mother and Theoctistus Logothete, a eunuch advisor to Theodora blocking his every move.

"You have to secure your reign and the Amorian Dynasty you inherited from your ancestors, by having a son with a reputable family," his mother and his parrot sisters kept on telling Michael. "Dekapolitissa is such a reputable family. You must learn to love her and have offspring with her for the good of the Empire."

Months after his wedding to Dekapolitissa, a woman he increasingly detested, Michael rebelled in frustration with help from his uncle Bardas. As Theoctistus was walking to his mother's chambers, Michael blocked his way.

"I am no longer a child!" he had yelled. "If you have any state business to conduct, come to me, not my mother!"

At this time Theoctistus, being a close advisor to Theodora, started yelling certain derogatory remarks that the Empress had stated about her son.

"You are still a child that cannot take care of the needs of your wife," Theoctistus yelled. "To become an Emperor, you must first become a man. You must assure that you are good enough in bed to have an heir son. If the Amorian dynasty depended on you, they are doomed."

Michael became furious and he tried to hit him. Theoctistus evaded him, but when Michael asked help from his Armenian friends, Theoctistus tried to run and escape to the hippodrome.

Michael realized how much his mother had brainwashed everyone in the court against him. As Theoctistus was yelling and running, he found himself blocked in his escape by Bardas, who gathered few friendly officers to back him up. Theoctistus immediately drew his sword, only to be disarmed by Bardas and his officers. Theodora heard the commotion and came at the door yelling at everyone to stop.

Immediately Bardas sent some men to lock her in her chambers.

"Let us bind this old fool and send him to exile," said Bardas.

Michael was red from fury. The words of Theoctistus rang in his brain, remembering the exact same words that his mother was yelling at him daily: "To become an Emperor you must first become a man. You must assure that you are good enough in bed to have an heir son to the Amorian dynasty."

He had to prove himself to the world, for the world to take him seriously. He was no longer a child, and anyone that said that from now on did not deserve to live.

"No! Kill him!" yelled angrily the now crazed, Michael, pointing to his mother's advisor and without thinking of any consequences to what he was saying. Theoctistus crawled under a chair to escape, but the captain of the officers ran him through. After seeing the bloody corpse of Theoctistus, Michael averted his eyes from it regretting his awful command to kill this poor servant of the Empress. He had seen dead bodies before, but none this close, and none by his own orders. He decided that he had a natural aversion to bloodshed.

For a while, mother and uncle Bardas kept on fighting, but a year later Michael was proclaimed the sole Emperor. Regardless of his status, Michael soon discovered that he did not know how to rule and make decisions daily. On this, he needed uncle Bardas. With Bardas' help, Michael ignored his legal wife and basically lived a care-free life with his friends. Michael's repeated attempts to live with his beloved Ingerina met with obstacles from Patriarch Ignatius, his mother and Ingerina's family. In frustration, he was surrounded with cronies who catered to his wishes, to alleviate his frustration. One of them was the rude, rough and totally uneducated Armenian peasant Basil. Basil was rough, but his Herculean strength and stature made him ideal for a bodyguard, an attribute that Michael wanted to use. The other attribute that attracted Michael to Basil was his remarkable skill with horses. Basil's family, like many other migrants had settled in Thrace, but taken prisoner by the Bulgarians and resettled to a region beyond the Danube, where several people from Macedonia had settled before thus naming the area "Macedonia." So, Basil, since his childhood had acquired the nickname

Basil the Macedonian, even though he had no Macedonian blood at all. He liked his nickname so much, that he refused to drop it. Michael for him represented a great opportunity to a palace life. To entertain Michael, he and others like him became the Emperor's clowns, dressed up in obscene outfits while carousing through the streets and wine shops of Constantinople.

Michael had to do something to alleviate his frustration. With help from his uncle he ordered Ignatius to personally shave the heads of his mother and sisters and send them to a monastery. When Ignatius refused, he got rid of Ignatius by exile and replaced him with Photius. At the same time, he sent his mother and sisters to the monastery. With his mother and Ignatius gone, Ingerina's family stopped their violent objections, opening Michael's road to Ingerina's bed. But now that things were becoming more to his liking, state business took a priority. Upon advice from Photius, Michael had to take on the Bulgars and stop them from attacking the Moravians. It took a few months before he could settle his affairs with the Bulgars.

Michael felt a pinch in his arm.

"Did you hear what I said Michael?"

He looked at Ingerina's beautiful face and lowered his gaze to her bare breasts.

"What is it about your breasts that drive men like me mad?" he murmured. He had tried to reason with his friends, why breasts were the sexiest part in a woman's body, but they all laughed at his rationale.

"I had told Basil once that we, men find breasts irresistible because we became brainwashed by our mothers when we were babies. That was the only place of nourishing comfort that was offered to us, while we were suckling after we were born. But after we grew up, our mothers closed their shop. Their breasts were barred and all we got was advice on how to become their tools of their ambition."

"Stop that and pay attention!" giggled Ingerina, covering her breasts.

"Now that I can enjoy my life with you," he murmured softly, "I find you apprehensive. What can I do to appease your fears?"

"Unless you can divorce your wife and marry me in church, we have no future." Ingerina repeated. "Any babies we have they will be declared as bastards and probably be killed along with me by either your relatives, or those of Dekapolitissa."

"Don't worry; I will protect you and our baby as long as I live."

		STAVROS BOINODIRIS PHD

"That is not enough Michael. I don't worry so much about us if you live. But you are an Emperor who goes and leads your armies in all sorts of God forsaken places, with enemies in front and behind you. All it takes is an arrow from a Bulgar, an Arab, or one of the paid assassins of your own Byzantine enemies to put both me and my baby in danger. It also puts in jeopardy your beloved Amorian Dynasty, and who knows who will take over the Empire."

"Now you sound like my mother!" yelled Michael angrily.

"I am sorry," whispered Ingerina with regret petting his face lovingly. "I do not want to be promised regalia and be thrown out, like poor Dekapolitissa. I saw her yesterday. She is quite a miserable woman."

Michael took a few seconds to calm down.

"Did you talk to Dekapolitissa?"

"Yes. She is quite miserable. She is an Empress only in name, tossed out and viewed by the world with pity."

"It is her own fault for coming on to me through my mother. Don't worry," he said finally. "I will not abandon you like her. I promise on my life to find a way to secure a future for you and our baby, whether I live or die."

Michael got dressed up and went to the door. Then he smiled, turned around and rushed back to Ingerina. He kissed her in the mouth and then sunk his face in her bare breasts.

"I am surely brainwashed," he exclaimed, as Ingerina pushed him away giggling.

"What was it that I just promised to her?" he asked himself as he rushed out of the door. He tried to erase his words from his mind, but without much success.

Full of thoughts, he proceeded towards a long corridor to a door and after opening it he walked at a fast pace to a conference room in Bardas' quarters. He had learned that Bardas was in a conference room with several high-ranking military men. A guard at the door opened the door for him. He found several men around a table, with Bardas at the head of the table. They all stopped their discussion and bowed as Michael entered.

"Please continue," said Michael after being seated in one of the chairs.

"I believe we can wrap this up," said Bardas. "What we heard is that we are not doing very well with the Saracens in the East. After taking Crete, they started fortifying themselves there at various locations. This may take them at least a year. We must prepare for a major attack this spring, before they can consolidate their defenses. You all know your assignments regarding the preparations. We have no time to waste. I need your detail reports before Christmas. Thank you."

All the participants rose and proceeded to the exit of the conference room. Bardas also waived to his aid to clear the room and close the door.

"Who is going to lead this expedition?" asked Michael.

"I guess that I am," replied Bardas, "unless you can take time from carousing with your Armenian bodyguard and your mistress."

"What is that supposed to mean?" said Michael in anger.

"Listen to me, nephew. Your close relationship to the unsavory character of Basil is becoming a threat to the State. People are talking about your carousing parties with him. Some rumors have it that you two have a homosexual relationship. I do not believe it, but the reputation of the State depends on public opinion. I fired your chamberlain, for not watching over you. I found him responsible for not preventing all these rumors"

"You fired him without asking me? Who is going to replace him?"

"I have not decided yet, but my point is that I highly suggest that you stop being close friends with Basil. What do you need him for? I can find you much better bodyguards than him."

"No, uncle; I do not want you to find me another chamberlain. I am now at an age, when I must choose the person that will sleep next to me and be my bodyguard."

Michael paused before continuing.

"As for Basil, he has his uses uncle. He is exactly what I need, for me to have some fun. You had no right to dictate to me who will sleep next to me at nights and who will be my friends. I need the kind of person that Basil is to free me from all the strict controls and punishments that I endured from my mother, and her puppets, like Theoctistus. Otherwise I will go mad. Yes, Basil is wild and rough, but he makes me feel free."

"Alright nephew, I will not interfere in your choice of chamberlain" said Bardas. "Yet I see only trouble in it. Do you know the legend of the young boy in Sparta? He was not allowed to keep any pets in his camp. One day, he found a kit in a cave. He took this wild baby fox and hid it in his tunic and brought it in the camp. There he was stopped by his trainer. Afraid to tell anyone he kept the kit in his tunic without saying a word. He kept silent even

　　　　STAVROS BOINODIRIS PHD

when the fox started eating him from inside his tunic. Finally, he fell, and his camp fellows found that the fox had devoured a good portion of his liver."

Bardas paused. "Basil is wild, like a wolf cub. Now he makes you feel free and you use him as a pet. But beware when the wolf becomes strong. When that happens, he may turn against anyone that is in his way, including you."

"I can control him uncle. Don't worry. As for the rumors about our parties, I understand your concern."

After a pause, Michael looked at his uncle with a pleading look. "If only I could settle the affair of my divorce…"

"Bad timing," interrupted Bardas. "I do not think that the Patriarch would allow it. It is too much of a scandal, after the killing of Theoctistus. Anyway, being busy with the business of State does not allow me time to pressure Photius to go through with it and sustain criticisms from the Ignatians, the Pope and your wife's powerful relatives."

"I need your support on this, uncle" said Michael, as he got up to leave.

"Be patient," Bardas replied.

Michael walked out of the room and proceeded to go into the palace grounds. There, he met with a young stable boy holding a horse, to be used by the palace residents. He climbed on it and rode to the palace stables, with the boy running after him. He slowed the horse enough, so that he does not tire the stable boy. He knew that he could find Basil at the stables at this time. He needed to gather as much information about everyone involved in his life and figure out what they were thinking.

He found Basil shoeing a mare at the blacksmith's shop. Basil was strong enough to shoe the horse on his own, by simply tying its reins to a post. He had two helpers that handed him tools and steadying the mare. When he saw Michael, he stopped what he was doing, bowed and smiled.

"How nice to see you; I hope you are well Highness."

Michael waived to the two helpers of Basil to leave them alone.

"Not as well as I hoped," replied Michael as the two men strolled along the stables, where horses were tied up eating. "I just came from a meeting with my uncle."

"Forgive me your highness, but your uncle seems to have assumed the place of your mother. He has taken over all affairs of state as if you are some sort of a weakling. How long are you going to keep this up before you can prove to the world that you are the Emperor?"

Michael stared at the face of this muscular Armenian peasant. He could sense the obvious ambition in this man, but one that was presented with a façade of illiterate peasantry, which made the ambition seem to be of minimal danger. He figured that he could outsmart this fellow, with his hands behind his back. That meant that he could control him if need arose. Then, the image of a young wolf cub, that Bardas had mentioned came to mind. After looking at the Armenian's face he dismissed the whole notion.

"How would you like it, if you became my chamberlain? My uncle fired my existing one and the position is open."

Basil was surprised. "But how can you do this? Isn't a chamberlain supposed to be unmarried?"

"The position is yours, if you divorce your wife."

"Does your Highness want me as a chamberlain?"

"I would not ask it, if I did not want you. What do you say?"

Basil thought for a minute about all the ambitious dreams he had in reaching the Byzantine throne, but this unexpected promotion was a gift he could not refuse.

"I will do whatever your Highness wishes."

"I will make the appropriate announcement tomorrow," said Michael." You better notify your wife Maria of your decision also."

"I will, Highness."

"Since you will be officially my chamberlain and my bodyguard, I could entrust you with some new developments. Bardas is preparing us for a major expedition to Crete next year against the Saracens. I am thinking whether I should go along with him."

Basil looked pensive for a few seconds.

"What for?" he replied. "If Bardas goes and he is successful, you might as well give your Empire away to him. Do you, or don't you want to be an Emperor that rules Byzantium?"

"What are you telling me?"

"If you go with him, while he controls all the officers in the army, you are vulnerable. All he needs is an assassin's arrow and he is the Emperor. Since he is organizing this expedition and assigned all officers in the field, you have no protection out there."

"I will have you to protect me Basil," said Michael laughingly.

"This is no laughing matter, my Lord. I would not be able to save you there, but if we go with him, be prepared to kill him before he does. On the other hand, if he goes and leaves you to govern here while he is gone, you can change things here in your favor. You can take out all his cronies that make him strong and put your own people in key posts, so that you can set your own policies. You can even force Photius and anyone that opposes you to give you the divorce that you crave from your wife."

Suddenly Michael felt danger. He was wrong about Basil. This illiterate peasant was hiding behind his seemingly placid face an insidious and dangerous character.

"I will let you know what I will decide to do," he responded, as he walked back towards his horse. Basil bowed and followed him. The two men were so absorbed in their discussion that they failed to see a young attendant behind a horse, who happened to be grooming a mare silently, listening to the whole discussion. The attendant was the nephew of Philotheos, the General Logothete and a friend of Bardas. Philotheos had posted the youngster in the stables as a palace trainee.

That evening, the nephew told what he heard to his uncle. The following day Philotheos approached Bardas with the news, as he heard it from his nephew.

"So, my immature nephew has found a partner to conspire against me. I do not think that he has the maturity yet to plan anything beyond having sex, let alone a conspiracy. But to make sure that he does not do something stupid, I better insist that he comes with me to the Cretan expedition."

Philotheos looked at Bardas with anxiety.

"Be very careful my friend," he uttered. "These two are unpredictable."

Bardas went to the window of the Great Palace and looked outside. At some distance, he could see the domes of several churches.

"With God's help, I may survive them both," he responded, listening to the church bells calling for the evening mass.

# Oath Declaration (Constantinople, Church of Panagia, March 25, 866)

The bells of the churches were sounding harmoniously this holiday morning. The liturgy of the Annunciation of the Theotokos at the Church of Panagia Chalcoprateia was attended this year by most of the Byzantine court. This church, about a hundred yards west of Aghia Sophia was built in the fifth century on the site of a Jewish synagogue, once used by Jewish coppersmiths. It was named as Panagia of the copper-market and was very revered, since it seems to have shared the robe of Virgin with Panagia of Blachernae.

Among the attendants was Emperor Michael with his friends, including Basil, whom Michael had given an unprecedented promotion to the rank of High Chamberlain, despite Bardas' displeasure. A Chamberlain had to be unmarried, so that he can sleep at night with the Emperor, guarding him. The title of Chamberlain, or Parakeimomenos in Greek, literally means "one who sleeps nearby," or personal guard and attendant. So, the price that Basil had to pay was to divorce his wife Maria, who at that time had Basil's baby, named Constantine. The previous High Chamberlain was discharged by Bardas because he had lost his temper with him, when Bardas leaned heavily on him for not watching out for his master's welfare. Michael jumped immediately on the opportunity and replaced him with Basil, infuriating Bardas unbearably.

The church attendants today also included Bardas with his entourage of secretaries. After the church service, the government officials gathered in a room adjacent to the church for refreshments. The Emperor posted a few of his Imperial guards at the door.

Wine, bread and some delicacies were already served as part of the customary luncheon. Emperor Michael rose with a raised silver cup full of wine.

     

"Let us toast and pray for my uncle Bardas and to his successful Cretan expedition."

They all rose, except Bardas.

"There will be no Cretan expedition!" Bardas yelled. His face was angry and flustered.

Flat silence followed. After a few seconds, Michael broke the silence.

"What is wrong, uncle?"

"What is wrong? You act as if you did not know." The response was loud and caused some of the audience to jump. "I do know what you and your sidekick Basil are plotting to do the minute I sail for Crete. I took out your previous chamberlain, because he did not watch out for you when dealing with people like your buddy Basil. So, you went over my objections and assigned Basil to his post, even though he was a married man. You even forced him to divorce his wife. I worked very hard to establish a prosperous government that works without snags. I am not going to allow you and your Armenian clown to tear it down."

Bardas looked at Basil, who became flustered, lowering his head.

Then, Bardas got up and took Michael by the hand to a corner where the others could not hear. He lowered his voice.

"I talked to Patriarch Photius about your plots. I also found out that Eudokia Ingerina is pregnant because of your infidelity to your legal wife. To avoid public scandal, Photius suggested that Ingerina leaves the palace and goes with her parents, something that I ordered immediately. After my session with Photius, I don't think that he will give you any dispensation to divorce your wife. Your plot and your infidelity will cost you Michael. It will cost you the loss of the Amorian Dynasty succession. I would not be surprised if the people look upon you as a lost cause and sooner or later someone deposes you for good."

Michael was dumbfounded. How did his uncle find out that Ingerina was pregnant? He only found out about it a few days ago. He must have spies all over the palace. Maybe Bardas has one of the servants spying for him.

"You are mistaken uncle!" he replied with a smile, looking at Basil, now raising his voice so that everyone could hear. "I swear that we never had any hostile intensions against you."

"I do not believe you!"

"Basil," he faced his Armenian bodyguard as both men returned to the table; "please tell my sweet uncle. Tell him that neither I, nor you have any hostility against him."

Basil faced Bardas. After a brief pause of surprise, he exclaimed:

"We formally swear that we have had no such hostility against you Sire. Your information must be an insidious lie." He waved his hand pointing to Aghia Sophia. "In the altar of Aghia Sophia, there is a vial with the blood of Jesus Christ. We are willing to sign this document of solemn declaration of no hostility to you with the blood of Jesus Christ. Will this persuade you?"

Bardas was silent. He paced back and forth, looking at Basil and then at Michael several times. One question was buzzing in his head: can he afford to show that he was afraid of his nephew, in front of so many witnesses? What would the people say if he stopped the Cretan operation, despite assurances signed with the blood of Jesus Christ?

"I want this document before I decide to resume preparations for the Cretan expedition. I also want both of you with me in my expedition. The Patriarch will look after the business of the Byzantine State while we are away. I do not want you to destroy the Empire by leaving you behind."

Michael meekly nodded affirmatively. Then he looked at Basil with a somewhat surprised look. *"Signed declaration with the blood of Christ? What is this man up to?"* he thought to himself.

Bardas called Philotheos Logothete and instructed him to prepare all that was needed for these men to sign. For the Byzantines, the title of Logothete was equivalent to that of a Secretary of State. Philotheos, accompanied by a guard hurried towards Aghia Sophia. Minutes later he returned with the guard, a bishop and two scribes. The bishop was carrying a small golden container, which had the remnants of a red liquid, which the clergy believed to be the blood of Christ. They sat down and wrote the declaration, as dictated to them by the Logothete. Then both, Emperor Michael and Basil, signed it by dipping the pen that was given to them in the red liquid.

After the document was signed, Bardas handed it to the bishop. Then he returned to the refreshments table and picked up his cup, raised it and made a toast.

"Let us now … toast and pray for a successful Cretan expedition."

They all gathered around the table and picked up their cups. None said anything except Basil:

"Let us toast to a successful Cretan expedition."

They all sat, drank their wine and ate some delicacies, prepared for the occasion. Michael, pretended to drink and eat, but he was doing neither. After all that commotion, he had lost his appetite. He was very apprehensive about the future. He could not afford to refuse to go along with his uncle. He had to go on the Cretan expedition. Otherwise, it would be an admission of guilt for the conspiracy that his uncle just accused him. That would certainly give his uncle the reason he needed to take over the Empire. Now that he signed with Christ's blood to go to this expedition that his uncle organized and controlled, who knows whether the Saracens or his uncle would permit him to survive the trip?

Michael decided to go outside to get some fresh air. *This is getting out of hand,* he thought to himself.

A cold breeze, coming from the Black Sea swept through his face and brought chills to his body. He noticed that the Byzantine banner was flapping strongly in the wind and immediately went back inside.

# The Cretan Expedition (Outside Miletus, Asia Minor, April 21, 866)

The spring breeze was blowing on the Byzantine banner and the flaps of the Byzantine army tents in a pleasant way. Inside his tent Bardas, was awakened by one of his attendants and after washing in a basin he sat on a table where the servant had placed a bowl of milk, bread, butter and honey for breakfast. He sat and realized that he had hardly slept, except a few hours in the morning. He was tossing and turning all night long. He reflected on what was bothering him and realized that it was something that Philotheos had told him the previous day.

Philotheos was very concerned about his safety. He heard something, but he had no solid proof of its validity. He had told him that both, Basil and the Emperor conspired to kill him, despite the oath they signed a month earlier. He visualized the clown-like, rude, peasant face of Basil, and laughed. "Not him!" he mumbled. Then he visualized his nephew, whom he raised to a man, trained him and taught him most of what he knew and shook his head, dismissing the whole idea. But something still was bothering him. It was enough to keep him up most of the night.

As he started to eat, he watched out of his tent flaps, between his two guards the scenery of the Byzantine camp. Tents were set along the mouth of Meander river and beyond it, the Byzantine galleons, as they were anchored, loading supplies for the Cretan expedition. As he was eating, Philotheos made his entry to his tent.

"Sire, we are expected at the imperial pavilion to order the embarkation of the men."

Bardas stared back at Philotheos with a blank look.

"I did not sleep well last night Philotheos. Do you suppose that there is something to what you told me last night?"

"I do not know Sire. It may be just rumoring among the soldiers,

   STAVROS BOINODIRIS PHD

especially after the declaration events of last month. It seems that the clergy have spread the news about the declaration that was signed with the blood of Christ to the people and the people are speculating on what will happen between you and your nephew. Anyway, we have no choice now. We are all committed to this expedition. Thousands of men are ready to embark. We must trust to God that your nephew has the Chamberlain under control, and they will support you against the Saracens, until this expedition is over. Put on your peach-colored gold cloak and face your enemies. They will scatter before you."

Bardas called for his personal servant and ordered him to get him his peach-colored gold cloak and prepare his horse. A few minutes later, after he was all dressed up in his bright uniform and sword, he rode to the imperial pavilion, accompanied by his trusted Logothete Philotheos, also in his uniform.

The imperial pavilion tent was full of army officers chatting among themselves around several tables. They all rose and stopped the chatter after Bardas entered. At the end, there was another table, where Michael, Basil and two secretaries were seated. One of them was Symbatius, an Armenian friend of Basil's with the title of Logothete of the Course. Behind them, there were three imperial guards at some distance. Bardas greeted everyone and sat next to his nephew. As he sat, he turned and smiled at his nephew. Then he looked at Basil, keeping his smile. He pointed to Philotheos to take over the meeting.

"We will now read this morning's report on all the supplies that have been placed in the fleet," said Philotheos with the esteem of a perfect book-keeper. Then he asked one of his secretaries to read the lists that included grain, animals, water, weapons, and other supplies. Bardas listened very attentively, while looking at his nephew, who started to show signs of fidgety boredom. When the secretary was finished, Bardas turned to Michael.

"Do you have any other suggestions or preparatory recommendations before the embarkation of men begins?"

Michael turned, looked at his uncle, half opened his mouth, but he did not utter anything. Then his head turned to Basil. Suddenly, Basil jumped up, his hand on his sword and with lightning speed he kicked his chair and leaped towards Bardas before his bodyguards knew what happened. In a single move he raised his heavy blade struck him to the ground, breaking his chair in the process. Then, one of the imperial guards attached to Basil came over and helped him finish Bardas off. The body of Bardas fell on the ground among parts of the broken chair.

Michael froze in his seat. He watched his uncle, with his blood-stained, peach-colored gold cloak, torn to shreds and immediately averted his eyesight away from it. He remembered how he felt after he had ordered the killing of Theoctistus and realized that simply the sight of blood made him sick.

He suspected that Basil was capable to do this act, possibly in some remote place, far away from his view, but not now, right next to him, in front of all the civil and military officials.

"All of you! Put your swords away," he shouted after taking out his sword and looking straight at Basil. Basil complied by dropping his bloody sword to the ground. The rest of the attendants that had reached for their swords placed them in their sheaths. Among those was Philotheos, who was surprised by Basil's speed.

"This meeting is over, until further orders from me," ordered Michael. "Philotheos, please make arrangements to clean up the imperial pavilion and take care of the body of my uncle." Then he pointed to one of his imperial guards that finished off his uncle.

"Arrest that man!"

The other two grabbed the third guard and disarmed him.

Then he turned to Basil.

"Come with me," he ordered, still holding the unsheathed sword. He guided Basil to the next tent, followed by the imperial guards. He ordered the soldiers of that tent out and posted the imperial guards outside the tent. Then, still holding his sword and pointing it to Basil came close enough so that the two can communicate in a low voice, low enough so that they could not be heard by the guards.

"What the hell did you think you were doing?" said Michael angrily.

"We had no choice ..."

"You could have waited for the overthrow to be done in a remote battlefield. Now, we are all exposed as assassins and as ones cursed by the Holy blood of Jesus Christ." Michael was genuinely concerned about the repercussions of the public execution of Bardas.

"We had no choice Your Highness," replied the Chamberlain. "Once we board the fleet, we would have been at his mercy. That is his army out there. They are his officers. We were suspects and as such, he could kill us and claim that we were killed by the Saracens. This was an opportunity that I could not pass.”

“How do you expect us to survive now? Except for few Imperial guards, we are in the middle of his army. How do we survive the wrath of the people in Constantinople, when they hear that you assassinated Bardas? What is the Patriarch going to say to these people about this event during his sermon in Aghia Sophia?”

“I am glad that you brought up the Patriarch on this. We must write to Photius. We must write to him and turn the tables on Bardas’ accusations. We must inform him that we discovered a conspiracy against the Emperor by Bardas and after closed hearings we found him guilty of high treason and summarily we executed him. A similar declaration can be made to the army. We must also isolate, discharge, or eliminate any close friends of Bardas’ friends, like Philotheos. Anyway, your conscience should be clear about your oath affirmation and signing using the blood of Christ. I did the killing. I will take the full responsibility on my soul in the afterlife.”

“Do not make jokes Basil,” said Michael tapping angrily the blade of his sword on Basil’s shoulders. “I am implicated, because you are my Grand Chamberlain. You work for me.”

Then both men stood staring at each other and thinking. Michael had stopped the tapping of his sword and he rested it on Basil’s shoulder. Basil looked at the Emperor, not knowing whether Michael would decide for him to live, or to lob his head off in this tent. He looked sidewise to the Emperor’s blade next to his neck, and although it made him somewhat nervous, he controlled his fear. He knew that the Emperor deep down would not do a killing on his own. He had read him over the years well and the odds of his survival, at least for today were good. If he came out of this alive, his chances to advancement and possibly becoming an Emperor himself were vastly improving.

Michael on the other hand was considering how to deal with Basil. The thought of killing him now, never passed through his mind. On the other hand, he could order his execution anytime Basil became a threat. But right now, the biggest threat was that of the people and the army. In order to appease both he needed Photius on his side.

"I reluctantly agree, Basil. We must inform Photius that we discovered a conspiracy against me by Bardas and after hearing this, my personal guards executed him. We must first though make the same declaration to the officers of the army, to avoid any rebellions. I want you to take the declaration yourself instead of Philotheos Logothete. If he appears, arrest him, but do not harm him."

"What about the Imperial guard arrested earlier. He was under orders from Symbatius to support me. Can we release him?"

"I will decide on his fate later; I must not seem to be very eager to forgive what happened and somebody has to pay for all this bloodshed. We will deal with him and you later, after seeing how events develop. Meanwhile we will state that he is under arrest and interrogation."

"What are our chances of avoiding persecution by the people and Photius?"

"Don't count me as being guilty in this murder Basil," said Michael. "You did the killing. As for your chance, I believe that we can count on the *willful blindness*[3] of our people. They do not like any disorder or conflict in their government. They want to feel safe, to avoid conflict and to reduce anxiety. Therefore, we can sell them a story that makes them close their eyes to the probability that we lied. But as for Photius, I am not so sure."

Michael sheathed his sword and walked to the exit. He called a few Imperial guards and gave them some instructions. Minutes later two scribes, after finishing the Imperial letter to Photius and to all officers of the army, were putting the imperial seal on them. Carriers then took them to their destination. Basil undertook the task of the Logothete, and he dictated the Imperial declaration in front of most officers.

"By Imperial Declaration, I assert that Caesar Bardas plotted against me, with the intent to slay me, and for this reason induced me to leave the city. Had I not been informed of the conspiracy by Symbatius and Basil, I

---

[3] Willful blindness, also known as conscious avoidance, is legally defined today as a deliberate failure to make a reasonable inquiry of wrongdoing (as drug dealing in one's house) despite suspicion or an awareness of the high probability of its existence. Among the first that recorded this human trait was Thucydides, in the "History of the Peloponnesian War" in the 5th century BCE, as he described it in the fall of Plataea. Also, see latest observations in "Willful Blindness: Why We Ignore the Obvious at Our Peril," by Margaret Heffernan, July, 2012.

        STAVROS BOINODIRIS PHD

should not be alive today. The Caesar was found guilty and brought death upon himself."

Hours later Basil assured Michael that the army was so confused, that showed no reaction to what was happening. A few days later, a reply came back from the Patriarch.

"The virtue and clemency of Your Majesty forbid me to suspect that the letter was fabricated or that the circumstances of Caesar's death were other than it alleges. I implore the Emperor, in the name of the Senate and the people, to return at once to the capital."

Now both, Michael and Basil knew from Photius' response that he definitely suspected a foul play on their behalf.

"I better kiss my divorce dispensation good bye!" he said to Basil. "You cost me a lot by your impetuous hurried actions."

"I did it all for your wellbeing, Your Highness," replied Basil with a smile.

A few days later they were back in Constantinople. The Cretan expedition was over before it began. All through his trip back, Michael was trying to think how to reassure Ingerina that everything was fine. She probably already knows from her sources, that a suspicious Patriarch Photius will not back down on Michael's request for an honorable divorce. Yet, he had to face her sooner or later.

Figure 1 The Assassination of Bardas (By Unknown, 13th-century author - History of John Skylitzes)[4]

---

[4] Licensed by Alamy Inc Invoice number: IY01109033.

# Michael and Ingerina (Constantinople, Saturday, April 30, 866)

Today was the day for Michael to face Ingerina. Michael had ridden his horse with only two bodyguards. He stopped by the market to buy some candied pumpkin sticks, some of which he shared with his guards and his horse. These sticks were made by taking pumpkin pieces and boiling them in spiced grape juice. He stopped in front of Ingerina's parents' home and dismounted. In his hand he had a pumpkin stick, half eaten. He ordered the guards outside, and before the servant that opened the door had any chance, he barged unannounced into Ingerina's quarters smiling.

"Good morning, Ingerina, my love;"

He immediately dismissed both of Ingerina's servants as they were trying to dress her up and comb her long hair by waiving the pumpkin stick at them. Ingerina turned around, as she was seated in front of a mirror.

"Good morning to you, too, Michael. It would have been a better morning though, if you announced your coming and allowed me to get properly ready to receive you, instead of seeing me in this condition."

Michael smiled. "That is exactly how I want to see you; in your worst. "He pointed to her with the pumpkin stick. "Stand up and turn around, "he ordered. She slowly got up in her silk night dress that flowed over her body, revealing all her curves. Although she was close to four months pregnant, she was beaming with beauty. Michael finished eating the pumpkin stick. He walked over to a washing bowl and cleaned the stickiness out of his hands. After that, he walked over and kneeled in front of Ingerina. He put his arms around her waist and his ears on her abdomen. Ingerina smiled, as he was trying to listen to the heartbeat of the fetus.

"That is my son!" Michael murmured. "That is my Amorian son, prince to the throne."

"Are you sure?" said Ingerina with a smile. "It could be a daughter."

     STAVROS BOINODIRIS PHD

"No, Ingerina, it is a son; I can tell."

Ingerina paused for a second. "Why do you always call me, *Ingerina*? My name is Eudokia, like your wife, the one your mother chose for you."

"I hate both, her and that name. No, for me and for all my friends you will always be called Ingerina; Inger's daughter." Michael rose, took Ingerina by the shoulders and took her to her bed. Then, he lied next to her without bothering to take off any clothes or foot-ware. He gazed at the ceiling thoughtfully.

"No, our baby is a son. I will bet my life on it. Sometime ago I had promised you something. Do you remember what it was?"

"Like it was yesterday," said Ingerina. "You told me not to worry and that you promised on my life to find a way to secure a future for me and my baby, whether you live or die. To tell you the truth, I did not think that you meant it. In fact, I don't know how you can pull it off, now that Photius refuses to give you any dispensation for a divorce. Why do you think he is so inflexible?"

"Patriarch Photius is a true politician. He gets input from all sorts of people, from peasantry, to high officials. Rumors regarding the assassination of Bardas point a finger at me and Basil, despite our attempts to tell the world otherwise. My stature as Emperor can only go so far in persuading people that Bardas caused his own death. This is especially true with Photius. He indirectly assured me that my marriage to Dekapolitissa is part of the penances, something that I must endure for implicating myself, directly or indirectly with the death of Bardas. So, there will be no divorce."

"So, do you take back your promise?"

"I wish I could," said Michael. "But Emperors cannot do that."

"What then?"

"I have a plan, but one that requires your help. This help must be based on absolute trust to me and my decisions, regardless of how crazy these decisions sound. So, for me to keep my promise, I ask that you swear on our baby and on the most holy personages you can think of that you will follow all my instructions without question."

Ingerina was now puzzled. How can Michael find a way to secure a future for her and her baby, whether he lives or dies? She was curious, but also apprehensive. It sounded too good to be true to pass it off and her curiosity was too big. After a few moments, she replied:

"I promise, on the life of our baby and the Virgin Mary to follow your instructions."

Michael took a deep breath. Did he want to tell her everything, or feed it to her a little at a time so that she is not overwhelmed?

"I want you to marry Basil."

"What?" yelled Ingerina; "Basil was married. His wife even has a baby boy."

"He has already divorced his wife to become my Chamberlain."

"I cannot believe this. Are you giving me up to him? In any case, I don't like him at all."

"No, you don't understand. Your marriage is a frontal show to the Church, to appease the pressure on you and our son. In fact, I want you to move into the palace. You must be next to me, so that I can keep you and our baby safe, right next to my quarters."

"What about Basil? Don't you think that after a while he will want to have conjugal affairs with his new legal wife that he marries in church, in front of everyone? I don't think that he will agree to all this."

"He either agrees to that, or I can have him executed for killing Bardas. I can talk him into doing what I say. He will not be my Chamberlain anymore and his quarters will be your quarters. He will leave you and my son in my care. Knowing also that he had hot ambitions of marrying my sister Thekla, I recalled her from the monastery of Gastria and ordered her to become his mistress. He will sleep in her quarters, not far from us. She would be happy, because she never wanted her head shaved to become a nun. Her hair would grow back, and she would find Basil very kind to her. This would also keep Basil happy and his sex life fulfilled."

Michael paused thoughtfully with a wry smile.

"We will do this to avoid any scandals of the ugly rumors spread by palace servants. You see my love, in the last few years I have been learning what I can or cannot do. I discovered that, as an Emperor I have no power to get a divorce from an unfortunate marriage arrangement that my mother concocted for me with the Church. She did not like your family because of their past, iconoclastic ideas. But, despite all that, I can very easily order or have arrangements made for mistresses or wives in my court for others."

Michael paused again in self-reflection.

"Isn't that something of an irony? I realize that my mother and the

Church inadvertently turned me into a pimp. Blast it! I hate them for that. I detest my misfortune for having been born into this, because I know it is not an honorable act. Yet, for us to be happy and for my son to survive, I am forced to compromise and do something dishonorable. I have to find my honor by staging a theater for the survival of our happiness."

"How long is this theatre going to last?"

Michael became silent. He did not have an answer, but he could not disclose this to Ingerina. He would let Ingerina digest what he had just told her, until another time. He kissed her passionately and walked out of the door.

"How long?" yelled Ingerina with frustration.

Michael climbed on his horse and he and the two guards rode back to the palace. After they arrived there, Michael dismounted and walked straight to Basil's quarters. He found Basil with a cup of wine, talking to Symbatius around a table. The two stopped talking, got up and bowed to the Emperor.

"I want to talk to you alone Basil," said the Emperor staring at Symbatius. Symbatius bowed again and hurried out of the door. Michael sat where Symbatius was seated earlier, pointing to Basil to sit.

"You know that I could execute you for murdering my uncle," he said to Basil.

"My life is in your hands, highness."

"Instead of executing you, I will let you live, provided you do exactly what I tell you."

"I am your obedient servant, Your Highness. I will do anything you wish."

"Well, you may not like it so much, after you hear my wishes. Now that you have divorced your wife, I want you to formally marry Ingerina, but keep your hands away from her. This wedding is only for show. She is my love and the mother of my son. If you touch her, you will lose your head."

Basil was awestruck. Michael saw that and continued:

"There is more. As you know, I have brought my sister Thekla back from the monastery of Gastria and placed her at the princess' quarters. You will move in with her. Then, I want you to bring Ingerina to the Palace, place her in your quarters and do all that without raising any scandals by the servant rumor leaks."

"As your Chamberlain, I am not allowed to move away from you Sire or to be married to another woman. Of course, you can demote me to some advisor ..."

Michael interrupted him smiling. "Since as a Chamberlain, you have limitations, we must eliminate such limitations. Instead of demoting you, I plan to promote you to a manager of the Palace, as a Co-Emperor."

Basil's eyes became wide. He could not believe his ears. Despite his divorce, what he was hearing from the Emperor's lips was an unbelievable forward move to his ambitions. He could not believe his luck. His ambition to get close to the throne was finally fulfilled. The transition from an uneducated, rough, Armenian stable boy to a Co-Emperor took him only nine years. All he had to do now is follow the Emperor's wishes and try not to foul his good fortune. He bowed deeply, hiding his smile. When he got his composure back, he found the courage to ask in a serious manner:

"Who will conduct the ceremonies, Your Highness?"

"I believe that the Patriarch will have to conduct the coronation. As for the wedding, I don't know. I will find out."

Basil bowed. "I am eternally your faithful and obedient servant, Your Highness. I hope to prove worthy of your expectations."

"I hope so," said Michael. "One of your first tasks as a Palace manager is to clean up this place from undesirable spies with big ears and mouths. I do not want anyone here that would blurb a word on all this to the Patriarch, or any member of the Senate."

"Your order is my command, Your Highness."

The Emperor got up and exited the Chamberlain's quarters. As he entered his own quarters, in the adjacent door, he was a bit apprehensive. He could not put his finger on the source of his apprehension, but he dismissed it by saying:

"The die is cast."

A servant appeared and helped him get into his sleeping gown. He was tired. As he fell asleep, he felt that he had accomplished a great deal today. Any apprehensions can wait until tomorrow to be resolved.

The next morning, Emperor Michael was having a private discussion with the Patriarch at his office, explaining what was to transpire. Photius listened attentively.

"Unless you have a change of mind on my request for divorce, the

     STAVROS BOINODIRIS PHD

business of the State requires that we do this in an expeditious manner," concluded Michael.

"The business of divorce cannot be reversed," said Photius. "As you know, Bardas' friends still hold a great deal of power, and they would want someone to pay for his murder. Regardless of all the assurances about your innocence on his murder, the people of this City are not sold on your assertions. They think of you, as an inexperienced and gullible ruler who is misled by Basil's conspiracy plots. As for Basil, they consider him as an evil person with ambitions to take over your throne."

"I know," said Michael. "But I also know that I cannot govern this State without Basil. My highest priority is to secure Ingerina and my baby and for that I need time. For the sake of this State, will you perform the coronation ceremony?"

Photius looked at Michael with a stern look.

"Since you say that you cannot govern without Basil, I have no choice. This has nothing to do with the Church and will be totally based on your decision. My oath to serve the people of this State takes precedence."

"Will you also conduct the marriage ceremony between my Ingerina and Basil?"

"This marriage is not based on a true commitment of love between those two, and you know it. Also, it has moral implications and has little to do with State operations. It only represents a means for satisfying your self-indulgence with Ingerina. My oath to God forbids me from carrying out such an act and since this marriage is not critical to the people's welfare, I must decline."

Michael looked at the Patriarch's truthful face, bowed and departed. He had gotten the answers he needed. All that was left is to order some priest, or bishop that owed him a favor to conduct Basil's marriage ceremony at Aghia Sophia.

# An Imperial Show (Ascension Sunday, May 26, 866 AD)

Figure 2 Coronation of Basil the Macedonian as co-emperor - Unknown, 13th-century author [5]

Aghia Sophia was filling with worshipers this Spring Day. The ones that were arriving early noticed something different inside the great cathedral. Instead of a single imperial throne in its usual place, there were two similar thrones, side-by-side.

"I wonder if the second throne is for the Empress Dekapolitissa," said one elderly woman in a black dress to another, much younger one, dressed in a similar fashion.

"I doubt it. I have never seen those two together in public. Something else must be going on."

A few moments later, a chorus of chant-men started chanting, while the bells of Aghia Sophia were playing harmonious melodies, calling the faithful. During this whole time, the faithful kept on coming. While the

---

[5] Licensed by Alamy Inc. Invoice number: IY01109036.

　　　STAVROS BOINODIRIS PHD

liturgy was proceeding and conducted by a bishop, the Patriarch appeared and sat in the Patriarchal throne.

At the time that the bishop was getting ready to start the Eucharist, he nodded to a guard at the door, who relayed a message outside the cathedral. Suddenly, a trumpet sounded, playing the Imperial Entry. As the trumpet sounded, the bells accompanied it harmoniously. A bit later, the people inside the cathedral saw the Emperor arriving in a procession from the Palace on a carriage with riders all around him. He walked in, but instead of moving to his throne, he climbed to the top of the ambo, a three-decker pulpit, made of multi-colored marble normally used for the reading of the Gospel.

Another trumpet was sounded and the hoofs of more horses. Basil mounted on a white horse was accompanied by his friends and advisors surrounding him. Basil dismounted and went inside the cathedral and was led to climb onto the middle level of the ambo. Behind Basil, a secretary followed to the ambo and climbed at the lowest level of it. Then the secretary took out a scroll from under his arm and started reading:

"I declare the following, in the Emperors name. Caesar Bardas plotted against me to slay me, and for this reason induced me to leave the city. Had I not been informed of the conspiracy by Symbatius and Basil, I should not be alive today. The Caesar was guilty and brought his death upon himself. It is my will that Basil, the High Chamberlain, who is loyal to me, who has delivered me from my enemy and who holds me in great affection, be made the guardian and manager of my Empire and should be proclaimed by all as basileus."

At that time, Basil descended, and a handful of eunuchs started dressing him up with purple leggings and imperial regalia. Michael then descended and approached Patriarch Photius. Michael handed the Patriarch his diadem. Photius blessed it and returned it to his head. At this time, Michael and his aides proceeded in front of the templon gate, followed by Basil. There, the Emperor removed again his diadem and placed it on the head of the kneeling Basil, while the chorus was singing hymns praying for a lengthy life to the participants. The coronation concluded by the ceremony of the Holy Communion, where both, the Emperor and the Co-Emperor drank the wine and ate the bread offered by the bishop. The liturgy continued, while both, Michael and Basil sat in their thrones, side-by-side.

At the end of the liturgy, a horse-drawn carriage came from the palace with Eudokia Ingerina, accompanied by her parents. At this time, the Patriarch decided to make his exit on a side entrance by another carriage.

Ingerina's company proceeded inside the cathedral and positioned themselves at the entrance. At that time, the departing Patriarch turned and looked at the procession. He smiled, looking at Methodius, who was next to him. Soon the smile faded, and apprehension covered Photius' face.

"I wonder if I made a mistake with this young Emperor," he whispered to Methodius. "Maybe we could have avoided all this fiasco, if I tried harder to protect him from himself."

Then Methodius heard the Patriarch recite from Sophocles' "Antigone:"

"Eros anikate mahan, Eros os en ktimasi pipteis …"

Methodius looked awestruck, realizing the Patriarch's irony. Sophocles' verse was: "Love, undefeated in any battle, love, conquering everywhere..." Yes, Michael's love for this woman and his own character caused this drama of switching places between best-man and groom.

"I wonder how Ingerina feels," said Methodius.

"How can she feel, other than helpless?" said the Patriarch.

A woman, close to the Patriarch had heard Sophocles being recited by the Patriarch. She turned to her husband and asked:

"Did you hear that? This did not sound like a hymn."

"I don't know Helen," her husband replied and grabbed his wife's arm pulling her inside to attend the wedding.

As the bride walked in, Michael rose and proceeded to guide the bride in front of the templon gate, followed by Basil, with Symbatius on his side. There, a priest appeared, and he conducted a marriage ceremony between Eudokia Ingerina and Basil.

After the ceremony, Michael kissed the bride passionately and whispered something to her ear. Basil, after seeing that, he turned his face away. After a simple hand shake between Michael and Basil, congratulating him, the Emperor, the Co-Emperor and his brand-new pregnant wife went outside and rode together on the Imperial carriage back to the Palace.

As they were departing, the woman that saw the Patriarch depart earlier turned to her husband as they walked outside.

"This is very strange. Why didn't the Patriarch conduct the marriage ceremony for Ingerina?"

"May be because she is pregnant," was the reply. "I don't think the Church approves of pre-marital sex."

The woman slapped her husband on his back, blurting a loud scream of laughter.

# Ingerina's Baby (Great Palace, Constantinople, 19 September, 866 AD)

Ingerina's screams were heard throughout the corridor of the palace.

Emperor Michael was sitting on a couch at the Palace corridor, drinking wine and listening to the birthing screams of Ingerina, as handmaidens were running around her.

"Where is that no good drunkard husband of mine?" yelled Ingerina.

"I am here, my love," was a low response from the corridor. Michael raised his cup of wine.

"I want my drunkard husband to come and see me. To see how much I suffer to give him a child," Ingerina screamed.

Suddenly the screams of Ingerina stopped and a small infant sound came out. Michael came close to the door when the head maiden Anna appeared. She immediately kneeled and declared:

"Excuse me Your Highness. It is a healthy boy. In fact, both mother and baby are doing well."

Emperor Michael's face lit up as he finished the decanter of wine he was holding.

"Give us some more wine. Let's drink to the young fellow."

As the young maiden was running to the kitchen of the Palace to fetch more wine, Michael turned to one of his attendants.

"Go and notify all of my close friends. Today we will celebrate the birth of my son at the hippodrome. Let the chariot organizer also know, that we will be there to see a special chariot race today. Just to show how happy this day is, I am in a forgiving mood. I believe that I will order my mother and my sisters to give up the monastery and come and see my baby."

The attendant took off, gathering other aids to organize the event. On his way, he found Basil on the corridor, hiding behind a column at a door entrance. Basil had heard the screams of Ingerina and came out of his office.

He saw Michael on the couch and did not want to attract attention from him, so he hid behind the column. After hearing the callous remarks of the intoxicated Michael, he froze. When the attendant saw Basil he kneeled. Basil silenced him with his palm.

"I know," he said silently. "Ingerina has a son." The attendant nodded positively and departed. He did not hear Basil's soft curse:

"Damn this monster. How can he treat this lovely woman this way?"

Basil returned to his office silently.

Meanwhile, the young maiden entered the kitchen of the Palace. There she met with her father-in-law, one of the palace cooks and her husband, one of the Palace Latin tutors, named Chariton Psellus. They were eating belatedly their lunch.

"Eudokia Ingerina had a baby boy. I need a pitcher of the Emperor's preferred wine."

Spiro, the cook asked with a smile:

"Whose is it?"

Both, Anna and Chariton jumped and faced the cook and looking around if anyone heard the stupid cook's comment.

"Hush," said Anna. "Keep your mouth shut and get moving with that pitcher."

Spiro went straight to a barrel and started pouring wine into a silver pitcher.

"Don't worry. There is no one else in the kitchen," said the cook.

After a small pause, he whispered:

"Well, whose is it?"

"Whose do you think stupid?" said Anna, coming closer to him. Spiro handed her the silver pitcher, with a silver cup attachment onto its handle. She took them and disappeared towards the guarded corridor of the palace.

A few minutes later she was back. She asked to be seated and served some of the same wine that the cook served to the Emperor. She was quite tired, being up all night and taking care of Ingerina. Now, after the birthing ordeal, Ingerina was asleep and the Emperor was drinking his wine and chatting with his attendants. The new quarters the way that the Emperor had arranged them were quite convenient for everyone. One chamber was kept for the Emperor, with a communicating door to the Chamberlain's chamber. Only, that chamber was occupied by Ingerina and her maids.

The next chamber was given to the Emperor's sister, Thekla, but Basil moved into the adjacent room to Thekla where her chambermaids were supposed to reside. None of the palace servants could talk to anyone about this arrangement, but Anna knew that eventually these secrets could not be kept secret for too long.

Not far away from the kitchen, at another chamber, the Co-Emperor Basil was sitting with Symbatius and a few secretaries and were having some baked quince, discussing the Empire's business, when a chambermaid appeared, kneeled and proclaimed that his "wife," gave birth to a boy son. Basil's face was blank as he nodded acknowledgement. Then, as the maid left, he immediately asked for some wine. Then he dismissed his secretaries. When the room was empty, he turned to Symbatius.

"I don't mind playing my role as a cut-up doll of a shadow theatre Symbatius, but we must end this soon. I am a patient man. I got my title as a High Chamberlain for a price. The price was that I had to divorce my wife Maria and let her raise my baby Constantine all on her own. Now I have the title of a Co-Emperor and all I must do is to wait. You and I must play the role of stupid, illiterate peasants in front of this imbecile Emperor, but we must do everything to keep this Empire afloat. The Empire must survive, otherwise we may inherit nothing. Since we are illiterate peasants, looking stupid should not be too difficult."

"But there is a limit to what you and I can do, Basil. It is hard to pretend to be stupid and do smart negotiations in keeping the Empire afloat. Your Emperor dumped all the responsibilities of governing the State to us. Meanwhile, all he does is get in bed with … I am sorry to say … your wife, while you are sleeping with his sister. Did you hear what she called him as she was giving birth to his child? She called him an immature, spoiled brat who visits her only to fulfill his need for sex. The rest of the time, he spends it drinking and having fun with his friends at the hippodrome. We are having serious political problems these days and we, the stupid, illiterate peasants are expected to solve them."

"Yes, I know. That is why we need to split roles. You will be my wise advisor, while I am the stupid, illiterate peasant." They both smiled, while Symbatius nodded his head.

"What is happening in Bulgaria?" asked Basil.

"It is bad. Many Papal missionaries are being sent to Bulgaria and I

          STAVROS BOINODIRIS PHD

don't think that Photius can stem their tide. The missionaries are spreading dangerous heresies, as a differentiating insult and to disrupt the stability of our Church. They insist on the celibacy of the clergy; this would have a very adverse effect on our parish priests, who are required to marry before priesthood. They will probably condemn them and maybe excommunicate them. But the worst storm that came out of Pope Nicholas was that for the first time his church changed some fundamental beliefs on the Holy Trinity. They are changing their Nicene Creed during the Mass. They say that the Third Person of the Holy Trinity, or the Holy Ghost was to proceed from The Father and The Son, adding the word "Filioque." This subject is now …"

Symbatius' sentence was cut short, because he saw Basil's face freeze, looking at the door. He turned and saw standing at the door Michael, with a silver cup of wine in his hand. Immediately Symbatius and Basil wondered how much of what was said went into the Emperor's ears.

"Are we now adding the word "Filioque," because I have a son?"

Basil looked at Michael, as they both got up and bowed. Michael seemed a bit drunk, but not drunk enough, for Basil to be less alert on his role-playing.

"We have serious problems, Sire," said Symbatius. "This requires the immediate attention of the Co-Emperor. This is what we were discussing."

"That is fine," said Michael "but don't take yourselves seriously with the title of Co-Emperor, now that I have a son. I suggest that you lay some of those responsibilities to the Patriarch."

He paused for a few seconds, looking at the pair of men.

"Since you two are occupied with your chit-chat, I will not invite you to the hippodrome to see the races."

He smiled and exited, tossing the empty silver cup on Symbatius' chair.

Symbatius went to the door and made sure that the Emperor was gone. He returned and saw Basil look at him with a stern, piercing look.

"I am not sure that I looked like a harmless illiterate peasant," said Basil. "Peasants don't talk about "Filioque." We must continue to be very careful around him, or we can both lose our heads."

"Now you see how hard it is to pretend to be stupid and also do smart negotiations in keeping the Empire afloat," said Symbatius as he was pacing on the floor of Basil's chamber.

Emperor Michael took off on a carriage with a bodyguard and half way to the hippodrome, decided to stop the carriage.

"Take me to the Patriarch's office," he ordered the driver.

Soon he was entering the office of the Patriarch, making a motion to his bodyguard to stay outside. Photius was on his desk, talking to a priest. They both got up and bowed.

"Highness, how can I be of help?" asked Photius.

"I need a moment with you in private."

Photius motioned to the priest to leave. When the door was closed, Michael sat on a chair and motioned Photius to sit down.

"I just had a baby boy."

"Congratulations! That is marvelous."

"I need to make sure that he is safe. I want him to succeed in taking the throne of Byzantium."

"I see."

"No, you don't. Right now, all my bodyguards are Basil's people. I do not trust them. Since I dismissed Basil as a chamberlain, I don't have one. I need one that I can trust."

"Why? Did Basil do anything to cause you to think that you are in danger?"

"Yes. I noticed that he methodically has assigned as guards, people that are under his influence. I cannot let this to continue."

"If I recall, it was you that have set him up as a co-Emperor and a manager of the palace."

"I need a trustworthy person as my Chamberlain, so that I can take the responsibility of assigning guards away from him. Can you recommend me someone capable?"

"I think that I can be of use to you on that," said Photius. He got up and started pacing on the floor, scratching his beard.

# Palace Friction (Constantinople, April 1, 867 AD)

This day Photius was again pacing on the floor of his office, where he had invited Leo the Mathematician for his periodic consultations. Leo was sitting on a couch, listening.

"I know that you are not a religious man Leo, but I want to hear your opinion on how you would handle this situation with Pope Nicholas. If we do not react at all and accept all this differentiating sales pitches of our religion to the Bulgars, our people would revolt and be in the streets yelling. If we do react, opposing what the Roman missionaries are doing and start teaching to the poor, misguided Bulgars of the error of the ways of Rome, we are talking about another religious war, splitting Christendom in two. We just finished a lengthy religious war, regarding the icons. I am not in favor of being the cause of another such schism."

Leo the Mathematician, or as some others called him Leo the Philosopher was in his late seventies. Even though very frail, he continued to appear at the University of Magnaura for lectures. His name was a legend throughout Byzantium and Photius had great respect for him. Leo spoke slowly, but clearly.

"From what you are telling me, all this conflict resembles a battle caused by two fishermen trying to sell their fish to the Bulgars, each one of them yelling the attributes of their fish. You and Pope Nicholas know very well that both of you are selling the same thing, from the same sea, but you say that your fish is the right fish while he says that his fish is the freshest. You both know that to the common people, the Bulgars and people like me, the word Filioque means absolutely nothing, one way or another. I suspect that the reason for this differentiation is because nobody understands it. Most of us have tough time rationalizing the concept of the Holy Trinity. But to you and Pope Nicholas it means a lot. If you allow his missionaries in

Bulgaria, you will lose control of all the churches there that could have been yours. Then, from Bulgaria, who knows where else they may pop up. So, your problem, although it seems to be a religious one, it is strictly a political one. It is also an economic one, if you consider the loss of revenue from the churches that you lose to the Pope."

Photius smiled. "I hope you don't repeat these things to your students, or some of my priests. Some of them are fanatics, especially on the Pope's insistence of celibacy."

"These thoughts are between us two, as close friends. As for the concept of celibacy, I agree with our priests. You cannot be a spiritual leader of both, men and women, by not knowing what makes them both what they are. If someone becomes a priest and has not experienced the joy of having sex with woman, the daily servitude that a woman must bear, their need to be viewed as beautiful, the agony of childbirth, and their daily frustrations with their husbands, what sort of a spiritual priest is he? I think that Pope Nicholas, in his eagerness to differentiate himself, made a great error. If they insist on it, it will haunt them for a long time."

"If I look at it politically," said Photius "I can act only on the bits of information that I am getting from the West. I hear that Pope Nicholas has aggressive and non-compromising stance on Church interests, which are also extending to other matters that made him some serious enemies. For example, he refused to allow King Lothair of Lorraine to divorce his wife and marry his mistress. He antagonized not only Lothair, but also his older brother, Emperor Louis. Nothing would give the two brothers greater pleasure than to see the Pope replaced by a more amenable one."

Leo started laughing.

"So, the Pope fell in the same trap that you did, huh? You still do not allow poor Michael to divorce Dekapolitissa and marry the woman he loved. Instead, we now have this brothel in the Palace, because you did not give Michael the divorce he deserved."

"I know Leo. But I had to do it. At the beginning, a divorce could have caused political friction and Bardas knew it. He advised me strongly against it. Then, as Michael matured, he goes and kills Bardas with the help of his Armenian hoodlums. He had to atone for his sinful act. Otherwise the moral ground upon which my Church and this Empire stands would be eating

 STAVROS BOINODIRIS PHD

on us and especially me eternally. I had to balance honor, based on moral strength and compromise, based on reality."

"I could hear similar arguments from Pope Nicholas," said Leo.

"Well," continued Photius. "We have sent Imperial emissaries to Louis's court. Basil who now speaks for Emperor Michael agreed to do it. In addition, I plan to form a Church Council here, to declare Pope Nicholas deposed."

"What do you think Louis could do, and why would he do it?"

"Well, he has the power to overthrow the Pope physically. I don't know whether he will do it or not. In return, I got an agreement from Basil, that the Byzantine government grants Louis Imperial recognition as Emperor of the Franks. I believe Louis would jump on this opportunity to be at the same status as his great grandfather, Charlemagne, who in 812 was accorded this same privilege."

"I think that such an act may not sit well with some people here, including the Emperor Michael. Emperor Louis is an insignificant prince in Italy. How can this prince be raised to the level of God's Regent on Earth, Equal to the Apostles?"

"This negotiation is secret and should not go beyond this room," said Photius. "Neither Michael or Basil know of these details. Presently, Michael is occupied with his girlfriend and his horses, while Basil is occupying himself with building a power structure around him. He has placed his own functionaries around the court, even though he still plays a subservient role in front of Michael, who is totally useless."

"Be careful," said Leo. "You are in dangerous waters. Eventually you will have to tell Michael what you are promising Louis. What then?"

"Then, I pray to God that I can persuade him of the rationale of my actions. Telling Michael would be last, because it would not be easy."

"Does Basil know what you are trying to do with the Pope?"

"No. Dealing with Basil is another story. Him, I may ask to oversee the Church Council, so that when we propose to depose the Pope, he would have a difficult time saying no, since he will be presiding over the Council and he would have already had contributed to that outcome through our envoys to Louis."

"Good luck!" said Leo the Mathematician as he put both his feet up on the couch.

# The Council of Photius (Constantinople, August 23, 867 AD)

Leo the Mathematician was reading a manuscript as he reclined on his home couch, when his housekeeper announced that he had visitors. She recognized one as Methodius, the noted Patriarch's emissary to Moravia dressed as a monk. In contrast, the other was in a military outfit. In fact, it was a naval uniform, but the housekeeper did not know the difference.

"Show them in," said Leo.

The two men came over and bowed to the elder philosopher. Leo ordered some wine and asked the two men to become comfortable on a couch, across from him.

Methodius opened the discussion.

"I do not know whether you know this officer, Master Leo. His name is Nicetas Ooryphas. He is droungarios, in charge of the imperial fleet. The Patriarch asked me to bring Nicetas over, so that he can be apprised of our decision, regarding our actions relating to the Pope of Rome."

Leo smiled and bowed to Nicetas, acknowledging him.

"How are things progressing at the Council that the Patriarch organized?"

"As far as I know, things are progressing as the Patriarch had intended. Pope Nicholas was declared a heretic by a majority vote and formally deposed from the Church as a Papal representative. In addition, the Council voted and Photius himself performed the ritual of anathematizing Nicholas. As you know, both, Michael and Basil were participants in the inauguration of the Council, but the Patriarch had not told Michael what he did today with the agreement and in the presence of Basil. They both declared that Louis and his wife Engelberta were now recognized as the Emperor of Franks. This now fulfills Photius' part of agreement with Louis, leaving Louis to fulfill his end, by physically removing the Pope."

"What about Emperor Michael?"

"That is the tough part. Emperor Michael has been so much out of this that he knows nothing. Photius thinks that he will blow up in a temper tantrum, but Basil assured him not to worry."

"Not to worry?" said Leo as he shook his head in disbelief. "I believe that now is the time to worry. I understand that he chose Basil, because it was a politically expedient means, but Basil's motives to support Photius are suspect. He must have some ambitious undertaking in mind. I would not put much trust in Basil to persuade Michael of something as important as this. Basil is a sneaky fellow and my advice to Photius is to watch his back."

"I will convey your thoughts to the Patriarch, Master." Said Methodius as he took a sip of wine and continued. "Meanwhile, Co-Emperor Basil had ordered a military operation in the Adriatic. Last year, the Aghlabids launched a major seaborne campaign against the coast of Dalmatia. They plundered several cities before they set their eyes on Ragusa. They lay siege on this city. The people of Ragusa managed to resist the siege for fifteen months, but as their strength declined, they sent envoys to Constantinople to seek assistance. Co-Emperor Basil agreed to help them, and equipping a fleet of about 100 ships, under the command of our friend here, Nicetas Ooryphas. Nicetas wants me to come with him, since we may need to open communications with the Slavic tribes there for better coordination."

"How do you feel about this operation, Admiral?"

"We are well prepared, Master," said Nicetas. "My officers believe in this new, assertive foreign policy in the West. As you taught us at Magnaura repeatedly, we are ready to follow the seven rules of survival of our State. We avoid wars whenever possible, but we are always prepared for war as if it might come at any time. We continuously gather intelligence on all possible enemies. We campaign vigorously, but always in small units, which patrol, raid and skirmish rather than mount an all-out attack. We replace battles of attrition with evasive maneuvers. Always strive to end wars by recruiting allies, to change the balance of power. We strive to use subversion in order to win and when everything else fails, we use tactics that circumvent the enemy's strengths and exploit their weaknesses."

Nicetas paused smiling to take a deep breath.

"The fact that the Slavic tribes sent us envoys, make me believe that my forces will be welcomed. Yet, besides the military, we will need to dispatch many officials, agents and missionaries to the region, to restore Byzantine governmental rule over the coastal cities and regions. The old theme of Dalmatia, destroyed by many raids, needs to be restored as a largely autonomous region. Also, a Christianization of these Slavic tribes would not hurt in this process."

"I agree with your assessment, Admiral. Good luck in your enterprise." At this time, Leo turned to Methodius. "Since ancient times, we humans struggled with our own shortcomings. Among us we have people that are well-disguised narcissists, or adult infants, like our illustrious Emperor Michael. These people are a major trouble to society. Philosophers talked about containing these people through education, traditions, group symbols, family loyalties, and basic respect for authority. We can add to this civil and church laws and a sense of the goodness, value, and special importance of your country, ethnicity and religion. Many people in this world, even educated ones lack the foundation of healthy self-identity. They either have weak identities or terribly overstated identities. So, when they are in a tough situation, they end up with some sort of "pick and choose" morality, leading to tragedies. Since we are unable to control all these characters that drag us all backwards, we must either wait until they see the error of their ways or see them die. When we find ourselves in a bind and see that waiting leads to nowhere, we decide to take these people down. This is where the function of Nicetas comes in. We need the Byzantine armed forces to be strong enough to protect us from external leaders with overstated identities, whether they are Saracen, Christian, or non-believers."

"What about internal leaders like our Emperor Michael?" said Methodius; "How do we stop the tragedies that they create?"

"That is a big problem, especially since we are all bound by our moral code of civil and church laws. Yet, one of us must have the courage, or be given legally and morally the obligation to eliminate such a threat, before it drowns us all. It is easy for humanists to describe remedies for raising healthy minds, but not very practical, since we all know that some minds will not be healthy and will drag us all down. In that case, we need armies and police that are obliged to break such laws as "thou shall not kill," and do it with clear conscience."

After a few minutes, both, Methodius and Nicetas departed, thinking about what Leo told them.

 STAVROS BOINODIRIS PHD

"Who do you think has the guts to take down an Emperor?" said Methodius to Nicetas.

"Only another Emperor," answered Nicetas.

Methodius left and went to meet the Patriarch. He found him in his office. There Methodius told the Patriarch of Leo's concern regarding Basil.

"I suspect that Basil is untrustworthy," said Photius, "but all I can do is to give advice to Emperor Michael to watch what he is doing. The last time I had talked to him, he told me that Basil was the problem. He also told me not to worry and if Basil did not control his egocentricity, he had a plan of his own to get rid of Basil."

"What?"

"Yes, he did. I don't know which one of those two is the biggest narcissist, but they are heading for each other's throat. Michael was a bit drunk at the time and I am afraid that he is careless with what he says. If Basil finds out any of this …"

Both men looked at the floor thinking.

"It could hurt us too, if Basil knows that I tried to warn Michael," said Photius thoughtfully. "I care less about Michael's future, as much as what Basil plans to do with Pope Nicholas. I don't think that Basil believes that the results of my Council are worth anything."

"Why not?" asked Methodius.

"From what I sensed, Basil thinks that an Emperor should be put higher emphasis on materialistic goals of acquiring and holding lands, rather than attracting people to a given faith. He would prefer conquering the Moldavians, instead of converting them. He believes in military solutions, while I believe in a peaceful, spiritual takeover. I am thinking of Basil because he is now running the business of the palace. I don't know for how long. I have my doubts that those two can find a way to peacefully coexist as Emperor and Co-Emperor."

"Why? What do you think would happen?"

"I believe that, although they were friends initially, now they are in a situation where they afraid of each other. Fear can be ignored, until one, or both feel that they are cornered."

The Patriarch rose and smiled at Methodius.

"Are you hungry?"

Methodius smiled back and nodded.

"I am also hungry," said Photius. "Let us go to the dining area and have something to eat."

They started walking to a dining facility used by the Patriarch at Magnaura. As they entered through the door, the aroma of cooked food and wine filled their nostrils. Several people noticed the appearance of Photius and bowed.

# Invitation to a Murder (Constantinople, September 24, 867AD)

The staff of the Imperial dining room of the Palace of St. Mamas stopped whatever they were doing and bowed as the two Emperors and Eudokia Ingerina arrived and sat at the head of the already prepared table. All the staff worked hard for hours preparing the dining room with all the royal trimmings and plenty of wine.

The cooks and servers were very busy in the kitchen preparing a banquet for the Imperial team and several officers and dignitaries that joined them. Among them was the Vice Chamberlain, a Patrician called Basiliscianus, who took the Chamberlain's role. He had assumed the duties of Chamberlain to protect Michael, since the Chamberlain was away on a mission. Next to Basil was his trusted friend Symbatius. Both, Basil and Symbatius seemed nervous.

A few days earlier, someone had confided to Basil that Michael and Photius had several meetings together. After a Chamberlain was assigned to Michael, and he was given responsibilities of reorganizing palace personnel, a rumor started around the palace that Basil is now out of favor with Michael. Finally, after several of Basil's people in the palace were dismissed by the new Chamberlain, Basil heard the rumor from one of those dismissed, that he was under suspicion of treason by the Emperor. Immediately, Basil's mind started racing with fear. The day before, he called for a secret meeting with Symbatius to secretly organize a counter-response to these allegations.

"We have no choice," he had told Symbatius. "We either take him now, or we end up being slaughtered ourselves. I have it from good authority that Michael is planning an organized uprising against me with the help of the Patriarch. I understand that he has sent his Chamberlain on a mission to bring armed men that he trusts into the Palace. If we give him time, he can do it. Fortunately, he is a bit occupied now with Ingerina, his horses and his drinking and we have an opportunity."

"How are we going to escape from the wrath of the people if we kill him?" asked Symbatius. "The Patriarch, the Senate and all his friends would be after us."

"I am counting on something that Michael himself taught me," responded Basil. "He called it *willful blindness* and it worked with Bardas. You see, the people do not like any disorder or conflict in their government. They want to feel safe, to avoid conflict and to reduce anxiety. Therefore, they will believe anything I tell them and most of them will close their eyes to the probability that their Co-Emperor lied."

"I hope that it works," said Symbatius

"I hope so too," said Basil, "but we have no other choice. We must go through with it. I want you to assemble a handful of our trusted men to attend the dinner tomorrow and finish up what we started. Among them, I want John Chaldos and my cousin Asylaion. And, for God's sake keep all this quiet. Our heads are on the line."

Today, Basil was thinking all that, as he was nervously sipping his wine. *"Was everyone ready and committed?"* he thought. Then, towards the end of the meal, Basil got up.

"Excuse me, but I have to relieve myself," he said to the Emperor with a smile.

"Be my guest," said Michael, with a slur in his voice. He was getting drunk fast, after consuming lots of wine.

Basil hurried to the imperial toilets. They were made of marble and had a stream of water running from under the seats, making a whispering noise. He raised his tunic and sat, not only to relieve himself, but to think his next move. Then, he got up and peeked out, making sure that no guards were monitoring his moves. He then proceeded to Michael's chamber. He looked at the door, which was like his own and took out a dagger from his belt. With it, he bent the iron tongue of the lock, so that it misses the latch, in a way that the door cannot be locked. In the process, the tip of his dagger broke and fell on the floor. He picked it up and satisfied, he placed his dagger back on the hilt of his belt. He then returned to the dining table.

It did not take too long until Michael, now blind drunk as usual, staggered

     STAVROS BOINODIRIS PHD

off to bed with the help of his Vice Chamberlain and fell into a deep slumber. Byzantine Emperors never slept alone, so the Vice Chamberlain prepared his bed, on the foot of the Emperor's and got ready to lock the door. The Vice-Chamberlain tried to lock the door unsuccessfully. After a while he gave up and decided to lay awake next to the Emperor, guarding him.

Meanwhile, Basil gave the signal and Symbatius went to a distant corner of the Palace where seven conspirators were gathered. Among them were Asylaion, Chaldos and Zautses. They walked toward Basil, and all together went in front of Michael's door and waited. The Vice Chamberlain heard their footsteps approaching the door in the dimly lit corridor and sat up. He immediately went to the door and peeked out. After seeing armed men, he slammed the door, trying to block their entrance with his body.

The weight of the attacking men hurled the door aside, pushing Basiliscianus, while a sword was thrust against him, wounding him seriously. Then, John Chaldos approached the sleeping Emperor with his sword. Seeing him, lay there helpless, he froze for a few seconds.

"What are you waiting for," said Basil behind him.

John then raised his fearsome heavy blade and in repeated moves hacked both Emperor's hands. Sickened by the sight, he then turned around and fled from the room, as the Emperor started yelling from pain. At that moment Asylaion raised his blade and hacked the Emperor into silence. The assassins then exited the Emperor's chamber, leaving him and his Vice-Chamberlain in a pool of blood. They walked briskly the dark corridor and went straight to the Golden Horn. There, they got on a boat and in the dark rowed to the Great Palace. One of the palace guards, pre-arranged by Basil let them in. There, they went to sleep.

The following morning, Basil conducted himself as if nothing had happened. When news arrived from the Palace of St. Mamas of the Emperor's death, Basil gathered the Palace staff, which showed little surprise.

"I want you," said Basil to one Palace official "to go to the Palace of St. Mamas, to arrange for a funeral appropriate for an Emperor. Make sure also that Empress Theodora and her daughters are available for the funeral."

As the official went to do what was ordered, Basil pointed to another one.

"I want you to arrange that Ingerina moves to the Imperial quarters. Also, bring my ex-wife Maria here at the Palace with my baby son Constantine. Then you move all my things there too. We have a country to run."

Basil turned to Symbatius. "Bring a scribe here. I want to send a decree to the Patriarch, stating that he is out of a job. I want you to take it to him personally. I do not want him to conspire against me, like he did with Michael."

As Basil was getting settled as the sole Emperor, the palace officials entered the imperial chamber, where they found the horribly mutilated body of Michael wrapped in a horse blanket, that someone covered it with. They arranged the funeral with minimal ceremony at Chrysopolis, on the Asiatic shore, where Theodora and her daughters were seeing weeping uncontrollably.



STAVROS BOINODIRIS PHD

# Basil (Constantinople, October 15, 867 AD)

Ingerina was sobbing, with tears in her eyes, when she and her maids heard a knock on the door. One of Ingerina's chamber maids responded and opened the door. When she saw Basil, with two guards she screamed in anguish. Finally, she turned and made an announcement mixed with her wailing.

"It is the Emperor."

Basil peeked inside and saw that the rest of the chambermaids were also in tears. Then he saw Ingerina, now in her eighth month of pregnancy, crying. When Ingerina saw Basil, she immediately rushed to one of her chambermaids and grabbed her young son Leo, a little over one years old. At that time, the chambermaid was feeding the toddler. She took him in her arms abruptly and faced Basil. The toddler started crying.

Basil turned to one of his guards and handed him his sword.

"Hold this for me for a while." The guard complied. Then Basil entered the chamber.

"Don't be afraid," said Basil with a calm voice. "I am not here to harm anyone. I simply want to have a private talk with my wife."

Ingerina waved her hand and handed the crying baby to the chamber maids. One of them grabbed the crying baby, while the other took the bowl of what looked like mashed cooked apples and went out, to the neighboring chamber. They were all whimpering.

"I don't understand. What is this?" said Basil. "Why is everyone afraid?"

"Why don't you get it over with," said Ingerina wailing at a loud voice. "You murdered Michael. When do you plan to murder me, my born and unborn son and whoever is a threat to your precious imperial throne?"

Basil looked at Ingerina with a stern look. He grabbed her by the shoulders and took an earnest look, staring her right in her blue eyes.

"Don't go crazy on me woman. No harm will come to you or your children." He paused for a moment. "That is not exactly why I am here. I hate what Michael and his mother made of this Empire, including you and me. I must drain the swamp that this dysfunctional family created in this Empire. All the hidden brothel activities must stop. You are legally now my wife and that is what you will be from now on. Your son is my son. You and your son are not to blame for all this filth and subsequent killings."

"Did you have to kill him?" asked Ingerina still wailing.

"Unfortunately, yes. I had no choice. Michael became dangerous to the Empire and to himself. Emperors do not have the luxury to deal with self-indulgent acts that break every law of morality. I saw that, before I was a Chamberlain and knew that I could do a better job as an Emperor any day. For the sake of the people of this Empire, I had to endure all sorts of humiliation, contrary to my honor. It was a sort of humiliating compromise, and I had to go through a lot of struggle to achieve today's results. I became a clown, I divorced my wife and my child, and I became implicated in the killing of Theoctistus and Bardas. I was forced to marry you, while you were having his children and being dumped all his responsibilities, while he was carousing drunk in the hippodrome and plotting his next assassination, this time of me. Michael had to die, for the good of the Empire."

Ingerina wiped her eyes. "Then, what do you plan to do with me?"

"That all depends on you," said Basil.

Then he turned around and exited her chamber. He picked up his sword from the guard and proceeded towards Symbatius' office.

As Basil was doing that, Photius was visiting the elderly Leo at his home. The two men were outside, in the garden. Leo was bundled up with a heavy, wool blanket, sitting on a wooden bench, while Photius was examining the fruit of a quince tree. The ex-Patriarch seemed to be somewhat upset with the developments, after his dismissal by Basil.

"I don't understand why Basil stabbed me in the back," he said. "I understand that he is concerned about me personally, even though all rumors of conspiracy against him were lies, concocted by certain friends of his, who were dissatisfied after losing their jobs in the palace. Regardless of my dismissal, he still must run the business of the Byzantine State. Our plans were ready to bear fruit. Pope Nicholas, God forgive him was out and dead since last November. Why did Basil reverse all our successes? Worst yet, I heard that he is considering bringing back the ultra-conservative Ignatius

     STAVROS BOINODIRIS PHD

as my replacement. This goes contrary to all I have been trying to do for months."

Leo was trying to calm Photius.

"Basil is new at this. He will try several approaches, most of them being wrong, but eventually will settle down. You must be patient with these Armenians. Eventually they will be tamed."

"Tamed?" said Photius laughing. "They may be tamed, but when, and at whose expense?"

"Unfortunately, we have to pay for it," said Leo. Then he looked at the sky. "I am getting a bit cold. Let's go inside. I will ask Theodore to light up a fire."

# The Two Brothers (Pannonia, Near the Danube, February 25, 868 AD)

Figure 3 Saints Cyril and Methodius in Rome;
Fresco in San Clemente [6]

The fireplace in the monastery of Pannonia was a welcomed luxury for the brothers. This monastery was no more than a small hut, very close to the Danube. The monastery was built by the local faithful in the middle of a forest, so there was plenty of firewood around to burn. The two brothers, Cyril and Methodius decided to rest there on the way to Rome.

The ruler of this region was a Slavic Duke, named Kocel, who was very accommodating. The Duke sent for them, while they were working

[6] Licensed by Alamy Inc. Invoice number: IY01109040.

in Moravia with an invitation by Pope Nicholas, the year before. But by the time the two brothers had finished their obligations in Moravia and were on the way to Rome, they found out that Pope Nicholas was dead. Then, it was decided to ask permission from the new Pope, Pope Hadrian, who had taken over. To sweeten the deal, the two brothers offered to bring with them the relics of St. Clemens to Rome. These relics were found in a monastery in Crimea by Cyril, while he was there.

St. Clement was the first of early Rome's most notable bishops, so his relics were of great value to the Pope. He was said to have been consecrated by Saint Peter himself and he is known to have been a leading member of the church in Rome in the late first century. Early church lists place him as the second or third bishop of Rome after Saint Peter.

According to church writings, Clement was banished from Rome to Kherson, Crimea during the reign of the Emperor Trajan and was set to work in a stone quarry. Finding on his arrival that the prisoners were suffering from lack of water, he knelt in prayer. Looking up, he saw a lamb on a hill, went to where the lamb had stood and struck the ground with his pickaxe, releasing a gushing stream of clear water. This miracle resulted in the conversion of large numbers of the local pagans and his fellow prisoners to Christianity. As punishment, Saint Clement was martyred by being tied to an anchor and thrown from a boat into the Black Sea. The Inkerman Cave Monastery marks the supposed place of Clement's burial in Crimea.

By the time the brothers got confirmation that their invitation to Rome was still valid, they were caught by winter storms. The guides that the Duke provided for them and their disciples decided that for their own safety they should spent part of the winter in this humble monastery, until the road conditions improved.

The two brothers were exhausted, so they rested in front of the crackling fireplace. Their disciples and guides penned the animals in the barn of the monastery and provided the party with wood for the fireplace for warmth. Their disciples set up some heavy wool blankets on the wooden floor of the monastery meeting room. Their guides also managed to hunt deer and rabbits for meat and fish from the Danube, which they cooked on the fireplace. The guides also transported with them two barrels of beer from a region west of Moravia, which was of excellent quality. After they got settled, they all sat to eat and drink some of the beer. Their disciples went out to feed the animals.

"How does this beer compare with our wine from Pangaion Constantine?" Methodius asked. The two brothers kept on calling each other with their baptismal names. Before he became Cyril to the Slavs, the eldest brother's name was Constantine.

"It is not a bad beer," said Constantine. "Yet, I would love to have some of our wine now to warm me up. This place is very cold; almost as cold as Cherson in Crimea, during my visit there that winter with Photius. Do you remember how long ago it was that we made that trip?"

"I believe it was about seven years ago. Unfortunately, we froze our behinds and had very little success."

"Yes. The Khazar Khagan had made up his mind already, so he imposed Judaism on his people as the national religion."

"I believe we lost that region because we were a bit too stiff. We did not understand very well the feelings of these people, based on the customs that made their life bearable on a day-to-day basis. We were novices at this business of understanding and compromising seven years ago. When it comes to dealing with these people, we must first listen, understand them and their lives and then offer them something better. What we offer must be better for them and not necessarily better for us. We must treat them like children. The honor of God is in slowly taking them by the hand and even compromising to some degree when necessary. We must do that especially when resistance is strong, in order to bring them gradually and patiently into the fold."

"I agree brother. You are talking as if you are describing a fisherman. Never resist the fish, but slowly and patiently bring it in the boat. We lost the Khazars, but you got something out of that visit. You learned their language and you taught it to a few of your students at Magnaura."

"That was just a small payment for my troubles. The biggest payment came by our failure. That failure taught us what not to do. I hope that these lessons we took help us in our trip to Rome."

"Our goals depend so much on politics and self-interests brother. I don't know what to expect. These people are not innocent children seeking guidance in the dark."

"Our goals are to reunify our Church and through a unified Church to

    STAVROS BOINODIRIS PHD

achieve our primary goal that Photius impressed upon us. That goal is to bring as many people as possible from darkness to Christianity through the knowledge of their language, customs and interests, whatever those interests are. Our friends in Rome may be a lot more complex to understand, but we must understand them nevertheless and must compromise, if necessary, in order to achieve our goals. If we need to work with the Pope to achieve our primary goal, so be it. We will and do it gladly. I am sure that Photius would agree with me."

At that instant, one of their Bulgarian disciples walked in.

"What is happening Brother Naum?" asked Methodius.

"We are all set up for the night," said Naum.

"Where are the rest of our people?"

"They are finishing up their chores. They will be here soon."

"Come and have some rest too."

Naum went to the corner of the room and took an oil lantern that was hanging in front of an icon of baby Christ in the arms of Panagia. He prepped it with oil, water and natural wick. Then he took a burning stick from the fireplace and lit the lantern.

"I lit the lantern, so that we can see at night, when the fire subsides," said Naum, as he lied down next to the crackling fireplace. Soon, the rest of the disciples and guides came and went to sleep, listening to the howling northern wind, as it was blowing through the pine trees that were near the monastery.

Naum's eyes slowly closed as he was watching Panagia hold baby Christ tenderly in her arms.

# Compromising Love (The Great Palace, Constantinople, September 868 AD)

Ingerina held her baby tenderly in her arms and started to swing it back and forth to stop it from crying. Then she opened her tunic and presented her nipple to the infant. The ten-month-old boy Stephen had been born the previous November and he was a handful.

A knock on the door made the maiden hurry there. She opened the door and bowed immediately.

"The Highness Emperor Basil is here," she announced.

Basil entered alone, waving to his guards to remain outside.

"I believe that it is time for young Stephen to get acquainted with the milk of a wet nurse. I have inquired and one of my cousin's wives can provide you with such a service. I asked you before that I have need of your services as a wife. Nursing a ten-month-old seems to indicate to me that you are still not over the death of Michael. I believe that I gave you as much time as necessary to get over this. I set you up in a separate bedroom with your maids, while I slept in another bedroom with my Chamberlain sleeping on the floor, next to me. I prefer to sleep with my wife instead."

"Are you saying that I cannot see my sons?" she said angrily, pointing to her suckling infant. Leo, the older, two-year-old boy was occupied, playing with the maiden in a distant corner of the room. He had a pot on his head and was wielding a long wooden spoon as a sword. The maid held the lid of another pot as a shield, deflecting his blows.

"Oh, no!" said Basil. "We can make arrangements to have your sons next door, with Chamberlains on their feet and maids and wet nurses to care for them. This would free you to go to Palace conferences with heads of states, sitting next to me. Your presence is valuable and provides us with added prestige and a sense of normalcy in our negotiations. During the past months I discovered that you have a keen mind. From time-to-time I want to tap that mind of yours and ask you for advice."

Ingerina looked at Basil with surprise. *"Is this the same guy that a year ago murdered the father of my children?"* asked herself.

"What about your wife, who lives a few doors down? Is your plan to have us both in your bed?"

Basil relaxed and sat on a chair, next to Ingerina's bed.

"We have to resolve this situation in a civilized and moral manner; anyway, as moral as we can."

Basil lowered his eyes.

"I know, I am not as handsome as Michael, but I am not as self-centered as he was. As an Emperor, I like to keep you as my wife and make you as happy as my position allows me. If you do not want me as your husband, because you feel enmity against me because I was forced to kill the father of your children, then I will ask for a divorce from the Patriarch, which I will have appointed. I fired Photius so that I can use a Patriarch who can do this for me. His condition of appointment would be my divorce. Then, you will be sent in a convent, where you may be allowed to raise your offspring."

Basil paused and looked at Ingerina before he proceeded again.

"So, I give you two choices. Stay as an Empress and be my faithful and obedient wife, as you swore at our wedding, regardless of how that wedding was brought on, or end up in a convent."

Ingerina laid the sleeping baby on the bed and after straightening her clothes over her breasts sat next to the infant.

"What about my sons?"

"If you decide to stay with me, Leo and Stephen will be raised as my sons. As far as the world is concerned, he is my son. Otherwise, he will disinherit any rights to the Palace privileges."

Ingerina took her hands out of her face and looked at Basil, to see his expression when she posed the next question.

"What about your previous wife, Maria and your son Constantine?"

"Again, if you stay with me, my ex-wife will be set to live, either in a convent, or some quarters, outside the Palace. My three-year-old son though will retain all rights to Palace privileges, including being an heir apparent to my throne."

Ingerina sought to find out whether Basil was earnest in what he was saying. She had a lot to think about. Basil saw her and interrupted her thought process.

"I do not want an answer from you now. This is a serious business. You must think about this carefully. You must decide though within a day. But if you decide to stay with me, there is no turning back. I expect you to be a faithful wife to me and fulfill all your duties as an Empress, both in the Court and the Imperial bed."

Ingerina was stunned. She could not believe her ears.

"I will do as you command," she replied.

Basil picked up her hand and kissed it gently.

"This is not a command," said Basil. "It is a recommendation that benefits us both. If you want added time to mourn your husband, that you, yourself could not stand, please let me know and I will grant you more time. There is though one problem with that. I may soon be needed to go out with my army for months on end. There is nobody else that cares about you that can give you the training you need in order to represent me, while I am gone."

Ingerina bowed and did not respond.

Basil left her with her sons and the maid. Ingerina tried to rationalize her feelings towards this man, who until a few years ago was her husband's clowning playmate. At that time, she was jealous of Basil, because Michael spent most of his time with him. She even thought that he may have had a homosexual relation with Michael and that made Basil a disgusting person in her eyes. What she saw in Basil since he murdered her lover was now forced by preservation for herself and her children to such a degree that turned into *willful blindness*. Her rational belief that Basil was a dangerous scum had to change in her mind, ignoring what she knew of him and hoping that she was wrong. Her honor and logic went by the wayside, in a willful compromise, to make room for the slim possibility that this rough, uneducated man that took the throne from the father of her children wants her to become his loving wife and advisor.

"What do you think of the Emperor's proposal Anna?" she asked her handmaiden after several seconds of thinking. "You heard what he proposed, didn't you?"

"Yes, my Mistress," Anna replied. "I don't know. It all depends on you

     STAVROS BOINODIRIS PHD

and your feelings about this man. I know that you did not like him in the past. The question is if you can truly and honestly stop hating him and start living with him in a civilized manner."

"I don't know."

"Tell me truthfully Mistress, did you really love Michael?"

"At the beginning, I was attracted to him. He was handsome. But after he started his drinking parties and his carousing with Basil's bunch at the hippodrome, I started hating him."

"Well, now you have a different road to take. You must see whether you can suppress your past disgust about Basil and find out the gentle and attractive aspects of him."

"I know. I also know that whatever Basil was doing in the past he did it because he wanted to take Michael out, and he did that successfully. Maybe, I need to play along with his proposal and see where that takes me."

"We are not perfect beings Mistress. None of us are," said Anna smiling. "There must be something you may like behind your new mate."

Ingerina started laughing, shaking the now sleeping baby Stephen in her arms. She handed him to Anna, who proceeded to place him in his swinging crib.

That same evening, Basil was entering Ingerina's quarters again. This time he did not bother dismissing her maidens.

"I know that I am acting like an anxious groom, but I came to see if you have decided."

"I decided to stay," said Ingerina, "not so much for my sake, as much as for my sons."

"I see. Do you understand your obligations to me?"

"Yes."

"I will give you all the time you need regarding your duties as my wife. I hope you get over any affection you had for Michael, if any. But I expect you to be by my side as an Empress, all the time from now on."

He came close to her and kissed her on the forehead.

"What do you think is the chance that we may be happy together, you and me?" asked Ingerina.

"It all depends on you, my sweet. Personally, I like you very much."

"What about your ex-wife, who lives with your children not far away from here?"

"I had to divorce my ex-wife Maria. I will admit that when I married her, I loved her. Now she is gone from my life, but my children from her will always be part of me. I will try to raise them as best as I can."

"What if some day some guard comes and announces that you have been hacked down by someone close to you?"

"That is part of the dangerous world of being an Emperor. Whatever will be, will be; it will happen as God wills it. Life has risks and you must take some risks yourself."

He kissed her again on the forehead and went out.

The next day, Ingerina decided with the palace staff to move her children and her child supporting maids to the next quarters. She only kept Anna as her own chamber maid.

Basil found out about the rearrangement and that night he took his bath in the Palace baths and entered her chamber dressed in his night silk tunic, while a custodian carried the rest of his clothes.

After the custodian left the clothes on a chair, he went out and Basil locked the door. He found Ingerina lying in her bed, with her chamber maid sleeping not far away. They were both awake but pretended to sleep. He smiled, lifted the covers on Ingerina's bed and placed his body next to Ingerina's without showing any intent of sexual advances. Ingerina opened her eyes and was wondering what is going to happen next. The same thoughts passed by the chamber maid's mind, as she turned and saw Basil being still in the dim light of the oil lantern. The two women stayed awake for quite a while, until they realized that Basil was fully asleep, breathing heavily. It seemed that Basil was in deep sleep.

Anna was the first to wake up the following morning. She sat on her bed, stretched her arms yawning and stared at the bed of her mistress. Ingerina was still asleep and so was Basil, each to their side of the bed. Anna got up and walked to Ingerina's side and put her palm on her shoulder. Slowly Ingerina woke up, looked at Anna and started to get up, when the reassuring smile of Anna, with a finger indicating to be quiet stopped her from getting up. She then listened to Basil's breathing next to her.

Slowly she lifted the covers of her bed and got up. She and Anna walked to Anna's bed where they sat, wrapped with Anna's covers, staring at Basil who was still sleeping.

"How was it, last night?" asked Anna. "I did not hear any commotion."

 STAVROS BOINODIRIS PHD

"Nothing happened," replied Ingerina. "He just plopped himself next to me and went to sleep."

The two women sat there. They were silent for a few minutes, until they heard a knock at the door. Anna immediately rose and unlocked it, finding Symbatius.

"Please tell Basil to meet me in the conference room. We have to meet with some representatives."

Anna bowed. Symbatius looked inside, with Basil in bed and Ingerina in the chamber maid's bed and laughingly turned around and went down the corridor.

Anna proceeded close to Basil and after kneeling she whispered:

"Your Highness, Symbatius was here. He asked me to tell you to meet him in the conference room."

Basil's eyes opened slowly. He looked at the maiden and yawned. He tossed his covers and looked around. Seeing Ingerina at Anna's bed he smiled.

He proceeded to undress in front of the women, taking off his silk night gown. His body was solid and stocky, with plenty of hair on his chest, matching that of his beard and groin. He was of an average height and his stocky heavy built muscles made him look like some statues of Hercules. With help from Anna he started to put on his Palace uniform, starting with his long cotton chiton, covered by the highly decorated chlamys. Anna then helped him with his foot wrappers, to keep his feet warm. Finally, he put on his sandals, tied around the calf.

As he stood up, all dressed up, he walked to Ingerina, kissed her on the forehead and then proceeded to the door.

"You must wonder my sweet wife," said Basil with a smile, "why I have not laid a hand on you last night. It is not because I did not crave for your beautiful, tender and warm body. No! I vowed though to respect your feelings. I will not touch you… not until you want me to do so and you are ready for me. You must lay a hand on me first, before I satisfy my craving for you."

Basil went out of the door, with both Anna and Ingerina staring at each other dumbfounded.

"What did he mean by that?" asked Ingerina, turning to Anna.

"He means to leave the next move up to you, my mistress. How do you feel about that?"

"I do not know this man," said Ingerina. "He is full of surprises. He divorces his wife with children, marries me for show, to bring me closer to my lover, kills my lover and father of my children and now lets me decide whether I want to make love to him, to have more children by him. Don't you see that something is wrong with all this?"

Anna pondered for a while. She picked up the usual clothes for Ingerina and she started dressing her up.

"I don't know," she replied after a few seconds. "Things may have gone wrong in the past because of reasons beyond the control of you or Basil. Maybe Basil is trying, in his way to correct what was awfully wrong up to now. Did you think that things were fine while Michael was alive?"

"Are you crazy?" said Ingerina with a loud, agitated voice. "I don't know how in the name of Heavens I ended up in the middle of this crazy family. You know very well Anna that I was barely fifteen when my widowed mother handed me over to Michael, knowing very well that Michael's mother hated our Martinakios family for being iconoclastic. What did I know about all the devious schemes for power that were waiting for me? Assassinations, one after the other, make belief weddings and all sorts of hidden dangers for me and my children followed one after the other. Can anybody straighten up this mess now?"

"Maybe he thinks that he can," said Anna with a calming voice. "Maybe he can fix the mess by being honorable, open and without any predisposed past biases and self-interests. Maybe he can fix it by starting to focus on improving the life of the people around him. We can only hope."

Anna picked up her own robe and put it on, on top of her cotton night dress.

"We will see," said Ingerina, as she walked towards the door. "I will start by focusing on my children next door. Are you coming?"

Anna followed Ingerina out of their chambers to the nursery next door. They entered the room trying to be quiet, so that they do not wake up any sleeping children. Unfortunately, the door to the nursery was somewhat squeaky, forcing Anna to open it very slowly.

# Palace Restructure (Great Palace, Constantinople, August 12, 869 AD)

A squeaky noise woke up Anna. She raised her head and realized that the noise was coming from Ingerina's bed. The squeak then turned into a louder creak, accompanied by gasps and pants. She sat on her bed and peeked across the dimly lit room, where she saw two bodies engaged in love making. It seems that Basil was lying down, having Ingerina riding him, while he was caressing her breasts. After several minutes of moaning and gasping, the couple stopped, and all was quiet.

*"I guess that Ingerina made her move,"* Anna thought as she plopped down to resume her sleep.

In the morning, Anna woke up first and helped Ingerina wash up on a basin. Then, Basil woke up and she helped him get dressed up. As Basil was putting his sandals on, he turned to an already dressed Ingerina.

"Eudokia, if you want to attend our staff meeting at the conference room, I would love to have you there. Just attend and listen to what is being discussed. We must decide how to approach the Papal delegates in fixing the problem of Church jurisdiction between East and West. We will start in two hours."

"How do you want me to get dressed Basil?" asked Ingerina.

"Why are you asking an oaf of an Armenian how to get dressed? Put something nice on and come on over. I am sure that even if you had a burlap sack on, you would dazzle them senseless."

The two women could not control their laughter. They were still smiling as Basil went out on the corridor, heading towards the kitchen for some breakfast. He was ravenously hungry. He found an old cook in his fifties, named Tryphon Psellus, sitting on a bench giving directions to a younger man to prepare vegetables for lunch.

"I will get your breakfast, Your Highness," said Tryphon getting up, as

Basil sat on the bench, right across from him. Tryphon went straight to the pantry, got a big platter, and filled it up with fresh bread, straight out of the oven, butter, honey and strained yogurt. He laid the platter in front of Basil and then went on the stove, where goat's milk was getting boiled and poured a ladle's worth onto a clay cup, presenting it to Basil. These two knew each other and treated each other with familiarity.

Tryphon had come to Constantinople from Amorium. He was a soldier under Theophilos, Michael's father. When the Saracens attacked Amorium, he was with the imperial troops at Dazimon, where the Byzantines lost the battle. This led to the destruction of Ankara and Amorium with many inhabitants being martyred by the Saracens. In trying to find what happened to his family, Tryphon Psellus ended up with the rest of the retreating army and the refugees from the East in Constantinople. Being a good food scavenger and procurer for the army, he was assigned as a cook to the palace by Theophilos. He was good in his job and the subsequent palace administrators not only kept him at his post but facilitated for his family to find quarters there. There, he married a woman chambermaid from Syracuse, Italy, named Marina, who, like him was also a refugee. Saracens from Spain had attacked her city in Italy. They had one son. His name was Chariton. Chariton got also a good education because of his father's connections with Palace personnel. When Chariton graduated from Magnaura, Bardas assigned him as a palace Latin instructor. Michael and Basil were very familiar with Tryphon's family, because they took good care of them when they came drunk back from the hippodrome.

"Tryphon," said Basil. "Make two more platters like this with milk and send them to my wife's room. Also, see if you can find some roses from the gardens and send them there too, with my compliments."

Tryphon bowed and went in the kitchen to muster more help for the task at hand.

Basil finished his breakfast and headed to the conference room.

The breakfast arrived at Ingerina's chambers as planned. Two young men laid two platters on a table and two bunches of roses on Ingerina's bed.

After the men departed, Anna turned to Ingerina smiling.

"You did very well last night Your Highness."

Both women started giggling.

Ingerina timed herself and entered the conference room while everyone was seated. She came in with Anna, who remained outside the door, where two guards were posted for security. She wore a white Greek stola, decorated with golden Greek-style embroidery. On top of that she had a purple paludamentum, also embroidered in blue and gold Greek style trimming. She also wore the imperial diadem, decorated in gold, pearls and emeralds.

As the staff saw her, they stood up, including Basil. Ingerina proceeded and sat next to Basil. Basil sat next and waved to the rest to be seated.

"We will resume where we left from last meeting," said Basil. "We know that Pope Hadrian will be sending us his emissaries this fall to the Council that we will hold here. I do not know how much enmity he bears on Photius, but I expect that he would insist on his excommunication from the Church."

"What does this imply?" said Symbatius. "Is this excommunication based on canons that we know, or those that the Popes apply in their domain?"

"In their domain," said a bishop sitting next to Basil "excommunicating Photius would be a formal act of public humiliation. It is sometimes accompanied by a ceremony wherein a bell is tolled, like it is done when someone dies. Also, the Book of the Gospels is closed, and candles are being snuffed out. This type of humiliation is called by the people as *condemnation with bell, book, and candle*. In order for the excommunication to be resolved, a declaration of repentance is necessary. This involves a profession of the Creed and an Act of Faith, or renewal of obedience by the excommunicated person. It also involves a lifting of the censure by an assigned priest or bishop empowered to do this. The absolution can be in the internal forum only, but in the case of Photius I believe they would insist on a public forum, especially since they may consider him as unrepentant."

"Who assigns the priest or bishop that has the power to resolve the excommunication?" asked Basil.

"In the case of Photius, it would be the Pope himself."

"What if we try to appease the Pope but do it with our canon laws?" asked Basil.

"Our canon defines two excommunications," said the bishop "a minor and major excommunication. Just like in the Latin canon, those on whom minor excommunication has been imposed are excluded from receiving the Eucharist and can also be excluded from participating in the Divine Liturgy. They can even be excluded from entering a church when divine worship is being celebrated there. The decree of excommunication must indicate the precise effect of the excommunication and, if required, its duration. Those under major excommunication are in addition forbidden to receive not only the Eucharist but also the other sacraments, to administer sacraments, to exercise any ecclesiastical offices, ministries, or functions whatsoever. Any such exercise by the excommunicated person is null and void. They are to be removed from participation in the Divine Liturgy and any public celebrations of divine worship. They are forbidden to make use of any privileges granted to them and cannot be given any dignity, office, ministry, or function in the Church. They also cannot receive any pension or emoluments associated with these dignities and they are deprived of the right to vote or to be elected."

Basil looked at his councilors in thought. "If we allow the Latin canon in our Church, it would mean that they can control us as well. What I do not like is that every time they excommunicate someone, they condemn him publicly and assign the jailer priest or bishop to decide whether and when to release him."

"What are you driving at Basil?" said Symbatius.

"Photius caused a split in our church," said Basil, "but he did it for political reasons, looking after the interests of our people. He is well educated and capable. I do not want to destroy him. In fact, I want him to work for me, sometime soon. So, in the proceedings of his excommunication I want to allow him to speak on his own defense."

Basil took a deep breath before he started talking again.

"On the other hand, I want to mend any differences we have with the Pope. Our people get very ornery when priests stir them up with fanatical sermons about another part of the same Church of our Lord Christ. Our people are simple, illiterate and easily manipulated into all sorts of acts of violence. Any priest that wants to win the souls and minds of our peasants would be tempted to exaggerate the benefits of his church in demeaning the church of his neighboring priest. I would very much like to have all our priests, reporting to Rome or Constantinople work jointly together to bring into the fold of Christianity all those idolatry worshiping tribes and villages that are stranded all around us."

"If that is what you want," said Symbatius "we must take control of the Council. That means that we must insist that they cannot preside on the Council, as they are assuming that they will do up to now. We must also

     STAVROS BOINODIRIS PHD

insist that the primary article of this Council, namely the excommunication of Photius would be executed based on our own Byzantine cannon law, rather than the Latin one. Who do you think is the right person to preside?"

"I will preside on the Council," said Basil. "I have to, in order to impress upon the papal representatives that they cannot escalate their demands anywhere higher. I would also need some help from Baanes, who will represent me in the day-to-day work of the Council."

"Does anyone have any more comments, or suggestions?" asked Symbatius.

The participants were silent.

"Well, I do," said Basil standing up. "I suggest that we all go for a stroll to the gardens and then go to the Palace kitchen and have lunch."

Everyone smiled and followed the Emperor, who took Ingerina's hand and walked out towards the palace gardens.

# Change of Rules (Constantinople, November 5, 869 AD)

The Palace gardens were without foliage this day in November and a cold northern breeze was blowing from the Black Sea through the bare branches. Photius walked with Theodore Santabarenos, one of his trusted followers towards the Church Council under the canopy of trees, huddled in heave, caped monk robes.

"I don't know how Pope Hadrian will take all this," said Theodore. "Ever since Pope Nicholas died two years ago, God Forgive his soul, Basil took you out, put Ignatius in your place and made all sorts of friendly overtures to the new Pope, which could be interpreted as a wish to heal the schism between the Pope and the Eastern Orthodox Church. Then Basil invites the Papal delegates to a Church Council here. The Pope accepts, hoping that his delegates would preside at the Council. Then, when the delegates arrive last month, they discover that Basil was not quite the lamb that they thought they had to deal with. They find out that Basil himself was planning to preside all along, selecting as the co-chairman one of his own men, Baanes. Then, when the Papal delegates came to the discussion of what to do with you, and they insisted on an immediate condemnation, without hearing, Basil cut them off. He insisted that you stand before them and speak in your own defense. Why did he do that?"

"I am sure that he had good reasons."

"You appeared, but you refused to say a word. Why?"

"Every word I would have said would have been used against me in that hostile environment," replied Photius.

The two men climbed up the marble steps of the Palace, where the Council was meeting. They entered and sat in the chairs assigned for the accused. Soon, all the delegates were seated. Then a trumpet was heard, and Basil made his appearance. Everyone stood up. He sat on the presidium

　　　STAVROS BOINODIRIS PHD

and waved his hands for all to be seated. The room was lit by light coming through the windows, but since it was a cloudy day, everything was dimly shown.

"The accused Photius is asked to rise," declared Basil.

Photius rose. Basil opened a small scroll and after glancing at it spoke.

"This Ecclesiastical Council has found you guilty of heretical thoughts, leading to acts that led to the schism of the Church of our Lord Jesus Christ. Therefore you are excluded from receiving the Eucharist and any other sacraments and from participating in the Divine Liturgy. You are also excluded from entering a church when divine worship is being celebrated there. You are forbidden to exercise any ecclesiastical offices, ministries, or functions whatsoever, and any such exercise by them is null and void. You cannot receive any compensation associated with your previous ecclesiastical post and you are deprived of the right to vote or to be elected. You are to be removed from participation in the Divine Liturgy and any public celebrations of divine worship. This decree of excommunication will be upheld without any means of appeal, until it is revoked. Therefore, you are expelled from the bosom of the one and only Church of Christ and we consider you anathema in the name of the Father, the Son and the Holy Spirit. Amen."

"Amen," the Council members repeated in unison.

The whole council room went quiet, everyone averting their eyes from Photius.

Basil then pointed to two Imperial guards. The guards went and escorted Photius and Theodore outside the building.

"What happens now?" Theodore asked.

"Absolutely nothing," said Photius. "Basil played his hand well. Byzantine and not Papal legal procedures were observed in every detail, leaving me no grounds on which to appeal. Also, he and not the Papal delegates delivered the verdict."

"I noticed," said Theodore. Both men walked quietly until Theodore changed the subject.

"What about Cyril and Methodius? What is to be done with their endeavors now that you are out?"

"Cyril and Methodius will be fine," said Photius. "I received a message that they are in Rome. It seems that the work they did in Moravia was found to be of value not only to our Church, but also to the Popes. I am very proud of them and the people at the Magnaura University that provided support for them. They wrote the first Slavic Civil Code, which was used in Great Moravia. Even the Roman clergy approved their work. They also translated portions of the Bible into Slavic. They started with the New Testament and the Psalms. These books seem to have been the first, followed by parts of the Old Testament. They also translated the liturgy, mostly from Greek, but also from Latin, with authorization from Rome."

"Are they now working for the Pope?"

"They are working for the Church of Christ. They were invited by Pope Nicholas to Rome. When he passed away, Pope Hadrian welcomed them there to congratulate them by formally authorizing the use of the new Slavic liturgy. The Pope himself ordained Methodius into priesthood. He, together with five more Slavs were made into priests and deacons. Unfortunately, Cyril died in Rome on February 14, after he decided to become a monk in Rome because of his deteriorating health. It seems that after all these years of tromping around the Balkans, Crimea and other places his body gave up."

"God forgive all his sins," said Theodore.

"God and all the Slavs will remember these brothers," said Photius. "All they cared about was to disseminate their knowledge to those that desperately could use it. They did not care whom they were talking to, or which sect they belonged. So, for them, there was only one Church, and Pope, or Patriarch should both join forces to its growth and spiritual enrichment. In fact, do you know what Cyril's first mission was?"

"No."

"Since Cyril knew Arabic and Hebrew, his first mission was to the Moslem leader Caliph Al Mutawakkil. He went there on a state mission to discuss with Arab theologians the principle of Holy Trinity, with the hope of closing the gap between Moslems and Christians. People like him are rare. They have ambition and the power to change things, power that emanates out of their thirst for understanding other cultures in the hope of uniting humanity."

Theodore shook his head affirmatively. The two men continued to walk, huddled in their robes, while the wind was whistling in the trees above. Finally, cold rain started coming down on them, turning into sleet.

"Let's find a shelter from this cold rain," said Photius. "I cannot stand it anymore."

# The New Co-Emperor (Imperial Palace, Constantinople, August, 869 AD)

"I cannot stand it anymore," yelled Ingerina. "You cannot have your ex-wife in the same house with me, your legal wife. Even Michael did not turn this palace into a harem."

Basil was at a loss. He wanted his eldest son, Constantine next to him, but he also did not want to upset Ingerina.

"I will talk to Maria," he responded. "I need to have access to my son and heir so that I can be assured that he succeeds me. There must be a smooth transition of government. He needs training from a young age, so that he can take over when time comes. That requires the best teachers and military trainers that I can bring in this palace."

"For God's sake, Basil, the child is only four years old. Why are you rushing things up? Let him grow up a bit."

"I need him now," responded Basil emphatically. "I have a problem with public image. Photius and Pope Nicholas have created a situation that split our Church in two. Meanwhile, the Saracens are ravaging Italy. The western Emperor in Italy, instead of fighting with us against them, he sees us as enemies. I need him as an ally. He has a daughter. I want my son to be promised to marry his daughter. That way we open up the road for the unification of the two Empires and the joint effort to expel the Saracens from Italy."

"How old is this Italian daughter of Louis?" asked Ingerina.

"I don't know," responded Basil. "Someone said that she is seventeen, but it does not matter. The point is that the marriage constitutes a political tool for an alliance."

Basil paused before continuing.

"You may think that I am acting in a selfish manner, but unlike my predecessor, I am dedicated to the interest of this Empire. I am willing to sacrifice the happiness of myself, my wife and my family to achieve that interest. So, when you come to me and ask me to quell your jealousy about my ex-wife and my son, I like you to think twice."

"Basil, this is not fair for me, your sons and your whole family," responded Ingerina.

"I know," said Basil. "But being Emperor has responsibilities that sometimes require unfair treatment of some people, especially those close to the Emperor. Yet, I will talk to Maria. Maybe I can persuade her to let go of her son."

"Then what happens? Her son becomes an emperor and kills or castrates my sons. Is that what you have in mind?" Ingerina was yelling at the top of her voice and was flustered red.

"What did you expect my sweetheart?" responded Basil. "That is the life your mother and Bardas chose for you when they brought you to the Palace. You have all the amenities in the Palace, but you have limitations on your freedom and that of your offspring. Yet, I would not despair if I was you. I need an heir. My son Constantine will be crowned as a co-Emperor and first in line to succeed me. But I want to have guarantees, that even if something happens to him, I will have a backup to fall on. So, nothing will happen to Leo or Stephen, if I see fit. Meanwhile, I set up the Patriarch tomorrow to crown Constantine as a co-Emperor. Yes, he is only four, but politics dictate that the people see him as my heir, and they perceive the Empire as stable. I will have all the teachers he needs in the Palace to keep him busy, so that he does not miss his mother. For my son's own good, I am considering sending her to live elsewhere."

Basil left the room, leaving Ingerina standing with her mouth open.

A short time later he was visiting Maria's quarters. He was telling his ex-wife the news. Next to her was the four-year old Constantine.

"Come to me Constantine," he told his son with a smile as he crouched down extending his hands for a hug.

"No; I don't want to leave my mommy," cried the boy.

After repeated attempts, Basil dropped his hands in frustration.

Maria stepped in. "You spent so much time away from us, that you know very little about children," she responded sharply but firmly. Then she lowered her voice, as she approached Basil. "I will bring him to the cathedral tomorrow for his coronation. If you insist to drag him by force, you will have a problematic son that hates you. The child needs some time to adjust. I promise that by next year, I will be out of the Palace, to the new place you set up for me."

Basil looked at Maria and rose up waving his hand. "That is fine by me. I will send some people to help you dress him up for tomorrow."

The next day, Maria led her four-year-old son, all dressed up in imperial regalia to be crowned as a co-Emperor by Patriarch Ignatius. Everyone was there. Basil sat next to his son. Ingerina sat next to him with her sons. Maria sat behind her son, calming the fidgety Constantine on his huge throne. The ceremony was typical, with the exception that Basil had to order a special gold crown that was suitable for the four-year old Constantine.

After the ceremony, Basil held a staff meeting, where a decision was made to send two emissaries to Louis, the Holy Roman Emperor to negotiate a marriage for his four-year old son with his daughter Ermengard, now seventeen years old. He did not know if this was plausible, but he had hopes of reunifying East and West politically and in affairs relating to the Christian Faith.

# Nicetas Ooryphas (Bari, Italy December, 869 AD)

Nicetas hoped that he had no adverse encounters from the Saracens, as he was heading to the beachhead outside of Bari. So far, these hopes were fulfilled. Nicetas' ships encountered no problems landing that morning. It was misty and damp, but the fog was moving away, as the winter sun was going up. He landed a short distance from the Bari city walls and could see the smoke of a few Saracen fires on top of the walls.

"Strange," he said to the officer next to him. "I do not see any smoke outside the walls."

He put that thought away. He immediately disembarked from his dromond and supervised the unloading of supplies and horses from the dromond holds, the cargo ships that accompanied the armored chelandia ships. As soon as the cavalry was in place, he gave orders to his infantry commanders to establish a fortified camp. Meanwhile, he rode towards the city with a detachment of his cavalry on a muddy path. He reached a short distance from the walls and saw not a living soul. He took his detachment around the city.

As he reached a clump of trees below a hill, he saw tents. He rode towards them, followed by his men. He saw no guards. He rode into the camp and went straight towards the largest tent. No one came out to challenge him. He pulled his sword out and cut the supporting ropes of the big tent, by riding all around it. His men looked at what was happening awestruck. The tent collapsed.

"What son of a whore did that?" yelled a voice inside the tent in a language somewhat different from the Latin that Nicetas was familiar with.

Several men came out of the collapsed tent with swords drawn and started yelling at Nicetas in a threatening manner. Several women also crawled out of the destroyed tent, yelling. Some men were naked above the waist. Others were trying to wrap themselves with skin or wool blankets. Nicetas noticed that most of the men and women were roaring drunk and their own yelling seemed to have given them a headache. Nicetas looked around to the rest of the tents. The same scene appeared there. Only a few men were alert enough to arm themselves against his cavalry fully armed with spears.

"Where is King Louis?" Nicetas yelled in Latin.

The men and women stopped their yelling.

"Where is your leader?" demanded Nicetas in Latin.

One of the men came forward. He spoke perfect Latin.

"I am Charles Martel, the commander of this post. Who are you?"

"I am commander Nicetas. I came by invitation, to provide support to the King of Franks, by order of Emperor Basil. He was supposed to be storming the walls of the city of Bari."

"We are the Franks you seek, and you are late."

Nicetas started laughing.

"It would take a lot of men to storm Bari. From what I see in your numbers and your disposition you could not storm an outhouse, even if you were sober. I could have cut you down to pieces with this troop alone. All the Saracens had to do is wake up and mow you down like weeds."

The Frank commander turned and looked at his men.

"We are here just to observe the city. On the other side of the city, another garrison led by Prince Adelchis is also on watch. We do not expect any problems from the Saracens. Emperor Louis is in the neighboring town at his winter quarters. He waited here until last week for you, but you were late."

"I came here as soon as our ships were ready. Ship preparation and weather conditions cannot be predicted accurately. We are ready to assist your Emperor in taking this city. I want you to take me to him."

The commander turned around and ordered six of his men to round up their horses that were grazing in the clump of trees. The seven Franks mounted their horses and went ahead. Nicetas and his men followed them. Behind them, the remaining Franks went to work, repairing the damage that Nicetas made on the tent. They were all yelling obscenities, raising their fists at the departing Byzantines.

"How many soldiers does your King have here?" asked Nicetas as he was riding next to the Frank commander.

"The Holy Roman Emperor has a few hundred. There are more, spread out in other towns in the area."

Nicetas was getting upset. *Why did this idiot invite us here in the middle of the winter all the way from Constantinople? To hold his hand while he is having good time at his winter quarters with the Italian whores of the region?* he thought to himself.

By the time they reached their intended town, the sun was shining brightly. Nicetas noticed that the town had only a few guards at the main entrance. The leading Franks took him towards a large house, probably commandeered by Louis. Most of the other houses were small, with pointed slate roofs, that the natives called trulli. Several Frank soldiers were moving around the town, mingling with the natives who spoke both, Latin and Greek.

*"There is no semblance of a Frank army,"* Nicetas thought. Most of the Franks were having a good time looting from the locals who were trying to scrounge some vegetables from their own gardens. A local woman was yelling at one of them as he came out of a door. The sound of a pot crushing against the door behind him showed how annoyed the woman was with the intruder. Two Frank soldiers were in a back yard chasing a pig, one of them with a dagger drawn. A little girl was crying, pleading with them to leave the animal alone. Another Frank was in all fours trying to fetch eggs from a chicken coup. He and several other Franks raised their heads, watching the riders go by, as they approached the large house.

The Frank riders stopped and dismounted. Their commander went in, while Nicetas and his men stayed mounted on their horses.

Shortly, the commander came out with a man, strangely dressed. The man had a yellow wool top above the waist, and he wore red wool stockings, pulled over his leather trousers. His leather sandals were strapped around the red stockings, all the way to his knees.

"Commander Nicetas, this is the Holy Roman Emperor Louis," said the Frank commander.

Nicetas looked at the man in front of him. Unimpressed, he did not know whether to start laughing, or to step down and bow at him.

"Are you Nicetas?" asked Louis.

 STAVROS BOINODIRIS PHD

"I am," said Nicetas. "I came upon request of Emperor Basil to help the King of Franks to take the city of Bari."

"I am the Holy Roman Emperor," said Louis. "Get off your horse! This is an order."

Nicetas became red with anger.

"I am not getting off my horse and I am not going to order my men to submit themselves under a non-existent command that endangers their lives for nothing. After I landed, all I found was a handful of whoring, roaring drunks that even the Saracens would not stoop down to bother with. After I woke them up from their stupor, I managed to persuade their leader to bring me here, only to find out that the King of Franks had not enough men to encircle the city, even if they were one hundred paces one from another. I have orders for support, but also to avert any operation that leads to our suicide."

It was now the Holy Roman Emperor's turn to be angry. He started spouting obscenities in French that Nicetas could not understand. He understood that they were obscenities only from the body language of Louis and his men, who chimed in laughing. Then Charles Martel said in Latin:

"Who do you think you are, you… Greek shit?"

Nicetas heeled his horse around. He took another look at the disorganized army and put his horse at a gallop.

"I am not going to waste my time with you," he said to the Franks. "Back to the ships," he ordered to his men. "We came here for nothing. We are going home."

As he was riding back, Nicetas was furious with his own behavior. *"I could have been somewhat more diplomatic. Speak when you are angry, and you will make the best speech you will ever regret, you idiot,"* he thought to himself. Nicetas, now angry with himself spurred his horse to go faster towards his ships.

# The Schism (St. Sophia,
March 4, 870AD)

Christopher, Basil's son in law spurred his horse towards Aghia Sophia, to be on time. He was not there only for the ceremony of Bulgarian consecrations, but also because Basil ordered him there for a meeting. Christopher dismounted, giving his horse to an attendant and entered the cathedral.

He found Emperor Basil sitting in his Imperial throne, with a pregnant Ingerina next to him. Ingerina was expecting her third child, the first with Basil. The congregation was watching the ceremony of the consecration of the Archbishop of Bulgaria by Patriarch Ignatius, which had just started.

When the ceremony was completed, Basil and Ingerina exited, while Ignatius continued with the consecration of several Bulgarian bishops. Christopher followed Basil, who signaled to Christopher to join them.

Basil and Ingerina got into an Imperial coach, asking for both, Symbatius and Christopher to join them.

"I don't think that you planned all this Basil, did you?" Christopher asked.

"No," replied Basil.

"We get what the Omnipotent brings on us," said Symbatius.

"I was trying to get in good terms with Pope Hadrian," said Basil. "I was even ready to give up churches in Bulgaria for Italian holdings. Then I find out that the King of Bulgaria, Boris became dissatisfied with the treatment he received from the Pope. Although he did not like Photius, because he refused him a Bulgar Patriarch, he was even more disappointed with the Pope, who not only refused him to have a Patriarch, but also refused him an archbishop. Meanwhile, his attempt to convert the Bulgars to Christianity almost cost him his throne, because some local boyars rebelled. So, when I asked the Patriarchs of Alexandria, Antioch and Jerusalem if they were ready to outbid the Pope, they agreed."

     STAVROS BOINODIRIS PHD

"It is amazing," said Christopher with a smirk in his face. "The whole affair resembles an auction where the souls of future Christians are sold to the highest bidder."

"Exactly," replied Basil. "Of course, the two Papal delegates that were here protested violently. From what I heard, they became so frustrated that they left for Rome in a hurry, to bring to the Pope the news of the loss of Bulgaria to the Eastern Churches. Nothing went right for them. From what I heard, their ship was attacked on the way by pirates. I also heard that the pirates are holding them as hostages. So, Boris got his autonomous Archbishop, but under the authority of the Patriarch of Constantinople."

"What about the Italian holdings?" Christopher asked.

"Nothing happened there. Last month I received a fuming letter from the Emperor of the West Louis. He claimed that he was insulted by Nicetas, after their encounter outside of Bari. It seems that Louis wants to be called Emperor of the Romans, instead of Emperor of the Franks. He claims as his possession all southern Italy, even though the Saracens still occupy places like Bari. Although my son was betrothed to his daughter Ermengard, after the visit of Nicetas the betrothal was annulled. He thought that my son was too young for her. To appease him, I offered another option, namely, to engage my friend Symbatius here to his daughter Engelberga. He accepted and sent his daughter here to Ingerina's court."

At this time, Basil started smiling, and then broke in laughter. "It seems that Engelberga had a tough time with Symbatius' name. So, we offered to change it to Constantine."

Christopher started laughing as well. Basil looked at Christopher, getting more serious.

"From what I hear though from Ingerina, the girl does not like us. I believe that her heart is somewhere else."

"So be it," replied Symbatius.

"Never mind Italy," Basil continued. "Christopher, you and I have some business in the East. We must prepare for a land expedition against the Saracens and the Paulicians. They both threaten this Empire. The Saracens are united under the banner of Prophet Mohammed. We have dealt with the Saracens in the past. On the other hand, we have the Paulicians, who are our own people. I am ashamed to say it since I am an Armenian. They are an Armenian Christian sect that does not adhere to our Orthodox faith and want to change it. After the iconoclasts lost, they joined forces with the Paulicians and captured several cities in the East. They maintain many Jewish traits. For example, they do not believe in the Holy Trinity and are avid iconoclasts. Their sect was named after a third century bishop of Antioch named Paul of Samosata. They are a major threat to the Empire because they want to enforce their beliefs by an armed rebellion."

Ingerina, who was listening to all this discussion decided to ask:

"How long are you expected to be gone husband? Will you be here to witness the birth of your child?"

"I hope to be here wife." Basil thought for a while. "But in case I cannot, and I have a son, I want you to name him Alexander."

"You promised me that my sons will be safe. You made Constantine a Co-Emperor. What would happen if something happens to him? Why can't you also make Leo a Co-Emperor, to assure that none else grabs that throne of yours?"

Basil looked at Ingerina with surprise, then turned and looked at both Christopher and Symbatius, searching silently for their opinion. They didn't seem to care.

"Good idea, wife," said Basil with a smile. He then turned to Symbatius: "Set things up! Tomorrow we will have young Leo crowned as a Co-Emperor, second in line to Constantine."

When the coach stopped at the Great Palace, Basil helped Ingerina out of the coach and handed her to Anna, her maiden that was waiting for them. When Ingerina was gone, he turned to his companions.

"Women!" he exclaimed. "They act like mother hens, wanting to protect the interests of their young ones." He shook his head with disbelief.

# Ignatius (Constantinople, May 5, 871 AD)

Chariton's father, old man Tryphon the cook shook his head with disbelief. "What do you know about Ignatius, son? This old man was something of a legend in his youth. I met Nicetas- that used to be his name before he became a monk- when he was a commander of the imperial guards. He was the son of Emperor Michael Rangabe and because of that he was forcibly castrated, to prevent him from seeking the throne. He survived all sorts of physical and spiritual ordeals."

"But father, he is an old man," said Chariton Psellus, the Latin instructor. "After all, he is a seventy-three years old man with all sorts of aches and pains in his body. Do you know the amount of work that needs his approval? Every day, missionaries send requests from every village and town in the Balkans for priests to be assigned, for churches to be erected and for liturgies, bibles and documents to be translated to their language. The seeds that Cyril and Methodius have planted in the Balkans are now growing faster by the day and the capacity of old Ignatius to coordinate harvesting all this bounty is beyond his capability."

"Then, why doesn't the University step in to help?"

"Because many people at Magnaura are previous students of Photius; they do not like Ignatius. Although Ignatius is now trying to support the vision that Photius had started, his students think of him as a non-visionary, stiff personality. I will admit that Ignatius works very hard; but he lacks the inspiring attitude that makes other people around him to work just as hard. I have been talking to some people at Magnaura and they think that I, being close to the Palace should talk to someone close to the Emperor, so that he knows what is going on."

"Why don't you talk to Symbatius next time he comes here?"

"That is a good idea father. I am glad that I talked to you."

"Good. Now I will need your help. I need to go to the market and get some supplies for the Emperor. Basil is going on an expedition and we are ordered to supply him with certain supplies for this trip. Can you hire a cart to do the hauling?"

"Of course; how big?"

"Big enough to feed twelve people for a month," replied Tryphon.

"Why twelve people?"

"Because that is the immediate support team of an Emperor," replied Tryphon. "They need these supplies tested and tried and brought over to the field from here. The rest of the troops will forage their food from the places that they will visit. But since that food can be scarce, or even poisoned, the Emperor and his staff must have a separate stash, carried over by boat and then cart and guarded continuously. That way they are protected from spies and infiltrators that seek to harm the soul and heart of the Byzantine army."

# Tephrike (Outside the City Walls, June 10, 872 AD)

The Byzantine army did not take long to surround the city of Tephrike.[7] The Armenian Paulician rebels that were raiding the area, all the way to Samsun were all forced to retreat inside this fortified city. The city was atop of a hill amidst a mountainous terrain. The leader of the Paulicians, Chrysocheirus fought a tough, hit and run battle, slowing the Byzantine army at every gulley and ridge, but Basil and his brother in-law Christopher knew the terrain and their techniques and anticipated their moves.

After a few days, the Byzantine army had built catapults from the local forests. Animals were confiscated and using oxen the machines were pulled up above the city fortifications. After that, Basil gave Christopher the task to direct the catapults and gave him the order for the bombardment to commence. Huge boulders were hurled at the walls of the city and the interior. It took several days of catapult bombardment and close watch by the surrounding army, until the city, now in ruins was running out of food. Well water was also scarce, since the boulders had destroyed most of the wells.

At this time, the gate opened, and an elder man appeared with a flag of truce. He approached the Byzantines. Basil signaled Christopher to stop the bombardment.

"I am Gregory," he said. "I want to negotiate terms to save the city from destruction. We are Christians too, and Christ would not want us to kill each other."

"You are a bunch of renegades, who went on a rampage looting and killing people," said Basil. "You defaced our Christian churches and killed our priests. I want you all to come out and swear that you will give up all

---

[7] Tephrike is today's Divrigi.

violent acts against any fellow Orthodox Christians. If you do that, all of you will be spared, except Chrysocheirus. Go back and tell that to your leaders."

The elderly man bowed. "Master Chrysocheirus is wounded by a boulder," he said. "He cannot move because a beam fell on his leg."

"Then, make a litter and carry him out!" said Basil. "You have one hour to comply, before the bombardment begins again."

It took close to an hour before the ragged citizens of Tephrike were piling out of the gate, getting searched by the Byzantines for any weapons and allowed to camp under the trees of a near-by forest, always under the eyes of Byzantine archers. Among them were many women and children, some in makeshift stretchers and hand-carts. Finally, the elderly man with the flag appeared, followed by two soldiers carrying a stretcher. Basil got on his horse and rode towards them, followed by two of his guards. He recognized Chrysocheirus, as he was lying down with a bandaged leg. Basil immediately stopped next to the stretcher.

"Put him down," he ordered. "Lay down your weapons."

The two soldiers complied.

At that moment, Basil dismounted. He took out his sword and pointed it to the two soldiers.

"You are my prisoners. If you behave, I will spare your lives. Otherwise..."

Suddenly he swung and hit the lying Chrysocheirus on the throat, killing him instantly. The helpless leader of the Paulician sect of Christians did not have time to react. His body was left there on top of the stretcher.

His guards tied the hands of Chrysocheirus' guards and led them to the forest where all the other citizens were gathered. Basil then turned to an officer.

"Search the city and bring a small detail to take this corpse and bury it in some remote location," he ordered.

The officer mounted on his horse and started shouting to his subordinates. They all had their orders to clean up this operation.

# Otranto (Fort of the City of Otranto, September, 873 AD)

Figure 4 Map of Byzantium during the Time of Basil I [8]

Nicetas Ooryphas had also his orders from Emperor Basil to clean up any Saracen presence in the Adriatic.

As he was entering the fort of Otranto with his troops after many days of siege, he was happy that the Saracens had decided to surrender. It was a tedious and lengthy operation with the limited Byzantine ships at his disposal.

His troops were rounding up the Saracen fighters and leading them to their ships. There, they were tied up in the hold of each ship and they were

---

[8] Licensed by Alamy Inc. Invoice number: IY01109046.

soon to be taken to Constantinople. The hard cases of these soldiers would face possible execution. Others would be released to farms and factories for servitude. Their families were taken separately to different ships that were destined to take them also into servitude in various Byzantine ports.

He not only had to deal with Saracens, but also had to chase and sink the numerous pirate ships that operated in the Adriatic Sea. After the papal legates to the Constantinople Council that excommunicated Photius were captured and stripped by pirates a few years earlier, the Pope blamed Basil for that. So, Basil's orders included continuous patrols along the Adriatic, to prevent such happenings.

Next to him, on a horse was the failed ruler of Benevento, a Prince, nonetheless. His name was Prince Adelchis of Benevento, a name that he had heard before, in Bari.

"What happened between you and the Holy Roman Emperor Louis?" asked Nicetas ironically.

Adelchis looked at Nicetas with a sour face.

"In spite of all the support I gave Louis, he came over to Benevento with his troops and tried to take it over from me. But he and his troops did not last long. I turned the tables on them, got them drunk and jailed them in my city. Instead of them eating me out of house and home, I took all that they had instead. Yet, after the Saracens landed with a big force, I was obliged to let them free, after he swore on a bible to never reenter Benevento with an army, or to take revenge on me or my people because of his jail term."

"Did he keep his oath?" asked Nicetas.

"That bastard is always full of tricks. Do you know what he did?"

Nicetas shrugged his shoulders.

"He went straight to Pope Hadrian on the 28th of May last year and the Pope released him from his oath. Can you believe that? How can anyone, including the Pope have such power, as to release someone who swears on a bible?"

Nicetas smiled. "That is unbelievable. So, did he come back to get you?"

"He did, but we found out about his intentions and stopped him. Nevertheless, we had some good people killed. That is why I sent an emissary to Emperor Basil and to you for help. Now that you and I are allies, I do not think that the bastard Louis will attack Benevento any time soon."

The two riders, leading a troop of cavalry reached a church in the middle of the city that the Saracens had converted to a mosque. They dismounted and walked inside to pray and thank God for their success in taking the city. As they climbed the steps to the church, Nicetas turned to Adelchis.

"Somehow I believe that we should stop fighting among ourselves and try to expel the Saracens out of Italy," said Nicetas with a smile.

# Magnaura Work (Constantinople, November 874 AD)

Photius walked into the University of Magnaura with a smile on his face. He found the events of the day ironic. He expected something was about to happen, but he never thought that Basil was as good as he proved to be.

While Cyril and Methodius had successes in the Balkans, they created an awful amount of work for Ignatius. First, they helped one of the Slav tribes to embrace Christianity. They found stiff Roman presence in Croatia, the northern end of the Dalmatian coast and in Moravia, but they worked their own deals with the Pope. But in Bulgaria, Serbia and Greece all the mountain tribes were slowly converting to Orthodoxy. What they found surprising was that besides the Pope, the hard-nosed Patriarch Ignatius also supported them in these regions. Despite his initial opposition to any enterprise that Photius initiated, when it came down to the interest of his Church, Ignatius encouraged the missionary work that Cyril and Methodius undertook. He encouraged it, even though he had difficulty managing it. He had to deal with enormous number of requests for establishing churches. Basil, with help from Symbatius saw the shortcomings of this elderly Patriarch and immediately realized that Ignatius could not handle all the administrative work required. He started helping him by promoting knowledgeable people to important administrative posts. But all these people had come out of the University of Magnaura and were close friends to Photius, or his students. But this was not enough to bring enough brainpower matching the task. So, one day, the frustrated Basil sends a message to Photius, requesting his presence to the Palace under guard.

"I want you to help the Patriarch," he said bluntly.

"How?" said Photius in a straight to the point manner.

"I want you to take charge of the University of Magnaura, where all educational and administrative support is provided for the leaders of the converted Slav and Bulgar tribes."

Photius smiled as he bowed.

"I will be honored Your Highness."

"That is fine. Now, what is this that I hear about you, conducting a genealogy research on me?"

"That is something that I bumped into by accident, Your Highness. I found a document that if true places your grandfather Maiktes to be a descendant of the Arsacid family of Armenia. As I am finding out, he was a descendant partly of ancient Parthian roots and partly that of Constantine the Great. We all know that Constantine was part Illyrian and part Greek. On the other hand, your mother, Pangalo's family, comes from a totally Greek background."

"That is very interesting, Photius. I want you to finish this work, write it and give me a copy for the imperial Library. All expenses for this work will be mine."

"It will be my privilege, Your Highness."

"Very good; I also have asked Patriarch Ignatius to resolve your excommunication publicly and he did so. As far as you are concerned, you are now a citizen without any restrictions and a public servant, in my service."

"Thank you, Your Highness."

"Now that you work for me, I want you to think about solving some problems of mine. Hire all the people you may need and see if in Magnaura you can come up with some solutions."

"Yes, Your Highness. Can you be more specific?"

"Our legal system does not serve us as it should, because it is too old. I am getting all sorts of complaints from my legal administrators that if they were to follow the guidelines placed on them by the Roman law that Justinian established, many cases would be unresolved and end up here for imperial arbitration. We need to upgrade our laws and to define the role of each branch of our society. We must define the role of the Emperor and the role of the Patriarch, so that each one knows what they can, or cannot do. I don't want to have a repeat of the past interferences, like those that incurred with previous Emperors and previous Patriarchs. Somehow, we need to have laws that can control citizens, senators, patriarchs and emperors. Maybe we can avoid governmental mismanagement, leading to discontent, violence and even assassinations. I don't want these to happen again in the future."

"That is a very noble objective, Your Highness. It is also a monumental task that I hope I can execute in my lifetime. I can promise you now that I will think upon it, discuss it with some key people and come back to you with what it would take, in order to start such work."

"That is fine, Photius." Basil paused for a few seconds and then smiled. "I always admired you and your fellow Greek intellectuals, Photius. I admired your knowledge and your capability to think constructively on different subjects at the same time. I also was very envious of your education, since my parents did not think much about my education. I trust that you do not have any ill feelings against me, based on my past conduct."

"On the contrary, Highness; I believe you have acted with the best interest for Byzantium in mind. We are not Greek, Italian, or Armenian nowadays. We are all fellow Byzantines, working for a common cause, to improve the life of our people."

Basil's smile was erased, looked at his guest trying to see in Photius' eyes how sincere he was. He saw nothing, but a person of academia immersed in thoughts.

"I am glad to hear you say this," he said passively.

He clapped his hands and a guard appeared.

Photius immediately got up and exited under guard. He exited the Great Palace full of thoughts, walking very slowly.

    STAVROS BOINODIRIS PHD

# University at Magnaura Work (Magnaura, Constantinople, May 875 AD)

Chariton walked slowly along the Magnaura University[9] corridor, followed by the two women in nun's habit. The women had their hair covered totally with a large black scarf but conspicuously they covered part of their face. He discretely led them into an auditorium, where Photius was to lecture his students on the relationship between philosophy and theology. The classroom was full of men, some with a monk's habit on and a few women, most of them in a nun's habit.

Chariton led his guest nuns to the last seats of the auditorium, and he sat next to them.

"Do you think that anyone noticed us?" asked Ingerina, hiding her face behind the nun's facial cloth in a low voice.

"No Highness, rest at ease," responded Chariton, the Latin instructor of the Palace.

At that time, Photius walked in. The room of about fifty listeners went silent. The only thing you could hear was Photius's sandals on the marble and the rustle of his black tunic as it was rubbing against a book and some manuscripts under his arm.

---

[9] The University of the Palace of Magnaura was built by Emperor Theodosius at 425 AD. Although some scholars consider it the first University of the World, others content that it lacked the structure that later defined the institutional character of the universitas of Western Europe. Nevertheless, for all intents and purposes, Magnaura had 31 chairs for law, philosophy, medicine, arithmetic, geometry, astronomy, music, rhetoric and other subjects, 15 to Latin and 16 to Greek. The university existed until the 15th century. Byzantine society overall was an educated one. Primary education was widely available, sometimes even at village level and uniquely in that era for both sexes. Female participation in culture was high.

"I want to remind you," said Photius "about the Lexicon work that we have compiled and now is available in our library. This work is an extensive reference that helps us read old authors, whose language and vocabulary may be difficult to read. Reading these authors is very important in understanding how we, in Byzantium managed to transition from the philosophical base of ancient Greece to Christianity, carrying into it most of the great moral and constructive values that our ancestors, like Plato and Aristotle have left us as a legacy."

He paused for a few seconds, staring at his audience. He saw the nuns at the last row, and he recognized Ingerina's face. He had seen that face many times and he was certain that he was not mistaken. Then, he saw a student come in. The student was one of his own, a novice monk named Nicholas. He tried to find a seat and after looking at Ingerina, he sat next to her. Photius smiled and turned discretely his face to the student in the front row, so that he does not betray any of his thoughts. Photius was pleased to see members of the Imperial Court attending his classes, but seeing the Empress there was especially pleasing.

"We will continue on analyzing the theological work of Amphilochia, where we examine many difficult points in the Scripture. As we have mentioned before, there were hundreds of questions that were addressed to Amphilochius, archbishop of Cyzicus and this work contains the questions and the answers. Today we are at question two hundred thirty-four."

Photius proceeded, by reading from his book. Ingerina and Anna listened attentively behind the nun's habits until the lecture was over, one hour later. Everyone stood up as Photius exited the room and all the students followed in an orderly fashion.

Chariton and the two nuns exited the hall at Magnaura and proceeded to walk towards the Great Palace. Behind them there were several students, all exiting and dispersing to various directions. This was the case until they started reaching their destination and made a turn towards the Palace Gardens. As they were proceeding among the hedges, they noticed one student in a monk's habit with a hood drawn over his head. The student had quickened his pace and was closing in. Chariton was alarmed, thinking that they were discovered by someone who was after the Empress with bad intentions. He immediately turned around to face the monk, by grasping a small dagger he had around his belt. He was not fast enough. The monk

     STAVROS BOINODIRIS PHD

grabbed his arm and as he twisted it, forced him to drop the dagger on the gravel of the walk path. The monk picked the dagger.

"Take it easy compatriot," he said. "I am on your side."

"Who are you?" asked Chariton. "Why are you after us?"

"My name is Leo," said the monk as he came up examining the dagger, "Leo Choirosphaktes. I don't know for sure why the name Choirosphaktes,[10] but I guess that one of my ancestors was a pig butcher in the Peloponnese." Leo smiled slyly, and Chariton followed with a smile.

Leo then became serious. "I am also a student at Magnaura, but this time I was on a special duty, to protect you and the Empress." After extending his hand, he turned the dagger around and handed it to Chariton. "Here. Take your dagger back."

"To protect us…? On a special duty to whom…?"

"To Emperor Basil; I am a secret palace official, a mystikos. This is a confidential position that Emperor Basil has created to monitor what is going on, get information and provide it on an advisory basis to the Emperor." Chariton took the dagger and placed it back on his belt.

"Is my husband spying on us?" asked Ingerina.

"Not directly, Highness. He knows that you are attending lectures at Magnaura and he is very happy to see you doing it. What he wants to know is simply how Magnaura proceeds with his projects there. But he also asked me to secure your safety."

"You called me compatriot," asked Chariton. "How do you know about me and where do you come from?"

"You are Chariton Psellus, the Latin Instructor and the son of the palace cook Tryphon, from Amorium," said Leo smiling. "I know that you have a Greek background. By the way, I met one of your relatives from a Greek Island. His name was Constantine."

"I don't know any relatives of mine by that name," replied Chariton.

"Maybe you will meet him one day," said Leo smiling. "My family is also Greek and comes from the Peloponnese. My wife is of the Karbonopsina clan and part of the court."

"I think that I know your wife," said Anna. "She is related somehow to

---

[10] The word "choirosphaktes" in Greek comes from "choiros," meaning pig, and "sphaktes," meaning butcher.

the Zautses family. Why haven't you introduced yourself to us before the lecture?"

"I wanted to keep your attendance secret," said Leo smiling, "just like you did. Next time you see me there, make as if you don't know me."

Chariton nodded. Leo covered again his head with the hood and turned back towards Magnaura, waving at the trio.

"Where are you going now?" asked Chariton.

"Back to work," said Leo, as he turned around the hedges.

"What a strange fellow," said Chariton as he joined the two nuns heading towards the Great Palace entrance.

As Leo headed back, he noticed another young man, dressed in the habit of a novice monk that was following them. It was Nicholas. He went past him and as he made a turn, stopped and turned around. Leo watched him as he was staring at the women and Chariton, as they were entering the Great Palace.

# Ingerina's New Happiness (Great Palace, Constantinople, June, 876 AD)

Chariton entered the Great Palace and immediately after he started walking in the corridor, he encountered Symbatius.

"We have few young students from Bulgaria here," said Symbatius. "They are from elite families, sent to us by their families to get educated. I ask that you take them, find them quarters and give them instructions on where to meet for their food and education."

"Yes Sire."

From that moment on, Chariton knew that he was not free to escort Ingerina and Anna to Magnaura. So, he informed them.

"That is too bad," said Ingerina. "I wonder if we could venture there unescorted."

"I don't know," said Anna. "It may be dangerous."

"Well," said Ingerina, "I am not going the get confined in here and miss out from public life."

So, Ingerina continued to go to Magnaura with Anna, finding freedom of thought and spirit. Since Chariton was occupied, the two women went unescorted. In her newfound freedom, she noticed a novice monk who followed them, and one time got the nerve to sit next to them. The three struck a conversation before the appearance of Photius.

"My name is Nicholas," he said. "How do you like these lectures?"

"We certainly do," said Anna.

"It is a pleasure to see such beautiful women interested in philosophy," said Nicholas. "I adore Photius. I am one of his students. What are your names?"

"I am Anna," replied the maiden.

"And … I am Eudokia," replied Ingerina. "We work at the Great Palace."

At that time, Photius walked in and after seeing Ingerina he proceeded to his podium. First, he smiled, but for some reason, the smile was erased, as he placed his notes on the podium and stared at Nicholas.

The lecture was about the historian Diodorus Siculus. He was known for writing history between 60 and 30 BCE. As Photius explained, his Bibliotheca Historica was arranged in three parts. The first covers mythic history up to the destruction of Troy, arranged geographically, describing regions around the world from Egypt, India and Arabia to Greece and Europe. The second covers the Trojan War to the death of Alexander the Great. The third covers the period to about 60 BCE.[11]

After the lecture, the two women were escorted by Nicholas to the gates of the Great Palace, talking and occasionally laughing about the lectures, especially about Helen of Troy.

"Do you think that Paris did an unwise thing when he abducted Helen?" asked Ingerina.

"No," said Nicholas. "If Helen was as beautiful as you are my lady, he could not help himself. It is not lack of wisdom that led him to his act, but the unavoidable destiny of human attraction between two sexes."

"You should not have thoughts like that," said Anna. "Not if you want to wear the cassock of a monk."

"That is true my lady," replied Nicholas. "My parents made a vow, to give their son to the service of God, which I am forced to honor. But God constructed me in such a way that I cannot yet discipline my brain from thinking these things. I decided to honor my parents, but also to honor God, by allowing such thoughts, as long as I do not act on them."

The two women giggled. This interaction continued day after day between Eudokia Ingerina and Nicholas, with Anna watching them flirt with an uneasy feeling. One day Anna asked Ingerina:

"Why are you so forthcoming with this student monk?"

"I don't know," replied Ingerina. "For the first time, I feel free. I like this young man. I like his company and his jokes. He makes me feel young again."

"What about Basil?" Anna asked. "What if he finds out?"

"What about him?" Ingerina replied. "He has not come to my bed for

---

[11]  To Photius, we are indebted for almost all we possess today on documents such as these. Among these are of Ctesias, Memnon of Heraclea, Conon, the lost books of Diodorus Siculus, and the lost writings of Arrian.

months. Who knows with whom he sleeps these days? Anyway, it is not as if I am going to bed with Nicholas."

A day later the two women returned from Magnaura, escorted by Nicholas. He was jovial and flirted back to Eudokia, telling jokes and the two were laughing loudly and holding hands, as Anna walked behind them. As they made a turn around the corner of a building, they came upon three men. One of them was Symbatius, who saw them as they were laughing gaily. He did not say anything. Instead, he hid behind the other two, who were his aides, so that he was not recognized by Ingerina. Symbatius turned around the building and stopped.

"I want you to discreetly follow these two women and the man that passed us," he said to one of his aids. "Report to me all their activities."

"Yes Lord," replied the aide, as he turned back.

Symbatius continued with his other aide, not noticing a monk, who passed them by, following the aide. Under the monk's hood was Leo Choirosphaktes, who was under orders from Photius to watch over Ingerina and her recent free behavior with Nicholas.

A few days later, both Photius and Symbatius were getting a report.

"Ingerina acted as if she was in love with a young novice monk, named Nicholas."

# Ingerina in Trouble (Constantinople, Great Palace, July, 876 AD)

"Ingerina acted as if she was in love with a young novice monk, named Nicholas," said Symbatius to Basil, reporting what his aides witnessed.

"Do you think that she is serious about him?" asked Basil.

"I don't know Highness. What is though at stake is your public image. What if this affair became public knowledge?"

"You are right," said Basil. "An Emperor should not be having such a scandal. People must view the Emperor and his family as a stable pillar supporting the Empire."

"How do you want us to handle this?" asked Symbatius.

Basil thought for a few seconds.

"I want you to arrest both when they are exiting Magnaura, preferably when they act in a familiar manner. Take the monk to a prison cell and keep him there. Take Ingerina to her quarters and immediately let me know that you have done so. I will wait to hear from you."

"Yes Highness."

Symbatius immediately set up his people to spy on Ingerina.

A day later, Ingerina and Anna were exiting from Magnaura, again dressed in nun habits. In a usual manner, Nicholas, the novice monk was following them.

"You are following us like a happy puppy Nicholas," said Ingerina. "What is in your mind?"

"I am just enjoying the beauty of your company," my lady. "If only I was really a puppy and you could take me with you in your chambers."

Ingerina started giggling, but her giggle stopped when she saw Anna's face. Anna had seen two men, simply dressed, behind them listening to their conversation and as soon as Ingerina started to giggle, one man gave a peculiar signal to the other. A second later these men rushed and grabbed

Nicholas, dragging him away from the women. Anna gave a small shriek, but before she could react, another four men, dressed as Palace guards grabbed both women.

"Come with us ladies," said one of them, who seemed to be the officer. The two women were taken to Ingerina's Palace quarters and two guards were placed at the door.

"You are under house arrest ladies," said the officer, as he left.

"Why is Basil doing this to me?" asked Ingerina. "We did nothing wrong."

"I don't know Highness," replied Anna.

A few hours later the two women heard a noise at their door. A knock on the door made Anna rush there to open it. In front of her was Basil. She bowed.

"Wait for us outside Anna," said Basil. Anna complied. Basil closed the door and walked towards Ingerina.

"You have broken your promise to act the role of my wife," said Basil. "Your indiscreet behavior in toying with this novice monk cannot go unpunished."

"What did I do?"

"It is not what you did, but what the people that see you think," said Basil. "Don't try to excuse yourself. It will not work with me."

The frustrated Ingerina sat on the bed with an angry look.

"We arrested the novice monk named Nicholas. I just came from his prison cell."

"Please don't harm this young man," said Ingerina. "He did not do anything indiscreet. Have pity on him."

"I know," said Basil. "I will be very lenient with him, because he would have not gone courting indiscreetly my queen, unless my queen encouraged him. I asked him to choose between his life and tonsure. He chose tonsure."

Ingerina started crying.

"You will not be under house arrest, but from now on, you will be watched," said Basil. "In fact, you are free to visit your boyfriend at his monastery, after he is castrated. He can even visit you here. Together, you both can pray for God's and my forgiveness."

Basil then moved and grabbed Ingerina by the shoulders and shook her violently.

"You better become a faithful queen, if you want to secure your sons' future," said Basil with an angry voice. "That means that you better keep your mouth shut. You cannot disclose any of this to anyone, including Anna. As far as the rest of the world and the Palace are concerned, nothing happened. We are a happy couple, with excellent relationship."

Before Ingerina could react to what Basil had told her, Basil turned around and exited from her quarters.

Anna immediately entered Ingerina's quarters and found her crying.

"What is wrong Highness?"

"I cannot tell you Anna. I am sorry."

Anna could only guess, as she was trying to console her mistress.

That same night, a scared Nicholas was led from his prison to a doctor's home, where he was castrated. News of the castration was made public. Three weeks later he was elevated to the rank of a stavrophore, jumping over the rank of rassophore because he endured a tonsure.

After all that, Basil pretended publicly as if he was in good terms with Ingerina and tried to bury any scandal.

Meanwhile, Ingerina decided not to visit Photius' lectures and Photius noticed it. He immediately summoned Leo Choirosphaktes.

"Both, Ingerina and Anna are absent from my lectures Leo. They used to come often with a young novice called Nicholas. After I noticed their absence, this novice was abruptly tonsured. Find out what happened."

"Yes, I shall."

Leo started going often to the Palace kitchen, where he could talk to Palace personnel, fishing for news on the subject. A few days later, Leo managed to meet with Anna.

Anna told him what she knew. Leo reached the same conclusion as Anna.

"It seems that Basil disciplined his wife from any farther scandals," said Leo to Photius. "I suspect that the young novice was tonsured on his orders. From what I also found out is that Basil does not sleep with Ingerina, for some time now."

"Good work Leo. Now I want you to focus on the work at hand, between the Patriarchate and my task force at Magnaura."

# Shortcomings (Great Palace, Constantinople, August, 876 AD)

"I want to introduce you to Leo Choirosphaktes," said Basil, looking at his staff in front of him. "He has been acting as a liaison between the Patriarch and the task force at Magnaura."

Then he turned to Leo.

"Are you telling me that Photius has placed all his people behind the efforts of the Patriarch?"

"Yes Highness."

"Yet, Patriarch Ignatius complains to me that he still cannot cope with the bureaucracy involved in his office? Why is that?"

Leo Choirosphaktes pondered for a few seconds before answering.

"Your Highness, it is not as if Photius does not want to help. He sincerely does so. And, it is not that Patriarch Ignatius refuses his help. He is also willing to do the best he can to work with Photius' people. But because each one personality has followers that clashed in the past, their people do not work with each other very well. An envoy that comes from Bulgaria and needs documents that Magnaura can provide has to go first through some of Ignatius' bureaucrat, who hates the bureaucrat of Magnaura. They both are needed to cooperate fully in order to complete the work. So, he sends an inefficient underling who is not known at Magnaura to ask for the work to be done. This takes time and it is inefficient. When I try to find out who is holding up the process, they blame each other."

"I see," replied Basil. "Nevertheless, I must have this work done fast before I get more complaints from Serbia and Bulgaria, with threats that they will seek help from Rome. Are there any recommendations?"

"We must bring Photius and his people back as a Patriarch," said Symbatius. "We have placed quite a few of his people out in the country, as missionaries, but Ignatius still has his own people at the Patriarchate that cause the bottleneck. Yes, Ignatius has many followers that will be upset. But so, does Photius, except that Photius' followers are more intelligent and efficient."

"I do not want to sack Ignatius," replied Basil. "He is a frail old man and I do not expect him to last long in this job. What I could do though is to replace just about everyone at the Patriarchate by people from Magnaura, but in a manner that Ignatius either doesn't know, or does not care."

"I have some ideas on how to do this, Highness," said Leo. "One way to do this is through the infrastructure building that Your Highness has undertaken in the past few years. Magnaura is known for the artists and architects that are part of its staff. We can assign these people in the Patriarchate to deal with the repairs of Aghia Sophia, needing urgent repairs after the earthquake we had seven years ago. Also, we must repair the Church of the Holy Apostles that is even in worse shape. Ignatius would not object to replacing some of his people with people that have the skill to repair our churches."

"Excellent idea, Leo," said Basil. "You and Symbatius coordinate this, tactfully and silently with Photius;" Basil paused for a second. "Talking about Photius, what is happening with the legal work that I asked him to work on?"

"The last time I talked to Photius," replied Leo "he told me that he was deep in work on a mighty purification compendium, that he called *anacatharsis*."

"When he is done, I want a copy of his work. It may be a bit over my head, but with the help of Chariton Psellus and other Palace instructors, they can explain to me and make me understand the legal terms, and any intricacies that are involved in the write up."

"Photius anticipated that you may have some problems Highness," said Leo. "So, he talked to me about creating an easy-to-read handbook, named *Procheiron*. He said that that book would contain a resume of the most important and regularly applicable legislation."

"Great!" said Basil with a happy face, "I like the way Photius can anticipate me, but I dare say that I am also intimidated by him. He is a formidable ally, but he can be a formidable enemy as well, if he decides to work against us."

"I am certain Highness that Photius is totally dedicated in support of Byzantium," said Leo.

Basil looked at Leo smiling. "Fine; I am going to Ingerina's quarters for lunch. Ingerina is waiting for me."

Leo turned his face, hiding a smile. Basil was lying, and Leo knew it. Leo, with his discreet source of Anna knew that Basil had not seen Ingerina for the last month.

Basil dismissed the meeting and exited towards his office. Leo left the Palace and headed for Magnaura. As he was walking through the marble paved colonnade of the Great Palace, he saw several children playing in his path.

# Sibling Rivalry (Great Palace, Constantinople, January 8, 877 AD)

Figure 5 A boy playing with hoops, depicted in the 6th-century mosaics of the Great Palace of Constantinople [12]

The marble paved colonnade of the Great Palace was the driest when this day in January finally the sun appeared after several days of rain.

"Keep your wheel straight as you run," said Leo. "Let me show you how."

Leo held the metal hoop upright with his left hand, while holding a long stick with a "Y" shaped tip on the right, guiding the hoop by the two prongs of the "Y". Leo started running with it along the marble paved colonnade, followed by his younger brother Stephen. The colonnade was covered and

---

[12]  Licensed by Alamy Inc. Invoice number: IY01109048.

protected the pavement from the rain that had fallen the previous days and it was the driest. Stephen watched carefully his brother, as he took off and then positioned his own hoop and stick and started running. He managed to go only a few steps, before he lost control and the hoop rolled to the left and fell on the pavement.

At some distance, sitting at a bench under the colonnade was Chariton Psellus, watching the children. He was bundled up with his winter, woolen tunic, wearing also a wool cap and wool foot wraps under his sandals, to keep him warm. The children were also dressed in winter tunics and wool covered feet under their sandals. He and the children were on a recess, after the first day of school and he finally took them out after several days of rain. He was their Latin instructor. The children got their presents on New Year's Day from Saint Basil, according to their parents. In fact, Ingerina asked Chariton to purchase the hoops and sticks from a local wagon builder, who typically used these metal hoops to strengthen the wooden wheels of carts. Yet, during the holidays, the wheel builder became a toy maker. Typically, the wheel builder rolled his wide steel hoop, loop it, forged it to a weld, measuring it to cover a wheel. Then he heated it to expand and fit over the wooden wheel. Finally, he had to cool it over the wooden wheel. Instead of that, he skipped several steps to make it into a toy. The toy hoop was relatively thin, forged into a weld. He sold enough of them at a reasonable price, so that his hoops were popular among children in most well-to-do households. The hoops and driving sticks were usually placed on the fireplace with the name of the child on the night before Saint Basil's day on New Year's Eve.

Ingerina had placed these toys carefully near the fireplace for both her sons. Both, Leo and Stephen became very excited, wanting to try their hoops as soon as they could.

On the other Palace quarters, Basil asked that a different present be given to Constantine, his eldest son and Co-Emperor. He told Chariton that Leo Choirosphaktes would take care of that. Indeed, Leo came through with not only a hoop, but with a hoop that resembled a light wheel and had small, noise making cymbals around its rim, so that whenever it was rolled, it made enough noise for people to hear and get out of the way.

Chariton watched as Leo and Stephen went to the other side of the colonnade and got ready to get started their hoop rolling run towards him. He noticed then that a little girl of dark complexion, which he knew appeared behind them, watching the two boys. The girl was Zoe, the daughter of Stylianos Zautses a man of a military Armenian family. Chariton also held Latin classes for girls and the 12-year old Zoe was in one of those classes.

The two boys started their run and held their hoops upright for at least ten steps, when Chariton heard the jingle of the cymbals behind him. He turned and saw Constantine, rolling his heavier hoop at a much higher speed and heading against the two upcoming boys. Upon hearing the jingles, Stephen lost his concentration, dropping his hoop, which got tangled on his foot, causing him to fall flat on the pavement. Leo on the other hand was a bit more skillful. He veered off to the side, picked up his hoop and went behind a column, letting Constantine go past him, straight against the fallen Stephen. The jingling heavy hoop caught Stephen on the forehead, making the 10-year old to start crying.

Seeing what happened to his brother, Leo started running after Constantine, yelling and shaking his stick.

"You are worse than an animal. Why are you doing this to our brother?"

"Don't call me your brother. Neither you, nor he are my brothers," said Constantine turning towards Leo. "When you hear me coming, you better vanish from my sight, you worm."

Before Chariton could get up from his bench to go and stop them, Leo and Constantine were fighting using their "Y" shaped sticks as swords. It did not take long for the 12-year old Constantine, trained in battle by expert swordsmen to hit Leo on his stick-bearing arm and disarm him.

"Stop it right now," yelled Chariton. But before he could reach the boys, Constantine managed three or four more whacks on the hands and feet of Leo, who was now in tears from pain.

Chariton took the stick away from Constantine and after grabbing him from his belt he forcibly dragged him towards the interior of the Palace.

"Let me go," yelled Constantine as he was been dragged, fighting the Latin instructor. "I am the Co-Emperor."

"You may be the Co-Emperor, but I am your teacher and responsible for all students in my class," said Chariton.

"You are fired," yelled Constantine.

"Not today," yelled Chariton, "turning and slapping Constantine on his bottom." Maybe you can fire me tomorrow, when you get permission from your father."

     STAVROS BOINODIRIS PHD

Constantine stopped. He straightened himself and followed Chariton, who after seeing two guards he yelled at them.

"Come on over. He was involved in a fight with his siblings. Keep him here safe so that I can take care of the other two. Take him to the Emperor's office."

The guards lifted Constantine and took him inside. Leo rushed towards Leo and Stephen.

Meanwhile, Zoe had approached the fallen boys. She helped Leo get up, wiped his tears with a handkerchief and to Leo's surprise, she kissed him.

*"Who is this angel that God sent for me?"* Leo asked himself, as his heart was beating at a much faster rate. The dark haired, dark complexion Zoe was beautiful, as she smiled back, watching the boy admiring her in awe from top to bottom. The awe-struck Leo stood there, while his brother was bleeding and crying flat on the pavement. As Zoe turned towards Stephen, Leo shook his head, grabbed the handkerchief from Zoe and rushed towards his brother. He applied the handkerchief on his brother's bleeding head cut.

"Don't worry Stephen, you will be fine."

At that time Chariton had arrived. He lifted Stephen in his arms and started taking him inside the Palace.

"How are you Leo?" he asked. "Can you walk?"

"Yes, I can."

"Zoe, please help him."

Zoe had already her arms around Leo, helping him walk. To his eternal surprise, despite all the beating he had received, Leo felt no pain. He smiled back at Zoe and put his arm around her, following Chariton to the interior of the Palace.

After hearing the commotion, Ingerina came out in the corridor.

"What happened?" she asked Chariton.

"Not a big deal," said Chariton, trying to calm the upset mother after she saw Stephen with blood on his forehead. "The siblings had a fight."

"Did you do that to Stephen?" she asked sternly to Leo.

"No mother; It was Constantine. He hit Stephen and when I went to stop him, he hit me."

"Where is Constantine?" Ingerina inquired.

"Two guards took him in, to Basil's office," said Chariton.

Ingerina led Chariton and the two boys in her room, where her servants went to work on bandaging the wounds of Steven and placing some curing ointment on the bruised arm of Leo. Chariton proceeded to Basil's office, where the two guards brought Constantine. One of them opened the door for him. What he did not notice was that Zoe was a few steps behind him.

As he entered, he saw Basil sitting behind a large table, and his son standing. Basil pointed to a chair.

"Sit down Chariton," he commanded." My son says that you should be fired, because you did not obey his commands. What do you have to say for yourself?"

Meanwhile, Zoe looked at the two scary guards, who closed the door on her. She went around to another locked door of Basil's office. There were no guards there. She looked around and saw none in sight. Then she stuck her ear on the wood and tried to listen. She was curious to see what the Emperor is going to do to Constantine.

"Your Highness" said Chariton with a hint of a smile as he sat down, "your son may be a co-Emperor anywhere else, but whenever he is in my school and under my care, he is my student and nothing more. I had to save Leo and Stephen from his vicious and unprovoked attack against the two boys."

"I understand," said Basil. "Thank you. That is all Chariton. Now let me talk to my son."

Chariton got up and left.

Basil turned to his son. "Tell me Constantine, why do you hate your younger brothers?"

"They are not my brothers," yelled Constantine. "Why does everyone want these bastards to be my brothers when they are not?"

Basil got up with a stern look and towered over his son.

"I think that you deserve a good whipping boy. You should learn to respect your elders and not raise your voice to them, especially your father, who loves you. These children are your brothers because I adopted them as my own. Why is it that you cannot abide with my wishes?"

Constantine turned around, away from his father, plopped onto a chair and hid his face.

"I hate them," he whimpered. "I also hate you from taking my mother away from me. What is so special about this woman, their mother, so that you can kick my mother away from us?"

"Because it was my duty to do so," answered Basil. "It was also the honorable thing to do. I do not expect you to understand my motivation, but I always had the best intentions in mind for the good of our people."

"Well, I am one of those people too," replied Constantine with tears in his eyes.

"No! You are not. Don't forget, I made you a co-Emperor and prepared a throne for you. Why can't you accept that you have responsibilities to serve our people, no matter how much hardship these responsibilities impose on you?"

"I don't want those responsibilities," said Constantine. "I did not want to be engaged to marry some older Italian woman whose name I cannot pronounce. Thank God that the engagement went sour and I was freed. How could you do that to your own son, father? How could you? Don't you have any feelings? I have had it. I want out."

"There is no way out for you my son," said Basil with a thunderous voice. "Both, you and I have responsibilities to uphold, no matter how much we dislike them. Get it through your head. I am training you for this role and your only choice is to follow through. I have taken you on a white horse, dressed for battle to Asia with me and trained you to use your sword, spear and shield, so that you can fight your own battles when the time comes. Don't tell me now that you want out. The only way out for you is if you die."

Constantine turned and looked at his father with disbelief. Basil immediately after he blurted his last words realized and regretted what he had said. He grabbed his son, lifted him up and hugged him tightly.

"Do you really mean that father?" asked Constantine.

Basil did not answer. He let his son fall back on the chair and rushed out of his office without saying anything. As he turned the corner, he saw little Zoe at the door to his office.

"Hey you!" he yelled. "What are you doing there?"

"Nothing Your Majesty, I was just going to my mother."

"Whose child, are you?"

"I am a Zautses child," said Zoe meekly.

"Go home!"

He knew Stylianos Zautses well. He was one of his Armenian compatriots and member of the Palace guards. He helped him numerous times, including the time when he had to assassinate Michael. Basil shrugged his shoulders as the child ran away from him and proceeded to the office of Patriarch Ignatius.

# Photius' Return (Office of the Patriarch, Constantinople, November 7, 877 AD)

The office of the Patriarch was very busy that day. It was a little longer than two weeks since Patriarch Ignatius finally expired, and the Emperor Basil asked Photius to become a Patriarch for the second time. The ceremony did not take long to organize and execute. Photius was well liked by all the other Patriarchs and his nomination was welcomed. When someone asked if there was need for the Pope of Rome to recognize him, he shrugged his shoulders, not caring whether the Pope did, or did not.

This day was special, because visitors from all the regions that Photius was interfacing with at Magnaura University sent their representatives to him for additional work requests, now that he was a Patriarch. Photius was hard pressed to assign his people at key posts to respond to these requests. On top of that, he was told that the Emperor wanted to see him on a private manner at the Palace.

Photius was accompanied by two of his students from Magnaura, dressed in a monk's habit. It was a rainy cold day and he had a heavy overcoat over the black garment and headgear of a bishop. He went there by carriage and asked his students to remain outside Basil's office door, keeping company the two guards posted at the door of the Imperial office.

"Good day Your Highness," said Photius.

"Good day to you Your Eminence. Please have a seat. I called you here to be updated on your work on the anacatharsis of the old legal system. I also have a personal problem that I need to discuss with you and need your advice."

"I am at your service Your Highness. Regarding the anacatharsis, its development is in progress. The old laws were collected, organized and where necessary improved to correspond to the needs of this time. What we are finding though, is that this work would take long time to complete and it would be very difficult for legal servants to follow, unless a much shorter, simplified version of these documents is issued, for commonly used cases on a day-to-day basis. I am suggesting that this handbook be started in parallel. It would require some additional resources, but these resources will bear fruit much earlier than the complete compendium."

"That sounds good to me Photius. Let me know how much more money you need to finance this project, but I hope you can trim it down to the minimum. You see, I am also involved in rebuilding our infrastructure here. As you know, Aghia Sophia was damaged from a severe earthquake. I had to spend money to repair it and add some mosaics. I also had to repair the church of the Holy Apostles. Several other smaller churches needed repair as well. As you know, now I am also building a new church, dedicated to St. Michael, the Prophet Elijah, Panagia and St. Nicholas. The people of course refuse to name all these names and they call it the "Nea" Church. Also, the Great Palace and the Magnaura need additional work. My resources are tight. To give you an example of how tight, I had to withdraw some ships from Sicily, to bring marble for these projects. This caused us to lose Syracuse to the Emirate of Sicily. I now have to redouble my effort to take that city back."

"I appreciate your problems Your Highness. I will endeavor to be very efficient in doing this legal work. What may happen though is that it may take much longer to complete it than previously expected."

"I understand," said Basil and paused for a while.

"Now let me come to some personal problems that I have. I am worried about my son Constantine. He resents me for all that happened in the past and does not seem to understand and forgive his father. I raised him into a co-Emperor, but he refuses to think like one. He rebels on every command I give him, and I am afraid that I am losing him. He acts carelessly and does not watch out for his safety. Can you advise me on how to handle him?"

Photius lowered his head in thought.

"Events that impacted that child in the past are not easily erased," he said. "I would not expect miracles to happen overnight, Your Highness. What I would suggest is that you switch a bit of your behavior to him from a commanding Emperor, imposing responsibilities for him to uphold, to a loving father."

"Do you think that I need to pamper him up? How am I to train him and make him tough enough to hold this Empire together when I am gone?"

"You must leave that for him to decide when the time comes. My Lord, you cannot have it two ways. Divorcing your wife, killing your predecessor, marrying his wife and alienating your children bear a penalty that must be paid. When you violate the morals of a society and the Church, for what you considered a good cause at that time, will eventually catch up with you and your children."

"I had to kill Michael for the good of this Empire, Photius. I am applying a new legal system, trying to deter situations where assassinations are needed to save the people from corrupt and ruthless state officials, including Emperors."

"I understand Your Highness. Yet, no matter how many laws you improve, nothing helps when you allow someone who assassinates an Emperor and takes his place. This happens because you allow him to  declare immunity for himself and his collaborators and get away with murder. What is needed is a balance of powers between a moral conscience and the practical needs of the state. This immunity from prosecution must stop. Others will think that since the Emperor could do it and get away with it, they should also be able to do the same. I am also worried about Constantine, now that you mentioned how careless he has become. His life may be in danger."

"What do you mean by that?"

"I would watch out for the company he keeps. Make sure that the people around him are trustworthy and are not trying to repeat what you did on Michael."

Basil got up from his chair and started pacing.

"If you are you trying to scare me professor, you are succeeding."

Photius smiled, after hearing the term "professor." He knew that he touched a sensitive subject with Basil, but that did not bother him.

"I will take your advice under consideration," Basil continued. "Thank you."

Photius got up, looked at the flustered Basil and went towards the door.

"Wait!" said Basil. "What would you suggest that I do, if … God forbid, something happens to my son?"

     STAVROS BOINODIRIS PHD

Photius turned and looked at Basil.

"I would think about his replacement," said Photius bluntly. "But I will also pray that nothing happens to Constantine."

Photius bowed and exited through the door hiding a smile. Basil mind started racing about his problem. He decided that he had a very busy day at his office and wanted to clear his mind, so that he can think better. Finally, he decided to just take an hour off, and go riding. He went to his office entrance and gave orders to the guard, to prepare his favorite white horse for a ride in the countryside. A short time later he and a small escort were riding through the streets of Constantinople, heading for the countryside.

# Zautses (Constantinople, September 878 AD)

Stylianos Zautses rode through the streets of Constantinople, coming into the City from the countryside. As he rode, he thought all about the events of the day. He was a commander of the junior regiment of Basil's mercenary bodyguard, called the "hetereia." This bodyguard was equipped as a heavy cavalry, part of the Imperial Cataphract.

The Imperial Cataphract was a heavy cavalry horse archer and lancer, who symbolized the power of Constantinople. The Cataphract wore a conical-shaped casqued helmet, topped with a tuft of horsehair dyed his unit's color. He wore a long shirt of doubled layered chain or scale mail, which extended down to his upper legs. Leather boots or greaves protected his lower legs, while gauntlets protected his hands.

He carried a small, round shield, the thyreos, bearing his unit's colors and insignia, strapped to his left arm, leaving both hands free to use his weapons and control his horse. Over his mail shirt he wore clothing of light weight cotton and a heavy cloak both of which were also dyed in unit colors. The horses often wore mail armor and overcoats as well, to protect their vulnerable heads, necks and chests.

The cataphract's weapons included a composite bow and the kontarion, or lance, short enough to be used as a javelin. They also had a sword, a dagger and a battle axe, strapped to the saddle as a backup weapon.

The lance was topped by a small flag or pennant, of the same color as the helmet tuft, overcoat, shield and cloak. When not in use, the lance was placed in a saddle boot. The bow was slung from the saddle, from which also was hung its quiver of arrows.

Byzantine saddles, which included stirrups, were adopted from the Avars. The Byzantine Empire also made horse breeding an important priority to the Empire's security. If they could not breed enough high-quality mounts themselves, they would not hesitate to purchase them even from the barbarians if the need arose.

Zautses had ridden all the way from Adrianople with his troop of these cavalrymen after a week's worth of exercises trying to train new recruits, most of them unable to speak Greek or Latin. He had to use translators, which were posted as lower rank officers of troops, but could speak both Greek and the language of the new recruits. As he was passing through the neighborhoods of Constantinople, he was dismissing each troop to disband to their residences, which were clustered throughout the city. The last troop with him was a Verangian one, consisting of blond warriors. Their neighborhood was close to his home. After he dismissed them, he took the street leading to his home, which happened to be near the Great Palace. He was tired.

His home was a modest place near a public cistern, consisting of several rooms, and a yard with a cooking oven, a stable and a storage barn full of chopped wood for fuel and stores of animal feed. He dismounted his chestnut horse, put his cavalry spear over some wooden hooks and hanged his shield over the spear. Then he took off his belt with his heavy sword and hanged it on another hook inside the barn. Slowly, he unburdened his horse from the bow and the quiver of arrows and the battle axe.

"Zoe, come on out here," he yelled.

He moved slowly, as he tied his horse in the stable. He took off the saddle and harness and hanged it over a railing, separating the horse stalls. There was another horse in the neighboring stall, a colt, making noises happy to see his mother. Stylianos gave the horse a pitchfork of dried clover from the storage pile. Finally, he took off his helmet and hanged it on a special peg.

"Papa is here," a girl's voice sounded from inside. A young girl of thirteen appeared at the door of the stable. Then she rushed over and hugged her father, still wearing his cavalry chain mail and uniform.

"Can you please fetch some water for our mare?"

"Yes papa." Zoe picked up a wooden pail and went to the cistern, where the neighborhood went to fetch water for everyday use. Meanwhile, his wife appeared at the barn door. She proceeded to hug and kiss her husband and without saying a word started unbuckling his breast plate and other parts of his uniform and armor.

"I heard something interesting today," she muttered smiling.

"What…?" Stylianos looked puzzled at his wife's enigmatic smile.

"The young prince Leo, Ingerina's son," replied Zautsina. "He seems to be taken by your daughter."

Stylianos' gaze turned towards the door, watching his daughter disappear around the corner house with the pail in her hands.

"What brought this about?" he asked with a faraway look.

"I do not know. The only thing that I gathered was that your daughter took Leo's side in a fight he had with Constantine."

Stylianos waited until he was freed from his heavy armor, picked it up and brought it inside the house. He carefully hanged it on a wooden post, especially constructed to support it and maintain it polished and dry. Then he went to the den and after getting a clay cup, he filled it with wine using a ladle that was dipped in a large clay jar. Then he plopped on a low sofa, covered with wool covers and lined with pillows.

His mind was racing. What would happen, if through some miracle Leo became an heir apparent to the throne of Byzantium? What if Leo married his daughter? This would open the door for him to ascend in the ranks of power, instead of being simply an imperial officer, training troops to guard Basil.

After all, Basil was an emperor that he helped put on the throne by participating in the murder of his predecessor.

*"What makes Basil a better ruler?"* he thought to himself. *"He is not as educated as I am, and he is an oaf in his manners. His approach to taking over the throne has made many enemies. As for soldiering, if it was not for his compatriot Armenians like me, he would not have made it as an Emperor. I bet Ingerina would hate his guts for killing her lover and then putting his disturbed son as Co-Emperor, instead of Leo. I bet that she is probably scared out of her mind when she thinks what would happen to her sons Leo and Stephen when Constantine becomes an Emperor."*

"Do you want something to eat?" Zautses' wife asked.

"I am starved," he replied, as he finished the rest of the wine in his cup. Then, Zautses got up and after refilling his cup with wine, he sat on a long wooden bench and table that the family used for eating.

His wife had already served a warm soup, made of grains, with some pieces of meat in it.

"It's time to eat Zoe," yelled his wife. "I don't know what is wrong with that child. She just lies on her bed and stares at the wall." She went in the next room pulled Zoe by her arm and led her to the table.

     STAVROS BOINODIRIS PHD

# Leo's Secret Love (Zautses Home, Constantinople, Christmas Eve, 878 AD)

Leo pulled Zoe by her arm and led her behind the bushes, outside her home.

"Hush," said Leo. "Keep quiet. I do not want anyone to know I am here."

They were both dressed in their heavy winter tunics. There was snow on the ground and the cold breeze was hitting their faces and turning their cheeks red.

"What is wrong?" asked Zoe.

"There is nothing wrong. I missed you. I need to be near you, but I do not want anyone to know that I am with you."

"Why?"

"Because my stepfather would be furious; he wants to dictate to everyone who they are to see, or not see. To him, I am a commodity to use for some expedient trade. He married my mother for expediency and divorced his wife for the same reason. He had plans to marry his dear son, the bully Constantine to an Italian girl, named Ermengard, so that he can secure an alliance with her father. She was much older, but he did not care. I don't know what he plans to do with a commodity like me. I want to get away from that unbearable Palace."

"I cannot believe what I am hearing."

"Is there a place, where we can go that none can find us? We need to get out of this cold."

"I sometimes go to our barn. There, on the loft, where we keep dry grass for the horses, I keep a chest with some of my spare clothes and things hidden. I even have a blanket there."

"Perfect; let's go there."

The thirteen-year-old Zoe took Leo's hand and led him to the barn from the rear entrance. Leo was a year younger than Zoe.

The two went up the loft of the barn climbing a ladder. There were two horses there and they tried not to make any noise. Zoe led him behind several bales of hay. She opened a wooden chest and picked up a blanket. Behind the blanket, inside the chest there were two, hand-made dolls and a summer tunic.

She laid the blanket on top of the straw. Leo immediately went under it and pulled Zoe next to him. He hugged her to get warm. In return, she hugged him and kissed him smiling.

"Are you now better?" Zoe asked, caressing his head.

"Much better," said Leo, closing his eyes.

Zoe kept on caressing him, until she realized that Leo had fallen asleep. She laid next to him, thinking of how nice it felt to have this boy in her arms, listening to the wind howling outside the barn. Soon, she was also asleep.

Inside the Great Palace, Eudokia Ingerina was panicky. She was looking all over the palace for her son, but she could not locate him. His brother Stephen saw him towards one of the garden exits. She did not want to ask for a guard, because these Verangians would inform Basil, and she did not want Basil to know. If her son was after a mischief, Basil would fall on him like a ton of bricks. So, she sought after Chariton Psellus, the children's Latin teacher. She found him in the Palace kitchen, where he usually spent his time with his father Tryphon. He was at the time slurping on a vegetable soup.

"Come with me now," she waved at Chariton as she approached him; "I need your help."

Chariton dropped his bowl on the table, wiped his mouth with the corner of his tunic and rushed up, following the Empress.

"Leo left the Palace. I need to find him. Stephen saw him go outside towards the garden in the snow."

Chariton and Ingerina went outside and tried to see the footsteps in the snow. There were several, going in and out, but all except one were of large, grown man's feet. One, going out was a child's footprint of a sandal, wrapped with wool cloth.

"That's him," said Chariton. "Let's follow the tracks."

"No!" said Ingerina. "We better get something heavier to wear first."

The two got inside and gotten two woolen, hooded capes. Then, they went back out and followed the footprints.

They walked slowly, trying to follow the distinct footprint path. It led them out of the garden gate, down to a neighborhood of military officers and finally led them towards a house.

"I know this place," said Chariton. "This is the Zautses home."

"I should have known," mumbled Ingerina, as she knocked at the door.

Several seconds passed. Chariton then started hitting the door with the back of his dagger. A few seconds later the door opened.

Zautsina appeared and immediately was taken aback, as Ingerina pulled her hood back and revealed her imperial tiara on her head.

"Highness," she exclaimed, as she bowed. "Please come in."

Ingerina and Chariton entered the modest entryway leading into a great room, where a fireplace was burning wood and keeping the place warm.

"Please be seated," said Zautsina." I am sorry for the delay, but I was back in the barn. My husband had just arrived from the winter exercises, and I was helping him with his armor."

"I came for my son Leo," said Ingerina, coming straight to the point.

"Leo?" asked Zautsina. "I have not seen him."

"We followed his footsteps from the palace, all the way to your home," said Chariton. "Maybe Zoe has seen him. Do you know where she is?"

"She was here earlier, but I hadn't seen her for a while," said Zautsina. Then she went towards the back door, opened it and started to yell.

"Zoe, Zoe…"

Suddenly she stopped yelling. A set of heavy footprints were heard. Stylianos Zautses appeared from the barn, still partially dressed in his uniform.

"Have you seen Zoe?" asked Zautsina.

"Yes."

"Where is she? We need to find out if she knows where Prince Leo is. The Empress is here looking for her son."

Stylianos bowed as he entered after tossing the snow off his wool cape.

"Do not worry Highness. I just went up to get some hay for my horse, and there they were, covered up with a wool blanket asleep. They are both asleep in the loft of our barn."

"What…?" exclaimed Zautsina. She was ready to barge towards the barn, when Chariton blocked her way.

"Why don't we all sit down and see how to handle this," said Chariton calmly. "There is a reason why Leo came here. Zoe happens to be his dear and only friend that supported him every time Constantine bullied him. He feels that being with Zoe is the only safe place to be."

"I want to thank that girl for taking my son's side," said Ingerina. "I have a nice gold bracelet, which I want her to have."

"There is no need for any gratitude," said Zautses. "Our family is in the service of the Emperor and his family."

"Yes," said Ingerina. "Nevertheless, I have a problem. Despite the nasty, bully behavior, Basil adores Constantine. Any infraction that Leo is involved with, counts against him. It means harsh punishment for my son. I implore you that this escapade will not be known by my husband."

"We agree, and your wish is our command," replied Zautses. Zautsina followed suit and nodded affirmatively.

"I would not ask for your secrecy, but I am very worried about the safety and well-being of my sons," said Ingerina. "Being a prince puts them in a precarious situation, since the politics of the state take precedence over them. As far as Basil is concerned, Constantine is his heir and my sons are dispensable. Any accusations of bully behavior or misdeeds by Constantine are much easier to forgive if Basil can show that the rest of the princes are no good."

"We understand, Your Highness; no need to explain any further."

Ingerina smiled. "Thank you."

Then she turned to Chariton.

"Chariton, can you go and fetch my son from the barn in a few minutes?"

"Certainly, Highness," replied Chariton.

"Just allow me a few minutes for me to return to the Palace. I would like gallant Zautses here, dressed in his uniform to escort me back. He can pass like a Palace guard. You bring Leo back discretely and don't tell him that I was here. Tell him that you came searching for him on your own initiative."

"Yes, Highness," replied both, Chariton and Zautses.

Zautses helped Ingerina put on her heavy cape on. Zautses got his helmet and his cape and the two left out of the front door for the Great Palace.

A few minutes later, Chariton had his half-asleep youngster under his own cape, as they walked towards the palace.

"How did you know where to find me?" asked Leo.

"Teachers know everything," replied Chariton, "especially how to track naughty children's tracks in the deep snow. Next time, I suggest that you ask your mother's permission before you go visiting your girlfriend."

The two stomped their feet to take out most of the snow before they entered the Great Palace.

# Constantine's Training (Great Palace, August 17, 879 AD)

"He is only a child," yelled Maria, stomping her fist on Basil's desk. "Are you trying to kill him?"

"Please Maria," uttered Basil.

"I have not seen my son but only fleetingly, here and there, between all the military training you assign to him. Please give him a rest."

"You are missing the point Maria," replied Basil with a stern voice. "Constantine is a prince, soon to take on the responsibilities of leading armies against those that want to cut our heads off. If we do not get ready, the Saracens will be here and do to us what they did to our people in Syracuse. He needs to be toughened and trained well in the arts of politics and war, so that we can all survive."

"The last time I saw him he was in tears," said Maria.

"Did he complain about his training?" asked Basil.

"No, but I do not like the people around him. Now that he is in the company of rough soldiers, who knows what wine shops and brothels they will introduce him to? This City is full of danger for a young man like him?"

"That is another reason for him to go and conduct military exercises somewhere far from here."

"Aren't you expecting too much out of my son?"

"No. He is my son and heir and he would need all the training he can get."

Basil barged out of his office and headed to a large room where military planning was typically held. There he found several mid-ranked officers. Leo Choirosphaktes was updating them on intelligence information regarding Saracen movements after they had captured Syracuse.

As Leo explained, the siege lasted from August 877 to 21 May 878, when the city, effectively left without assistance by Basil's central Byzantine government and was sacked by the Aghlabid forces. Leo was stating facts on what he knew from first-hand reports.

"Most of the population of the city was massacred during the sack. Among the notables alone, over 4,000 were killed. The Arab commander had the commanding officer executed a week later, while the seventy men left with him along with other prisoners were reportedly taken out of the city and beaten to death with stones and clubs. One of the defenders, Nicetas of Tarsos, who during the siege had insulted the Arab commander daily, was taken apart and tortured to death. Only a few soldiers from the Peloponnese, along with some soldiers of the garrison were able to escape and, reaching Greece, inform admiral Adrianos of the events. The city itself was pillaged and practically destroyed. According to the sporadic news arriving from sailors, the Arabs remained there for about two months after the sack, before returning to their base, leaving the city in ruins."

Leo paused, when everyone stood as his Emperor took a seat on the table. Basil sensed a hesitation by Leo to continue and he interrupted Leo's presentation.

"For what happened in Syracuse, I accept the responsibility. We simply reacted with too little, too late. We were caught by surprise. I diverted our fleet from Italy to haul some marble for the 'Nea' Church, unaware of the pending attack. So, when news came of the Saracen attack, an inadequate Byzantine squadron of ships tried to save the city, but it was driven off. At that battle we lost four ships."

Basil stopped and waved to Leo to continue. Leo was relieved that Basil took the responsibility to announce his short sightedness, instead of letting him dance around, trying to justify the Byzantine defeat in some elegant way.

"What we are finding out now," Leo continued, "is that the Saracen commander did not enjoy his victory for long. Last year, he was killed by two of his slaves, at the instigation of his uncle and his brother, who then usurped the governorship. This shows that we have a period of internal strife among Sicilian Muslims, which could be advantageous to us. By reinforcing our forts there, we can hold them back."

"I have already assigned that job to the Cappadocian commander Nikiphoros Phokas, the commander in chief of the Byzantine armies in Italy," said Basil. "We must not repeat this mistake in the future. So, I am getting ready to train a whole new detachment of cavalry, ready to fight a fast reaction battle against the Saracens, in Italy, or in Syria."

Basil paused, looking at Leo. "I want my son, Constantine to be part of that training, but because he is so young, I want you, Leo to act as his bodyguard and protector. I want at least one thousand new trainees to participate in this training exercise."

"Your Highness," replied Leo, "I am honored to participate. May I ask who is going to lead this exercise? My reason for asking is that I am not an expert on cavalry tactics."

Basil looked around the room. "Which one of you is a cavalry commanding officer?"

One person stood up. It was Stylianos Zautses, who was sitting at the end of the table.

"Ah!" said Basil. "Zautses should be quite qualified for the job. Can you describe your last assignment commander?"

Zautses bowed.

"It was cavalry training of about three hundred trainees at Adrianople, Highness."

"Good enough," said Basil. "Let's start with three hundred and repeat the training until we have at least one thousand trainees as expert cavalrymen."

"Highness, in order to train the cavalry," said Zautses, "I will also need an equal number of infantry soldiers."

"That is fine," replied Basil. "There is a detachment of infantry, training in the Amasea region. I will order their commander to let you have some of his men. The Amasea region is also convenient because from there you can send me periodic signals of your progress along the coastal signaling towers. I am also entrusting you Zautses with my son's wellbeing and hold you responsible if something happens to him."

Zautses bowed.

"I will guard him with my life, Highness."

Basil stared at the group.

"I will leave you to make your plans. Let me know if you need anything."

The officers in the room all stood up and bowed as Basil exited the room.

Zautses turned to Leo Choirosphaktes. "It is nice to finally meet you

Leo. I have heard of you from my wife. You are married to one of my distant relatives."

"Yes," replied Leo. "I heard of you too."

"I presume that you are coming with us Leo."

"Of course; I have to guard the young prince."

"I don't understand Leo; how is the prince going to become a cavalryman, when he has a babysitter restricting his movements?"

"Don't worry. He will learn over time. I know my business. I hope you know your business training all these men."

# The Training Exercise (Amasea, September 5-8, 879 AD)

Zautses knew his business. He organized the training of three hundred heavy cavalry men, called the Imperial Cataphract Numerous. With him, he had also acquired another three hundred infantry men. With these troops, he can go through a full training exercise of coordinated cavalry and infantry tactics.

The Byzantine cavalrymen and their horses were superbly trained and capable of performing complex maneuvers on the drill field and the battlefield alike. While a proportion of the Cataphracts appear to have been lancers or archers only, most had both bows and lances and were trained to be equally deadly with either. Their main tactical unit was the Numerus of 300-400 men.

When in battle, the Numeri were usually formed in lines 8 to 10 ranks deep, making them almost a mounted Phalanx. Zautses recognized that this formation was less flexible and more cumbersome for cavalry than infantry but found the tradeoff to be acceptable in exchange for the greater physical and psychological advantages offered by depth. Yet, when traveling in the countryside, he made the troops to travel by column of twos.

The Byzantines usually preferred using the cavalry for flanking and envelopment attacks, instead of frontal assaults, and almost always preceded and supported their charges with arrow fire. The front ranks of the Numeri would draw bows and target the enemy's front ranks; then once the foe had been sufficiently weakened, they would draw their lances and charge.

The back ranks would follow, drawing their bows and firing ahead as they rode. This highly effective combination of missile fire with shock action, put their opponents at a dangerous disadvantage- If they closed ranks to better resist the charging lances, they would make themselves more vulnerable to the bows' fire, but if they spread out to avoid the arrows, then the lancers would have a much easier job of breaking their thinned ranks. Many times, the arrow fire and start of a charge were enough to cause the enemy to run or rout without the need of a close combat or melee.

A favorite tactic when confronted by a strong enemy cavalry force, involved a feigned retreat and ambush. The Numeri on the flanks would charge at the enemy horsemen, then draw their bows, turn around and fire as they withdrew (the Parthian Shot). If the enemy horse did not immediately give them chase, they would continue harassing them with arrows until they did. Meanwhile the Numeri on the left and right rear would be drawn up in their standard formation facing the flanks and ready to attack the pursuing enemy as they crossed their lines. The foes would be forced to stop and fight this new unexpected threat, but as they did so, the flanking Numeri would halt their retreat, turn around and charge at full speed, lances at the ready, into their former pursuers.

The enemy, weakened, winded and now caught in a vice between two mounted phalanxes, would break, with the Numeri they once pursued now chasing them. Then the rear Numeri, who had ambushed the enemy horse, would move up and attack the now unprotected flanks in a double envelopment.

When the Byzantines had to make a frontal assault against a strong infantry position, the wedge was their preferred formation for charges. The Cataphract Numerus formed a wedge of around 400 men in 8 to 10 progressively larger ranks. The first three ranks were armed with lances and bows, the remainder with lance and shield. The first rank consisted of 25 soldiers, the second of 30, the third of 35 and the remainder of 40, 50 and 60 adding ten men per rank.

When charging the enemy, the first three ranks fired arrows to create a gap in the enemy's formation then at about 100 to 200 meters distance from the foe, the first ranks shifted to their kontarion lances, charging the line at full speed followed by the remainder of the battalion. Often these charges ended with the routing of enemy infantry. At this point infantry would advance to secure the area and allow the cavalry to briefly rest and reorganize themselves.

When facing opponents, such as the Vandals or the Avars with strong heavy cavalry, the cavalry was deployed behind the heavy infantry who were sent ahead to engage the enemy. The infantry would attempt to open a gap in the enemy formation for the cavalry to charge through.

Zautses planned that the first training that both, cavalry and infantry had to receive would be to travel on the countryside fast and quietly, while protecting each other.

Cataphracts adapted their tactics and equipment in relation to which enemy they were fighting. But in the standard deployment, four Numeri would be placed around the infantry lines, one on each flank with one on the right rear and another on the left rear. Thus, the Numeri were not only the flank protection, but the main reserve and rear guard as well.

Zautses partitioned his cavalry into four parts, all four of them, flanking the infantry, front and back. The front infantry also had the task of scouting ahead.

"I am assigning you Constantine and your babysitter on the left-front cavalry company," yelled Zautses, as he approached Leo and the prince, riding towards them.

"I do not need a babysitter, you … impudent rascal," said Constantine.

"Calm down," said Leo. "Learn how to be immune to provocations, from both friends and foes. Also, don't forget your manners. He is your commanding officer."

"He can go to hell," said Constantine and spurred his horse towards the left-front cavalry company.

Zautses turned his horse around smiling and gave the order for the whole regiment to proceed in the heavily forested mountainous terrain of Amasea.

After the first day of riding with the cavalry company, Constantine started to complain about his horse to Leo. His favorite horse had acquired a leg problem, for some unknown reason. Leo, acting as his bodyguard immediately sent a rider asking for a horse replacement from Zautses for the prince.

Zautses appeared with the rider.

"What is wrong?" he asked.

"Constantine's horse is lame," replied Leo. "We need a replacement and make sure that it is in good condition."

"I will have someone bring you a replacement from the support group in the rear," said Zautses, as he galloped away towards the rear.

The following morning, a Verangian appeared with a horse, all saddled up, as the trumpet for the battle formation march was sounded. The left-front company was mounted and started moving, leaving Leo and Constantine behind.

"What about my saddle?" asked Constantine, looking at his new, saddled mount.

"We do not seem to have time," said Leo, as he gave a quick check on the saddle. It seemed fine. Then, he turned towards Constantine. "We don't have much time. Get your weapons on this horse with the saddle it has on."

Constantine mounted his new mount and Leo handed him his weapons. Constantine then started moving ahead, trying to catch their company.

"Wait for me," said Leo, as he hopped on his horse. He tried to catch up with Constantine so that they both could join the rest of the company, now riding in column of twos at some distance ahead.

Meanwhile, Zautses and his aides, including the trumpeter joined the right front flank. Suddenly, Zautses leaves the right flank and with the trumpeter and goes ahead of the whole column. He then orders the trumpeter to sound "enemy sighted." Upon this sound, the frontal cavalry columns were to gallop on a scouting formation. So, Constantine's column goes on a gallop over a ridge, with a deep ravine to the left towards a forest.

"Let's not follow them," yelled Leo to Constantine, who was several horse lengths ahead of him. "We do not know what kind of danger lurks in those woods, especially with a horse that you are not acquainted with."

Constantine hesitated for a while, allowing Leo to dismount. He stood there mounted as he saw his company galloping farther and farther ahead.

"This horse says that I have to go," he yelled, as he spurred his horse. So, his horse took off to a fast gallop.

Leo panicked. He tried to jump back on his horse to catch up with Constantine, but Constantine's horse seemed to be extremely fast. As Leo tried to catch up, Constantine's horse was swallowed by the dense forest growth. Leo followed yelling:

"Constantine, stop!"

Leo entered the forest, looking left and right. Then he saw it. First, he saw the shield strewn on top of a bush. Then he saw a spear and a helmet, but they were to a path through the trees to the left of where the rest of the cavalry seems to have gone, based on the size of the trail opening. He recognized the helmet as that belonging to Constantine. It was smaller than normal and had the red tuft of the troop. So, did the spear.

Leo started yelling for help, as he pushed his horse into the smaller path. It led down to a ravine. Four riders, at the rear of the column heard him and turned around. They went on a single file down to the ravine with Leo. Soon the forest gave way to a clearing. Leo followed the tracks which now turned right, heading back into the forest, in front of the regiment's position.

Constantine did not know what had happened. He ignored Leo because he had to prove to him that he did not need a "babysitter." As he had trotted ahead of Leo to catch up with the rest of the troop, he took a short cut over some rocky outcrops. Suddenly he felt his saddle snap, slipping from under him, and his head pointing downwards. He remembers being dragged by his stirrup over the rocks before losing consciousness.

He woke up, half dazed, finding himself in a peculiar position, one foot hanging on the stirrup of the saddle, which was on the side of the horse. His head was bleeding profusely. Then he heard a rustling. At the corner of his dazed vision he thought that he saw a rider. He tried to raise his arm, to ask for help, when all darkness came upon him.

Leo and the four cavalrymen went into the forest, following Constantine's trail. After half a stadium's distance they see the horse, with Constantine's leg hanging on the stirrup. Immediately Leo jumps off his horse and rushes to check the child out. Constantine was dead. Leo saw a gash on the back of his head and another one, on his right eye.

"He must have hit a branch on his right eye," said one of the riders that surrounded him after dismounting. "Then, he must have toppled over, hang himself on the stirrup and hit his back on the rocks."

"That is probably what happened," said the other rider.

"You two, go and get the commander," Leo commanded two of the riders. "Tell him what happened. This is serious. Tell him to sound recall. I would hate to be the one to tell the Emperor that his son and heir is dead." He saw the riders still hanging around and decided to take command, pointing to each one of them. "Don't just sit there! You, with the black horse, go straight into the woods from here. Try to find the main body and the commander. You with the chestnut horse, go back the way we came, making sure we find the main body. The commander should be somewhere around there. Tell him to sound recall."

　　　　STAVROS BOINODIRIS PHD

The two riders mounted on their horses and rushed to the paths that Leo suggested.

The cavalryman with the black horse looked around and to his surprise he saw a path along the dense woods, made by some animal. He did not think at the time to check the footprints, because of the seriousness of the situation. He followed the path and within minutes he was out of the forest in an open field, face-to-face with the main body of three hundred infantrymen.

In front of them was Zautses giving orders to his officers. The cavalryman on the black horse runs to his commander with the news of the event.

Zautses immediately orders his trumpeter to sound recall.

While all this was going on, Leo examined Constantine's horse and saddle. He discovered something that he had missed earlier. One of the saddle straps had an obvious knife cut on the inside of the strap around the belly of the animal, something that none could have seen, unless the saddle was taken off the horse. Then he noticed that the horse had a gash on the rump. Anyone that spurred with sandals the animal there would cause extreme pain to the animal, enough pain to make it run amok.

*"Something is not right,"* he thought.

With these thoughts in mind, Leo started walking towards the path that the rider with the black horse took. He stooped down and examined carefully the horse hoof-prints. He noticed that there were hoof-prints traveling both ways. He returned to Constantine's body and examined it carefully. Then he sat on a rock, thinking, as he waited for help to arrive.

Meanwhile Zautses ordered a contingent of support personnel to follow him and the cavalryman with the black horse into the forest, to retrieve the body of Constantine. There, using their battle axes, Zautses ordered that they made a litter. With it, the men brought the body back onto the clearing.

"What now?" Leo asked Zautses when they reached the clearing.

"First of all," said Zautses, the exercise is postponed indefinitely. "Next, we bring the body to Amasea with all the troops and signal Constantinople of the accident and ask for instructions. This signal would take a day to arrive at the Palace and another day for instructions to arrive here. There, while we wait for the instructions, we investigate, which will give us enough information to present to the Emperor when we arrive there in two weeks."

Leo nodded.

It took another day before the troops with Constantine's body reached

Amasea. That night, on the 6th of September, Zautses sent a tower signal, using fires on towers. The signal was simple.

"Zautses exercise cancelled due to accident. Co-Emperor Constantine is dead"

The message was repeated with light signals. It went to Amisus and from there to Sinope, Amastris and along the coast of Pontus all the way to Constantinople. By morning, the following day a cavalry messenger was presenting the scroll to Symbatius, Basil's chief information officer.

Symbatius came to the Palace and presented the message to Basil at his office.

Basil was shocked. His shock turned into silent weeping. Then he blew up into loud weeping.

"I don't know how to tell Maria," he yelled crying. "I lost my son and heir."

Then he became quiet. At that time Symbatius asked him for instructions to Zautses and Leo.

"Tell those bastards that killed my son to come here at once!" Symbatius realized that Basil's grief was turning into anger. This anger could lash at everyone around.

So, Symbatius exited Basil's office at once. He rode straight to the tower and scribbled the following message to Zautses:

"Zautses and Choirosphaktes are expected at the Palace as fast as possible to report on the event."

While Basil was thinking on how to face Maria, he also was fuming on the incompetence of Leo to prevent what happened.

"I specifically sent him there to act as a bodyguard," yelled to Symbatius. "I was warned that something like this could happen. Something stinks of an assassination conspiracy and I want the heads of those responsible."

"I suggest that you go and talk to the Patriarch," suggested Symbatius. "He can help you ease the news to Maria. He can also be useful in digging out the truth behind any possible conspiracy."

Basil nodded, but he was unable to recover from the shock. He immediately ordered his coach to take him to the Patriarch.

"Is this the way God punishing me for my sins?" he asked Photius whose advice he sought after he arrived at his office. "I tried my best to atone for my sins by building churches, fixing churches and giving splendor to the houses of God. Why is it that God cannot forgive me?"

Photius had in front of him a wreck of a depressed Emperor, who lost his anointed heir to the throne, just when he was coming of age. What do you tell this person in this condition?

"I will ask God for His mercy," Photius said. "I will also intercede and try to convey the news to your wife Maria. You do not need to distress yourself with such a painful task."

While Basil was running out of his mind in Constantinople, Zautses, Leo and all the witnesses were participating in an investigation on how Constantine was killed.

"Why weren't you with him in the woods Leo?" Zautses asked.

"I told him to stay put when the rest of the troop went into the forest," Leo protested. "I told him that it was not safe, with the new horse. I thought that he would listen to me and would dismount, when I did. Then for some strange reason he bolted as fast as he could in front of me. I suspect that it was the teasing you gave him on needing a "babysitter." When he bolted, I panicked and jumped back on my horse but could not catch him. Then I saw his shield, helmet and spear and started yelling for help. Four of your soldiers appeared and we followed his trail down to a ravine. After quite a distance we saw the horse, with Constantine's leg hanging on the stirrup. I jumped off my horse and rushed to check him out. Constantine was dead."

"We saw it too," said one soldier that witnessed it. "There was a gash on the back of his head and another one, on his right eye. We could justify the wound on the back of the head, because he was dragged on his back."

"What about the one on his eye? What could be the cause?" asked Zautses.

"After some thinking I thought that he must have hit a branch on his right eye," said another witness. "Then, he must have toppled over, hang himself on the stirrup and hit his back on the rocks. I told the rest of them my thoughts at the time."

"That is probably what happened," said Zautses.

"Did anyone see a sticking branch with blood on it?" asked Leo.

No response came from the group.

"It seems that this particular branch could have broken off and after all the riders that came through these paths, that branch could have been buried in mud somewhere." said Zautses. "Cavalry accidents are not uncommon, especially when they involve heavily armored men." He paused for a few seconds. "Are there any other observations by anyone?"

The soldiers and Leo shook their heads negatively.

"So, the consensus of this investigation has arrived at the conclusion that it was a freak accident. Do we agree?"

This time the soldiers and Leo shook their heads affirmatively.

The next day Zautses assigned a new commander to continue the exercises as best as they could. Soon after, Leo and Zautses were on their way to Constantinople, accompanied only by the four witnesses, to face the wrath of an Emperor in grief. It would take about ten days to arrive there by horse.

    STAVROS BOINODIRIS PHD

# Basil's Grief and Wrath (The Great Palace, September 20, 879 AD)

Basil sat on the head of the tribunal table that was instructed by him to find out what transpired to bring the death of his son and heir. Across from him were Leo Choirosphaktes and Stylianos Zautses, and the four soldiers that witnessed the alleged accident. Next to Basil was Patriarch Photius and Archbishop of Euchaites Theodore Santabarenos, a good friend of Basil.

Leo went first and described the events. Then the witnesses were asked to describe what they saw.

When the witness that rode back to get help finished his testimony, Photius asked:

"Did you say that you followed a path through the woods?"

"Yes Eminence."

"Did you see any tracks on the path?"

"I did not pay attention Eminence. The urgency of the event made me hurry up to reach the main body."

"I see," said Photius.

Basil grabbed Photius and asked him to come closer.

"What are you leading to?" Basil whispered on Photius' ear.

"Nothing Sire," replied Photius in a whisper. "I simply cannot preclude the possibility of someone from the main body meeting with the wounded prince and finishing him off."

"Whom do you suspect the most among these men?" Basil whispered.

"I would suspect anyone that has something to gain from your son's death," whispered Photius. The only ones among these men that I would suspect the most are those with some inkling of jealousy or gain. Yet, based on what we heard, we have no solid proof for any of this."

"I do not need solid proof to get rid of the ones that were responsible for my son's safety," replied Basil, this time in a loud voice.

He turned to Leo Choirosphaktes.

"I find you, Leo Choirosphaktes negligent of my son's safety. Yet, you are found not guilty in any complicity of assassination. You are henceforth relieved of any functions of mystikos of the Palace for one year."

Then he turned to Zautses.

"I find you, Stylianos Zautses negligent and responsible for my son's death. As a commander, you are totally responsible for whatever happens in your units. You are therefore demoted from the rank of commander to a lower rank and you are to be re-assigned to a distant region that I will decide later."

He then turned to the rest of the witnesses.

"All the rest of you are found innocent of any charges. This meeting is at an end."

Basil got up and asked Photius and Theodore Santabarenos to come with him to his office.

Basil sat down on a chair in front of a desk and pointed to his companions to get seated across from him.

"Now what?" he said. "I am out of an heir. My ex-wife Maria does not want to see me without vomiting. I heard that she may join a convent. Ingerina tells me to put her brat Leo on the throne, something that I detest, but I may have to do. I can see her and her son conspiring against me to take over the throne. I wonder whether Zautses and his daughter will also be part of such a conspiracy. For me, losing Constantine was like losing my own life. I want advice from you to appease God for my past sins."

Theodore spoke first.

"Your son deserves all honors that our Church allows. I suggest that his soul to be appeased, a special liturgy to be held in a special place, where his close family and friends hold a vigil in his honor."

"That sounds good," said Photius. "I will also hold special Masses in honor of Constantine at Aghia Sophia for the soul of Constantine, who sacrificed his life for the good of the Empire. I suggest also that you continue your work with the building and reparation of the churches that you have started. This would keep your spirit dedicated to God and will relieve some of the guilt you may have bottled inside of you. As for your heir, you are right. You may not have any choice, but to set Leo as your new heir. I do not like the idea also. Yet, there is time to shape him up to your standards."

 STAVROS BOINODIRIS PHD

"What do you suggest?"

"I suggest that you isolate him from his mother and anyone he knows up to now. Remove any close friends of his, so that any conspiracies planned by anyone of them backfire and they do not benefit by his ascend to the throne."

Basil nodded and got up. So, did Photius and Theodore.

"I will talk to you later," he stated as he walked out of his office. "Thank you for your support."

As Photius and Theodore were also exiting Basil's office they saw him going straight to Ingerina's quarters and closing the door behind him.

He found Ingerina and her maiden Anna, both in black, dressing her boys, Leo and Stephen to go out and play.

"I need to talk to Ingerina privately," he said abruptly, looking at Anna.

Anna bowed, handed up the remaining boy's clothes to each boy and she grabbed the boys by the hand and exited the room, closing the door behind her.

"Where are you taking us?" Ingerina heard the whine of Stephen, as Anna was closing the door.

"I grieve about our loss," said Ingerina, dressed in black. "How can I be of help to you?"

"You certainly can," Basil responded. "I have a conditional proposition for you. I can make Leo a legitimate heir to the throne, if you agree to certain conditions."

"Conditions?" said Ingerina inquisitively. "What conditions?"

"First condition in becoming a Co-Emperor is that I train him. He has to be trained in hardships, so that he can defend himself and can lead his armies when the time comes."

"But…" Ingerina started to say.

Basil looked at Ingerina sternly as he interrupted her. "You have kept Leo very close to your apron strings and up to now he has shown no athletic capabilities whatsoever. In fact, I doubt that he can even ride a horse. My people say that you, madam have allowed your son to turn into a bookworm, spending all his time reading books, instead of practicing with a bow or a javelin."

Ingerina was silent.

"The second condition," Basil continued, "is that he will have nothing to do with the Zautses family. The Zautses family is suspect to a possible conspiracy against us. I am going to send the father to the East, but I want no contact of Leo with anyone in that family, including his girlfriend Zoe. Is that understood?"

Ingerina nodded affirmatively.

"The third condition is that he will need a wife-to-be. Forget about anyone connected with the Zautses family. I will leave this up to you, but I will have to have the final approval of your choices. I like to see you choose a wife for your son that is a Church-going, God-fearing, child-bearing woman with all the attributes that can steer Leo to God's path."

"Is that all?" asked Ingerina.

"No," replied Basil. "But before I go to the next condition, do you agree to these?"

"Yes, I do," said Ingerina after a small pause.

Basil scratched his beard before he continued.

"Assuming we are successful with this untrained boy, we have to secure his throne from internal strife. That means that his brother Stephen will have to be tonsured, so that he cannot have any children of his own. We will think about him as to when to do that and what role in the government we should assign for him."

Ingerina's eyes became moist and she started crying.

"If your son is to take the throne," Basil continued, "you must protect him by agreeing to this last condition. Otherwise I cannot make Leo a co-Emperor, for he will always be in danger of being overthrown by someone that conspires against him and using his brother as a way in. Do you agree to all these conditions?"

"I have no choice, do I?" said Ingerina as she was sobbing. "Is there no end to my suffering here? You have taken all the people that I ever loved and either killed them or made them eunuchs. I wish I never laid eyes on this palace and the misery that it brought me."

"Do you agree?" Basil bellowed at Ingerina, towering over her.

"Yes!" responded Ingerina with tears in her eyes and by nodding her head.

"Thank you," said Basil, as he turned around and exited from Ingerina's quarters.

In the days that followed, he attended all the Masses Photius had for him at Aghia Sophia in honor of his lost son. He had to deal with his heavy depression and took Photius' advice on that. He immersed himself into the spiritual peace that religious ceremonies offered him.

Every day, Symbatius, who was always by his side, would ask:

"How are you feeling today, Highness?"

"I am coping with my depression friend, but it is still too heavy on my soul," would be his response.

# A New Co-Emperor (Aghia Sophia, October 10, 879 AD)

"These things are too heavy for me mom," complained the thirteen-year-old Leo. "I can hardly move."

His mother, Eudokia Ingerina was a thirty-nine-year-old beautiful woman. She looked at Anna, her maiden, as she was struggling to dress her son with the imperial regalia for his coronation as a co-Emperor.

"Then, don't move my boy," Ingerina commanded sternly.

Anna meticulously dressed Leo with the red shoes, his chiton and finally the heavily jeweled Imperial purple loros, or pallium that developed from the trabea *triumphalis*, a ceremonial colored version of the Roman toga. The loros was a long, narrow and embroidered scarf, which was wrapped around the torso and dropped over the left hand. It was one of the most important and distinctive parts of the most formal and ceremonial type of imperial Byzantine costume. It was worn only by the Imperial family. This loros was wrapped over the child's white silk chiton. It was a custom that purple was reserved for the royal family. This took some effort on the side of Ingerina, in procuring the right material for the palace tailor to have her son's outfit ready for his coronation.

After Anna prepared his upper body, Ingerina turned and grasped a thin golden crown, designated for a co-Emperor and placed it on her son's head. Leo made a face that showed his discomfort.

"This is your day, my son," said Ingerina after she removed the thin crown. "You should be glad and smile, showing how happy you are to be chosen as the top servant of your people."

She turned to the guard at the entrance.

"Is the Patriarch's coach here yet?"

"Yes, Highness," the guard responded. "So is your Imperial coach."

Ingerina led the young Leo to the Patriarch's coach and helped him climb in. The weight of the jeweled loros made Leo stumble, but with his mother's help he made it in and sat next to Photius.

"I want you to come with me," Leo whimpered at his mother.

"I cannot do that my boy," said Ingerina softly, kissing her son. "Your father ordered that you become tough and stand on your own two feet. I will be in the next coach and will see you at your coronation."

Leo looked at her, with moist yes.

Ingerina averted her eyes from her son and returned to the door of the palace where Anna was holding young Stephen's arm. The twelve-year-old boy, all dressed-up for church was watching the commotion in the palace, wondering what it was all about. Ingerina and Anna led Stephen to the imperial couch and waited for Emperor Basil to arrive.

Basil arrived with some of his close advisors. He then turned to one of his guards and gave an order. Then he approached the imperial coach.

"I and some of my advisors are coming by horse," he said to Ingerina. "You may proceed. We will catch up."

Ingerina then ordered the coach driver to proceed to Aghia Sophia. Two mounted guards led the procession, followed by the imperial coach, the Patriarchal coach and several coaches filled with servants. After a few minutes the convoy of coaches was joined by the cavalcade of the Emperor and his advisors.

As they were traveling, Photius struck a conversation with Leo inside the coach.

"I see that you love your mother a lot," said Photius. "Do you love your father?"

"He is not my father," said the youngster. "He killed my father and he is full of hate for me. He took away any good friends I ever had."

"Whom did he take away?"

The youngster hesitated.

"Well?" insisted Photius.

"My good friend Zoe, and …"

"Zoe Zautses?"

"Yes."

"Maybe he had his reasons," said Photius. "Yet, you owe him allegiance and support, for he is the Emperor. Don't you think so?"

"If you say so…."

"I do say so. And, if you are to succeed him you must obey his every wish. He intends to be your teacher, military trainer and advisor from now on. Do you think that you can be good on following all that?"

"I have many good teachers that know a lot more than he does. In fact, I have read more books and manuscripts than he has ever seen. All my teachers praise me for how much I have learned. As for being a good soldier, I have never tried it and I do not think that I will be good at it, no matter how much training I get."

"Have you ever ridden a horse?"

"No."

"Do you know archery, by aiming an arrow with a bow and hitting a target?"

"No."

"Have you ever thrown a javelin?"

"No."

"Do you know how to use the large cavalry sword on a horse?"

"No. I told you I am no good on these things. I have never done any of these, ever."

"Give yourself a little time. You will soon be trained on being a soldier. It is a primary requirement for an Emperor-to-be."

Soon the coach stopped in front of Aghia Sophia. The two mounted guards dismounted and took position at the entrance. Photius helped the thirteen-year-old Leo to the cathedral and seated him at his throne. Soon Ingerina and Stephen arrived and took their seats behind Leo. Finally, Basil arrived with his advisors. He sat next to Leo and waved at Photius to commence the ceremony.

There was little fanfare on this ceremony. The liturgy was typical, the bells rang harmoniously and finally Leo was declared a co-Emperor and the thin golden crown was placed on Leo's head. After the ceremony, Leo, Ingerina, Anna and Stephen took off with a coach and returned to the Palace. Leo immediately shed the crown in the coach and could not wait to shed the rest of his heavy clothing as they entered their private quarters.

While they were getting back, Basil had a private consultation with Photius in front of Aghia Sophia.

"You may have a few problems with Leo," said Photius. "He is a very bright boy, and he does not like you. For some reason, he will never forgive you for separating him from Zoe Zautses.”

“He will. I will make sure that he does. I met a wealthy merchant, Theodore Gutzuniates. Do you know him?”

“Yes, I do. He is in his thirties and he just lost his wife on childbirth.”

“Yes, that’s him. I made a deal with him to find him a suitable wife, if he finances part of my project of building the ‘Nea’ Church. The bride I have in mind is Zoe Zautses. She is only fourteen, but by marrying Theodore to her I get a church, Leo stops seeing her and Theodore gets a young wife. What do you think? This way I can train Leo the way I want.”

“You may not find that part very easy,” said Photius. “I don’t know how he will take it with Zoe, but he also has no aptitude for military skills whatsoever, something that is required for a co-Emperor.”

“All that will change, starting today,” said Basil. “I do not want him to like me. I want him to obey me. Every time he doesn’t, he will be severely punished.”

Photius lowered his head pensively.

Basil took off and rode back with his advisors to the Palace. On his way back, he was contemplating on the proper military trainer for Leo.

He went straight to Ingerina’s quarters.

“Where is Leo?” he asked Anna.

“He is inside, reading one of his books.”

Basil pushed Anna aside and went inside the library, where he found Leo sitting on a desk with a manuscript. He grabbed Leo by his belt. Leo dropped his manuscript as Basil led him outside. Anna and Ingerina just stood, watching and keeping quiet. Stephen was scared and uttered an “aah,” but his mother silenced him.

“It is time to drop your reading and start training to be a soldier,” said Basil. He handed a whimpering Leo over to a guard. “Take the co-Emperor by horse to the stadium and deliver him to the imperial trainers that I have assigned for him. Tell them to start with horseback riding. I will be joining you in a while.”

The guard took hold of Leo and placed him on a saddled horse in the stables. Then he mounted behind him and sped to the training grounds of the stadium. There he delivered him to three burly imperial soldiers who immediately started laughing at the site of the whimpering and scared Leo.

"The more you whimper, the tougher your training will become," said one, as he was leading Leo to a small, but spirited colt. "I want you to climb on this animal and ride all around the stadium."

"How?" replied Leo in a whining voice. The soldiers roared laughing. The one that held the horse grabbed Leo, brought him close to the horse and put his left foot on the left stirrup.

"Grab the saddle and put your right foot over the horse… you idiot," he yelled.

Leo tried, but his right leg did not clear the horse's saddle. He was ready to roll back down until another soldier pushed him onto the saddle.

"You are supposed to put a bit of a spring and jump on the horse," he commented.

"Now take the reins and kick its ribs with your heels. Then steer it by pulling the left or the right strap of the reigns," said the horse handler.

Leo did give a kick, but nothing happened. He did it again and again nothing. His feet were not long enough, and his kick was so mild that the horse thought he was petting it.

Frustrated, the third guard came and slapped the horse on its rump. The horse immediately took off catching Leo by surprise. He tried to hold on, but the horse bounce was too much for a thirteen-year-old. It took less than fifty paces for him to be thrown on the sandy ground of the stadium. He raised his face from the sand and spit out to clear his mouth from it. His nose was red, and his left elbow was scraped. The guards rushed to his aid, raised him up and took him to the stadium baths, where they washed him, wrapped his elbow and put ointment on his nose.

"I want to go home," said Leo.

"Not a chance," said the lead guard. "I have orders to keep you here until you learn how to ride. Then, another group will teach you how to throw a javelin and use a bow. You will go through all the requirements of the basic training, by order of the Emperor, your father."

"He is not my father!" yelled Leo crying.

"He is my Emperor," said the guard;" and if he says he is your father, he must be your father. You sleep with us in the stadium barracks until we are told otherwise."

# One Wedding and a Tonsure (Great Palace, December 10-15, 879AD)

"Your son is sleeping in the barracks from now on," said Basil, when Ingerina visited his office, inquiring about Leo.

"I see," said Ingerina placidly. "How is Leo's training coming?"

"I am afraid that he is very inept as an athlete, but my people are working on him at the barracks. Hopefully, he will not embarrass us, as a co-Emperor."

"When am I to see him?"

"He will have some leave during Christmas, but he is going back to training in the field after Theophany Day. He has a long way to go in his training."

"I see."

"Now, let us come to the main subject of the day," said Basil. "I talked to the Patriarch and he suggested a very good monastery that will accept Stephen, starting next month, provided that he is tonsured now. My doctor said that it is a simple procedure and he is available to come here with his aid this afternoon. I would like you to prepare him for it. He will bring you a potion that he prepares from poppy juice. You give that to Stephen. It will put him to sleep. When he wakes up, the doctor would have already finished the tonsure procedure."

Ingerina nodded, held her palm on her face and started crying.

Basil looked at her with mixed emotions of pity and anger.

"I am sorry, but I have to go to Aghia Sophia to attend Zoe's wedding to Theodore Gutzuniates," said Basil, changing the subject. "I promised them I would."

"Did her father accept this wedding?" replied Ingerina.

"No!" replied Basil. "Not at the beginning. But I gave Zautses no choice. I told him that he either gives his blessings to this wedding, or he stays in the rocky deserts of the East all his life. He finally agreed when I told him that I would even allow him back in the imperial guard, so that he and his family can be close to his married daughter. I told him that he could move here, as long as he and his daughter stay away from Leo."

"I see," said Ingerina and then she exited from Basil's office.

Basil immediately took off, went out and joined his guards and advisors on horseback. They all rode to Aghia Sophia to witness the wedding of Theodore and Zoe.

After leaving Basil's office, Ingerina went straight to her quarters. She was instructed by the doctor not to tell anything to the twelve-year-old Stephen about what is to happen. She was to give him the potion after the sunset. The doctor and his aid that would execute the tonsure procedure would be waiting outside the boy's chambers until she told them that he was asleep. Ingerina decided to do this all by herself, so she gave Anna her night off.

She served Stephen the potion with warm milk. It did not take long for Stephen to fall asleep. She called the doctor in, who immediately went to work making the proper incision. Then he removed the testes through the incision, which is then stitched and after disinfecting it with wine, it was bandaged.

Stephen slept through the whole night, with his mother, sleeping by his side. He woke up in the morning with a pain in his scrotum and started crying. Ingerina joined him in his crying, only silently.

"It's alright my son," she said as she held him in her arms. "It is all a bad dream. The doctor had to operate on you, but everything will be fine now."

Stephen was not able to move around for a couple days. During those days Ingerina stayed by his bedside, helped him with his bowel movements and comforted him. The third day, Patriarch Photius appeared with Leo Choirosphaktes and a fifteen-year-old youngster.

"We came to see young Stephen and to provide him with some comfort and courage," said Photius to Ingerina. "You know Leo Choirosphaktes, from my staff. The other youngster is a student of mine from Magnaura. His name is Simeon. He is a prince, son of Boris of Bulgaria from the Krum dynasty. He has been with us for about two years and he is a very good student. He can speak Greek fluently and he likes rhetoric of Demosthenes and Aristotle."

"Thank you for coming," said Stephen in a moody tone as he rose from his couch.

"We also brought you a present," said Leo Choirosphaktes, as he reached behind him and produced a basket. Strange yelps were heard from it. He brought the basket forward and opened the lid. Inside, there was a pair of barely weaned puppies.

"Puppies!" exclaimed Stephen. Suddenly, the moodiness disappeared, and his eyes sparkled. "Mom, can I keep them?"

"I do not know if the monks of your monastery would allow them to stay with you," said Ingerina.

"You can keep them," said Photius. "I will talk to the abbot and ask him for a special dispensation."

"They are of a special ancient breed," said Leo. "I brought their parents from the Peloponnese. The breed is that of a Greek shepherd dog. They are blue eyed, pointed ear and fierce in defending the herd, or their master."

Stephen picked up one of them on his couch and started petting it. Then he laid it in the basket and picked the second one. "One is male, and the other is female," he exclaimed. "I wonder what name to give each one of them. The white one, with black spots is the male. I believe that I will call him Apollo. The tan one with black spots is the female. I believe that I will call her Artemis."

"Don't forget to feed them with lots of goat's milk," said Simeon. "They will grow fast."

"Mom," said Stephen. "Can you ask Anna to fetch me some goat milk from the kitchen?"

"Is it for you, or the puppies?" said Simeon.

"It is for us," said Stephen smiling.

Photius, Ingerina, Simeon and Leo Choirosphaktes left for the kitchen, where Anna was instructed to bring two bowls of milk for the puppies and Stephen.

"I believe we should be leaving soon," said Photius.

"Thank you very much for coming Eminence," said Ingerina.

"That is the least I can do," said Photius. "Now tell me. How is Leo?"

"I haven't seen him for quite a while," replied Ingerina. "I hear that he is in training exercises and when he is not, he lives in the barracks with other soldiers and trainees."

"I see," said Photius. Then, he turned to Choirosphaktes. "What do you know about the whereabouts of Eudokia's son?"

"He is being trained, Eminence," replied Leo. "He has good trainers. They are quite rough at the beginning, especially to a youngster like Leo, but I believe they will be careful and watch over him."

"I want you to keep a discrete eye on his progress and his well-being Leo," said Photius.

"Thank you both Eminence," said Ingerina, who immediately bowed and kissed Photius's hand.

Photius pulled his hand away smiling. "It is not necessary to thank us. Prince Leo's well-being is the responsibility of all of us."

     

# Chasing Zoe (Constantinople Market, June 30, 881 AD)

Prince Leo and his three trainer guards rode into Constantinople, coming from a training exercise near Philippi, in Macedonia with a contingent that Stylianos Zautses was commanding. Several days earlier Leo had presented himself to the commander. The commander was very happy to see him.

"How is Zoe?" Leo asked Zautses. Zautses immediately dismissed his aid and made sure that they were alone in his tent.

"I am sorry Leo, but thanks to Emperor Basil, Zoe was forced to marry an old, rich merchant," said the commander.

"Where is she now?"

"They live in the Galata[13] neighborhood. I have not seen them since the wedding. I can tell you though, that she is not very happy."

"That makes two of us," Leo responded. "Thanks to my stepfather, I am on training exercises since last October, with very little rest."

"Well, let me see if I can help with that. Your escorts have direct orders from the Emperor to get you involved in day and night reconnaissance operations. I can shorten them a bit, and assign them to do them in the plains, rather than the mountains."

"Thank you," Leo responded smiling.

"After the reconnaissance exercises, I hope that the cavalry brings some wild boar from the mountains in the north. We usually roast them on a spit and have some of the local bread and wine with it. I want you and your trainers to come and enjoy yourselves. But don't tell your trainers anything yet. They may have misunderstood my intentions. You see, I am not even supposed to be talking to you directly."

---

[13] Galata was a neighborhood opposite Constantinople (today's Istanbul, Turkey), located at the northern shore of the Golden Horn, the inlet which separates it from the historic peninsula of old Constantinople.

"Why?"

"That was the condition with your stepfather, in order to allow me to return to my family. So, don't tell anyone of this meeting here."

"Sure; thank you again," said Leo.

So, his training exercises were much easier this time. At the end of the week, Zautses had all four of them outside his tent, roasting a wild boar and drinking some of the best wine from the slopes of Pangaion.

The now sixteen-year-old Leo had a good time. So, did the commander, who took care so that the two were not communicating directly. As the banquet was ending and everyone went to their tents, Zautses signaled Leo to meet him in a small forest, outside the camp.

"I always dreamed that one day, you marry my daughter," said Zautses. "I believe that she loved you and had the best words to say about you."

"Zoe is an exceptional girl," said Leo. "I loved her too, but my stepfather hates her. Do you know why?"

"No, I don't," replied Zautses. "The only reason that I can think about, is because of me."

"Why you?" said Leo.

"Because he considers me responsible for his son's death; of course, he has no proof that I had anything to do with his death. Everyone told him that it was an accident".

"Why would he have suspicions that someone would harm his son?" asked Leo.

"Because he thinks that way; for whenever something goes wrong, there is some conspiracy of evil people, planning to overthrow him and his family by assassinations, like the one he planned and executed on your father."

Leo stared at the commander in horror.

"I don't want to talk about him," he mumbled.

"Soon you will be going back to the City," said Zautses. "I will have to stay here a little longer."

Leo nodded and walked back to his tent and went to sleep.

In the morning, the commander and his officers were gone back to the mountains.

Leo was thinking about all this as they rode on the cobbled pavement of the city. He also thought of Zoe, and how she felt, being married to someone she did not know or loved.

# Leo's Dire Position (Great Palace, August 2, 882 AD)

"He does not know her at all," said Ingerina, "and he probably will hate me for my decision."

"I concur with your decision wife," said Basil. "Theophano should make the perfect wife for Leo. I will set the wedding for next month, after Holy Cross Day."

"The one he really liked was Zoe," said Ingerina.

"Zoe is also out of the picture now that she is married," said Basil. "Based on what I hear, Theophano is a saintly girl that believes in devoted marriages and will probably straighten him out of any thoughts of adultery."

"I hope you are right."

"Have you told him of your decision?"

"No."

"Never mind, I will tell him. I will see him at the barracks."

Basil left Ingerina and with his bodyguards he rode to the barracks next to the stadium. Leo had just finished practicing archery, mounted on his horse and was putting the animal at the stalls.

"I have some good news for you Leo," he said smiling.

"What news…Highness?"

"First, I have learned from your trainers that you are getting better on your military skills. I asked them to allow you more leisure time."

"Thank you … Highness."

"This leads me to the second good news, on how to spend your leisure time. Your mother and I decided that you should marry. We planned your wedding for next month. You are to marry Theophano, daughter of Constantine and Anna Martinakios."

"I will not … Highness."

"What did you say?"

"I refuse to marry this Theophano. How can you expect me to marry someone I do not even know?"

"You will know her, and you will marry her because your Emperor orders it. If not, you will go straight to the imperial jail for disobeying a direct order from me."

"I don't care. Do what you must, but I will not marry the person that you choose for me."

Basil was red with anger.

"Guards!" he yelled at the top of his voice. Immediately, several trainers and his body-guards run in front of him with swords drawn. "Put this upstart prince in bondage and take him to the imperial prison. Do not hurt him but put him in the deepest dungeon we have there."

The trainers were confused. The person that they were supposed to imprison was by now their friend. The imperial body guards though did not hesitate. They grabbed Leo, tied his hands and feet, strapped him over a horse and took him to the imperial prison, below the palace.

Basil was quite furious because his stepson dared to disobey him. He took off with his remaining guards and rode to the Patriarchate.

Meanwhile, Photius had a meeting with Leo Choirosphaktes, who was going over his deductions from his investigation on Constantine's death.

"That is very interesting," commented Photius. "Yet, I would not say any of this to anyone. Keep it to yourself, until the right time. Basil would go crazy and many innocent heads may roll, including that of the prince … and yours. We do not want that."

"Why the prince…?"

"Because, from what you told me… he would be under suspicion. Don't forget Zoe."

"When do you think would be the right time to bring the guilty people to justice?"

"You will know it, when the right time comes. Meanwhile, on my behalf, keep trailing the prince in his training and his outings. Report to me anything unusual."

As they were ready to go out the door of Photius' office, Basil arrived for a meeting with Photius. He had to tell him what happened with the prince.

"Calm down Highness," said Photius. "It is natural for Leo to object on your choice of a bride. Especially, since he was in love with Zoe, now a married woman."

"If he disobeys me and I cannot rely on him being an obedient heir to the throne, I must prevent him from ever wrenching the throne from the person that I will choose to do so," yelled Basil. "I am thinking of ordering him to be blinded."

"That would be a fatal mistake Highness," said Photius with a calming voice. "First, you don't have any ready male offspring that would fit the requirements of a prince. Second, by the time you get one, you are vulnerable to assassinations and may lose the throne to some devious usurper. This usurper could be one of your closest friends, or a member of your own bodyguards."

"What do you recommend?"

"Let me talk to Leo and explain to him what he gains and what he loses by deciding one way or another. I know that he is very bright. I may have a chance to persuade him to change his mind."

"Fine," said Basil. "But until he does, he stays in the dungeon. Thank you for your services my friend."

Basil turned around and exited the Patriarchate, waving to his guards to bring him his horse.

Photius and Leo Choirosphaktes stood and faced each other.

"Alas poor Leo," said Choirosphaktes.

# Alas Poor Leo (Great Palace, November-December, 882 AD)

*"Alas poor Leo,"* was a common sentence, heard in Ingerina's quarters. It was a squawking parrot.

"My poor son," said Ingerina. "I am hearing that Leo is in really bad shape in prison. He was dirty and was losing weight because he stopped eating the prison food. He is on a hunger strike."

Anna, her handmaiden was trying to console her. She saw that Ingerina was depressed for months, so she had tried to lift her spirits by bringing her distractions, like a pet dog and the pet parrot. Now, she even taught the parrot to repeat the phrase *"Alas Poor Leo,"* something that Ingerina asked her to do.

Meanwhile, Photius had visited Leo several times in prison. He usually sat on a chair that his aids brought outside the cell that Leo occupied. He always ordered all his aids and the jailers out, so that he can speak to Leo privately.

Several days had passed, with Photius trying to talk some sense into Leo. Then, he received news that Ingerina had fallen ill.

Photius went to see her just in time to give her last rites. He received her confession and he gave her the Holy Communion. She died a short time later in Anna's arms, while Photius was reciting the prayers known as *"the Office at the Parting of the Soul from the Body."*

The following day, Photius went to see Leo again in prison. This time he brought his chair inside the cell.

"I came to tell you the sad news that your mother, Eudokia Ingerina is dead. We will have her funeral this Sunday."

Leo started weeping.

"Your stepfather is determined to keep you in prison," said Photius, "unless you meet his conditions. I begged him to let you out for your mother's funeral, but he is very upset with you."

Leo kept on crying. He stopped his wailing for a while to utter: "Basil is a vicious bastard…"

"Tell me Leo. What do you gain by staying in jail?"

"My self-respect," was the reply.

"That is very honorable. Supposedly I told you that you can keep your self-respect by marrying Theophano and restoring your status as an heir to the throne. Your stepfather maybe an old bastard, but he is getting old; if you keep your sanity, he will soon be dead, and you will be the Emperor. What if I can promise you that all of these inconveniences to your self-respect are reversible and that you and I can work to reverse them?"

Leo looked at Photius with doubt.

"How do I know that you will be able to reverse them?"

"You don't. Neither do I, but I promise you that I will do my best. After all, what is your alternative? Rotting in prison? Think about it."

Photius got up from the chair and started walking to the exit.

"Wait!" shouted Leo. "What do you want me to do?"

"I want you to promise that after the Theophany Day, you will marry Theophano of the Amorian Dynasty. I will pass this message to your stepfather and try to persuade him that you are earnest. I will also try to take you out of here for your mother's funeral. I cannot promise you anything more for now. Do you agree to do this and to not antagonize your stepfather anymore?"

"Yes, I do."

"Now, I have a question for you. Did you have any conversation with Zautses about your relationship with Zoe?"

"Why?"

"Because Zautses can use you to conspire against your stepfather," said Photius with a stern look.

"We may have discussed Zoe, but there was no conspiracy. I simply missed his daughter's company because I like her. Anyway, Zautses is an old friend of the Emperor; why would he conspire against him?"

"You are not to have any such relationships with Zautses or his daughter," said Photius. "If I get a hint of that, our contract about reversing your marriage to Theophano or supporting you in front of the Emperor will be over. I will oppose you and Zautses in any conspiracy, regardless of whether you are innocent or not. This barbaric series of assassinations must stop."

Leo was silent.

Photius took off and asked for a meeting with the Emperor.

After Photius pleaded for Leo, Basil agreed.

"I will let him out to attend his mother's funeral," said Basil, "but after that he will be under a short leash. I also hope that Theophano puts another leash on this ungrateful upstart."

"He is young, Highness. He is also in love with a married woman. Give him some time. He will get over it."

"If I had to go through the ordeal of a forced marriage, Leo better learn to bear it too. We all have to make sacrifices for the good of Byzantium."

Hours later Photius returned to the prison and handed the jailer an imperial order.

The jailer opened Leo's cell and led him out.

"The Emperor gives you a conditional pardon," said Photius. "You are now under house arrest. If you keep your affairs clean as we discussed, he may allow you to participate in parades. Nevertheless, you are obliged to do is to go with me to Theophano's home, during her name-day celebration and meet her family."

Leo simply nodded smiling. He was happy to be out of this damp, dirty place with a stink of urine and feces. The two men slowly went through the filth of the dungeon up a staircase into the fresh air and sunshine of Constantinople. As the two men came out, several people saw them and started clapping their hands and waved at them. Leo waved back at them with a smile.

# Theophano (Great Palace, Constantinople, January 30, 883 AD)

Leo waved at people from the imperial coach as the parade of the Emperor and his advisors were passing through the streets, on their way to Aghia Sophia to celebrate the Synaxis of The Three Hierarchs: Basil the Great, Gregory the Theologian, and John Chrysostom.

Next to him he had his new wife, Theophano. She was the same age as he, seventeen years old. To Leo's eyes, she was a peculiar girl. She was a beautiful woman with a well sculptured body, but she dressed very conservatively and had an obsessive religious nature. She woke up early every morning, washed her face with an urn and spent at least an hour every morning praying in the small palace chapel before she did anything else. Then, at night, she spent another hour praying before she went to bed, fully dressed. Leo restrained himself for saying anything to her after their wedding. He had made up his mind to smile a lot and bear this forced wedding of his, if he could.

Yet, after several days of enduring his new wife's behavior, he decided to intervene. "Do you find pleasure in praying so much and getting very little in return?" he told her jokingly with a smile.

"I have faith that God will provide me with all the satisfaction I need in this world," she responded sternly.

Leo tried to entice her to open herself sexually, but he found that it was as if he was trying to get a reaction out of a beautiful marble statue. He spent so much time trying to undress her in bed, that after that he was too tired and too frustrated to continue. Yet, being faithful to his promise to Photius he gave it a good try. Finally, he managed to have sex with this "marble statue" a couple of times.

A few days later, after one such frustrated attempt, he stopped. He threw on his tunic and went to the palace kitchen to find something to drink.

There he met a familiar friend and Latin instructor of his, Chariton Psellus, helping his father Tryphon in feeding the personnel of the palace.

"Are you alright prince?" Chariton asked. This was the first time he had seen Leo in the kitchen at that hour. The imperial family was served in a separate dining area first, sometime earlier. At this late hour, the only ones there that ate were the kitchen staff, and almost all of them had eaten and left.

"Oh, yes; I am fine."

"How was your wedding?"

"It was fine."

"How is your new beautiful bride?"

Leo could not hold himself. He looked around and saw that none was there to listen, other than Chariton and his father and then burst into a mix of laughter and weeping.

"One thing I can say about her; she is beautiful, but she is no Zoe."

"Zoe? Zoe Zautses?"

"Never mind Chariton; as my stepfather keeps on saying, we in the imperial family have to endure and sacrifice everything that a human being holds dear for Byzantium to survive. We must sacrifice our honor, our bodies, our loved ones and even our manhood for all the rest of you, lucky souls. Can we change places?"

"What?"

"Never mind my friend; just bring me some of the best wine you have. Also bring me some salty delicacies, if you have any."

"At once prince," said the instructor and went to the kitchen. He soon came back with a pitcher of wine, some bread and some pickled mackerel in olive oil.

The two drank and talked until midnight. Leo got enough drunk to spill his frustration.

"I don't understand my mother," said Leo. "You know, she is the one that chose Theophano for my bride. Why did she choose an ice, cold hermaphrodite for me? Is she trying to pass me a hidden message?"

"I am sure that you will figure it out," said Chariton.

"I felt sorry for my poor mother," said Leo. "She was very depressed and that sent her to her grave. I hardly saw her before she died. She was left all alone. I was in the army and then in prison. My brother was castrated and sent to a monastery. I am in desperate need of friends like you, teacher…"

Leo grabbed Chariton's face by the cheeks and tried to focus on his eyes. He couldn't. He let go and grabbed his cup of wine and emptied it. Soon, Leo's head started to bob. Chariton lifted him up and led him back to his chambers.

Leo walked to his bed and lifted the covers. He saw that Theophano, whose clothes he had peeled off with great effort, was fully dressed again in bed. He raised his arms in frustration and then became curious. He lifted the covers close to her feet and saw that this girl had also put on her socks. That is when he dropped his shoulders and let himself fall next to her with an exasperated moan.

"Oh, God; give her what she wants and prays for."

Today, as the carriage was pulling into Aghia Sophia, Leo's mind tried to put away all these memories of the past few weeks. As they stopped, he got up and helped his "marble statue" to get out of the coach.

# New Players (Great Palace, February, 883 AD)

Chariton took a coach to Ingerina's memorial services. He did not like how his student Leo felt about the situation. Chariton went to the monastery, where Ingerina was buried. In the forty-day memorial procession he saw Co-Emperor Leo and his brother Stephen in a monk's habit there. They were both in mourning. At the end of the funeral he approached them.

"My condolences on your mother's loss," he uttered to both.

The brothers thanked him. As he was ready to depart, he saw Zautses approach the boys. He took Leo by the arm and went behind the monastery, away from the crowds. Chariton waited until Leo returned next to Stephen. That is when Chariton noticed that Leo had switched from the sorry look he had earlier, to an uneasy and agitated state. For some peculiar reason, Leo became nervous and his face was white as snow. He soon made an excuse that he was not feeling well, got on his horse and raced towards the Palace.

Chariton felt sorry for Leo. He wanted to help him get over his depressed state, but he did not know how.

Then, the following day Leo Choirosphaktes arrived in the palace kitchen during midafternoon, for a late lunch.

He had not seen him in the kitchen for quite a while, and his presence was a surprise to him.

"What are you doing in the palace, officer?" Chariton asked. "I have not seen you for quite a while."

"I was sent away," said Leo. "I went to my home in Peloponnese and had some rest, after my wife died. I needed some time off, to recuperate."

"We are very sorry for your loss," said Chariton. "Anna said that she was a good woman."

"Thank you both! Now I am back, I am doing some chores for the Emperor and the Patriarch… chores that I cannot talk about."

"I understand," said Chariton. "I wonder though if you can help me with my problem, which eventually may become yours as well."

"What problem is that?"

"My problem is that I cannot help Prince Leo with his deep depression. He is all alone and without any support from his stepfather. I know him well as my student. He is very intelligent, but how is he to grow up and become a good Emperor if everyone badmouths him? I am afraid for his wellbeing and as a result for our own future."

Choirosphaktes smiled. "Bring me my food and wine and we will discuss Prince Leo. What do you have today?"

"My father has prepared rabbit stifado to die for, with plenty of pearl onions. We also have some wine left. We have some red and some retsina wine. What do you prefer?"

"Retsina, with some fresh bread…"

Chariton went to the kitchen to prepare Leo's lunch.

In a few minutes, Leo was enjoying his wine and food, with Chariton sitting across from him on the bench, waiting. As Leo paused, he whispered.

"I know all about the prince's frustration," he uttered. "I know that he loves the Zautses girl, Zoe, but he was given no choice by his stepfather. His mother suggested Theophano, knowing very well the girl and expecting that her son, in his own time will rebel against Basil and eventually kick her out of his bed.

"But why…? That was her son. Why make his life miserable?"

"Because she did not want her son to forget what his father had suffered … in the arms of a woman, other than the one he truly loved."

"That is unbelievable."

"Normally, yes; a normal woman would seek the happiness of her son. But in Ingerina's case, you can expect the unexpected. Think about it. She becomes the mistress of Michael, probably because she fell in love with a dashing prince, frustrated with his mother, who married him to a woman he despised. Then Basil, Michael's best friend comes and kills her lover, only to propose her to be his Empress, even though she had two sons with Michael. But instead of putting her son on the throne, he wants to place his own son, from another woman on it. This woman had been going through a continuous trauma all her life. I am surprised she held her mental and physical health as long as she did."

"What are you saying Leo? Are you saying that Ingerina was crazy?"

"She would have been fine, if Basil's son lived; but as fate had it, he was killed, when he was under my guardianship, under mysterious circumstances."

"What mysterious circumstances? I heard that it was an accident."

"Maybe…."

"But who would want to kill Constantine?"

"I cannot say," said Leo. "Things started going downhill when Basil and Ingerina separated. She found another man to love, but soon, Basil struck her happiness again down. He castrated the man and sent him packing to a monastery. Let me ask you. How much could a woman take?"

"I don't know."

"Well, she took it all very well, until the day of Constantine's death. After Basil heard of his son's death, it led to events that made Ingerina lose her mind. First, he set her son as a Co-Emperor; then, he force-married his girlfriend to a much older man. Basil then took her second son, castrated him and sent him to a monastery. Finally, he put the new Co-Emperor in prison and threatened to blind him. Leo was saved by the Patriarch from being blinded."

"Poor Leo…"

"Poor Ingerina…," chimed Leo. "I believe that drove the nail to her coffin."

"Can we do something to help Leo?" asked Chariton.

"We cannot do much, as long as Basil is alive; and Basil hates Leo."

Chariton looked at Leo with fright.

"I saw the prince at the memorial yesterday," he said in a low voice. "Zautses came over, took him behind the monastery for a while, and when Leo came back his face was white, and he was very upset. He said that he was not feeling well and took off on his horse to the Palace."

"That is interesting," said Leo, scratching his beard. "That is mighty interesting."

Then suddenly Leo got up, leaving the rest of his lunch untouched. "And, if you want to help Leo, please don't repeat what you saw there to anyone." He grabbed the towel that was hanging on Chariton's belt, wiped his mouth, and rushed towards the door.

"Where are you going?" Chariton asked in surprise.

"To talk to some of our friends," replied Leo as he went out of the kitchen.

It did not take long for Choirosphaktes to reach Prince Leo's quarters. He was not there. They told him that he was in the Magnaura Library.

He found the prince in the Library reading a scroll of ancient Greek Drama. It was Antigone, by Sophocles.

"Can we speak Prince Leo?" asked Choirosphaktes.

The prince got up and the two went out in the gardens. They sat on a bench.

"What is it?"

"What did Stylianos Zautses want of you?" asked Choirosphaktes in a direct manner. He caught the prince by surprise.

"What? Why are you asking?"

"Because the Patriarch and I want to keep you safe and away from any future accusations of conspiracy against the Emperor," said Choirosphaktes. "Your conversation with me is strictly between us. I know that he talked to you during your mother's memorial. Did he propose anything to you that may be interpreted as a conspiracy?"

"No. Not really. All he said was that he was eager and able to help me in any way possible."

"What else…? Statements like that do not make you so agitated as for you to lose all your face color and to run away from your mother's memorial by calling yourself sick."

"Why are you involved in this? This is not your affair, nor that of the Patriarch for whom you work."

"The Patriarch made it my task to help you."

Prince Leo pondered for a few seconds, whether to trust this man.

"Zautses told me that he vowed to my mother before she died that he would see me become an Emperor soon. He also told me that he would see that I divorce my wife and marry Zoe."

"Did he say anything else?"

"No. Isn't that enough?"

"Did he indicate how he plans for these things to happen?"

"No! But, just hearing that my mother and Zautses had such a conversation made me scared. What if Basil finds out? By telling you this, I am putting my life in your hands."

"Calm down prince. Basil will not find out; not from us, anyway. The

Patriarch is on your side. I hope that Zautses keeps his mouth shut, on his end."

"Thank you," said Prince Leo. "I feel relieved for telling you this. I have not talked about this anyone, including my brother."

"Keep it that way," said Choirosphaktes, as he got up to leave. "With your permission, I have to inform the Patriarch of this. He may come up with a plan to help you stay out of trouble."

As Choirosphaktes was leaving, Prince Leo also got up and went back in the Library. Choirosphaktes took a few steps and pondered what Photius would do, after hearing about Zautses' statements. One think was certain though in his mind. Photius would be certain to assign him the task of tailing Prince Leo very closely.

     STAVROS BOINODIRIS PHD

# Scandals (Great Palace, Mar 23, 884 AD)

Choirosphaktes tailed Prince Leo discretely whenever he could. Prince Leo was not allowed to wander around the city, except for the times that he was involved in parades or military exercises. When he returned from one exercise close to the Dardanelles, Choirosphaktes managed to track the cavalry troop that Prince Leo was with.

Prince Leo had an escort of a dozen riders with him, as they were riding on the cobblestone streets of the City.

As they passed some open market stalls, Prince Leo's eye caught a very familiar figure of a woman. It was Zoe.

"Give me a minute," he said to his escort, as he dismounted and handed the reins to his horse to one of them. He walked through the crowded market and approached Zoe.

"Hello," he said as he tapped her shoulder.

Zoe turned and, in her surprise, dropped the basket with eggs on the ground. The Prince picked it up and handed it to her. Half the eggs were broken.

"I don't have time now, but I want to see you," Leo whispered. "Can we meet at your father's barn at sunset?"

She nodded. "I am now married," she whispered back.

"I know," said Leo. "Your father told me. I will see you later at our usual rendezvous place, on the loft."

Zoe nodded.

Meanwhile, in the next stall, the commotion of dropping the egg basket drew the attention of another person. This person turned and saw the Prince talking to Zoe and smiled. This person was the other Leo, Leo Choirosphaktes.

Prince Leo went back to his horse and suddenly his eyes fell on a stall where they were selling uniforms for priests and monks. He immediately went there, and he purchased a hooded habit of a monk. Choirosphaktes saw this and immediately set upon to follow the prince.

"It is for my brother," the prince said to his escort trainers, as he came to his horse. "He is a monk."

The four rode to the barracks, where he changed from his military uniform to that of a civilian, but he donned the monk's habit over his tunic. As he was changing from his uniform to the monk's outfit, he did not notice Theophano in the next room peeking and finding the whole scene suspicious.

Anna, the hand-maiden that served Ingerina was out of a job after Ingerina died and Theophano had chosen as her own hand-maiden, a nun, who was at that time in her near-by monastery. Meanwhile Anna started helping her father-in-law in the Palace kitchen and some of the maintenance duties of the Palace.

Theophano was so quiet in her prayers, that Leo did not notice she was there. When he finished getting dressed up as a monk, Leo tried to walk quietly out of the Palace, trying to be as inconspicuous as possible. He walked through the streets with his hood on and headed to the neighborhood where the Zautses residence was next to the Palace.

He did not notice that Choirosphaktes was tailing him. But worse, he did not notice that a woman, dressed as a nun, was also tailing him as well. The woman was Theophano, who got dressed up in the habit of her hand-maiden and decided to track her husband.

Prince Leo went to the barn and climbed the ladder to the loft. There, he saw Zoe with blankets on top of the straw, waiting for him. Without saying a word, Leo took off the habit and lied next to Zoe, hugging her and kissing her passionately. The two covered themselves, like old times and started making love.

Choirosphaktes thought of what he witnessed. He immediately left the scene and rode to the Patriarchate to report what he saw.

A few minutes after Choirosphaktes left, after witnessing the love affair between the Prince and Zoe, Theophano, dressed as a nun entered the barn. She slowly crept up and saw Prince Leo making love to some woman. She did not recognize who she was. With tears in her eyes she returned to the Palace.

When Choirosphaktes walked into the Patriarch's office and reported the scene to Photius, he did not seem surprised.

"Do you think that Zautses is behind this love affair?" asked Photius in a calm voice.

"I don't know, Eminence, but I would not be surprised if he had arranged all this. From what I gathered from the troopers, Leo was at the Dardanelles training with some other units."

"Let's keep an eye on Zautses. I don't want to be surprised by another assassination plot."

"Yes, Eminence," replied Leo Choirosphaktes as he departed. He had to find out more pertinent information on Zautses and the imperial family. His best bet on getting such information was the kitchen in the Great Palace.

# Leo's Punishment (Great Palace Kitchen, Mar 25, 884 AD)

The kitchen of the Great Palace had a special dining area for the Emperor and all his family. Basil was having his lunch, when Theophano approached him with her nun, hand-maiden. She stood in front of him and told him exactly what she witnessed in Zautses' barn with her own eyes.

"He did what?" yelled Basil, in a booming voice. He got up and faced Theophano with a wild look.

"My husband was dressed as a monk. He went to a house with a barn and was making love to a woman," said Theophano, without any hint of intimidation by the towering Basil. "I saw him with my own eyes."

Basil flew in fury, entered Prince Leo's room, while he was asleep and using his belt, he started beating the eighteen-year-old prince with his sword belt. Fortunately, he did not have his sword, for he could have killed him. Yet, the belt buckle did quite a bit of damage. Blood was coming out of Leo's skin as he managed to outrun Basil out in the corridor, half naked.

Basil ordered his guards:

"Capture him and put him in prison again…" he yelled. "He needs to be blinded this time."

The frightened Prince Leo ran out of the Palace.

A few steps from the gate, he bumps into the arms of Leo Choirosphaktes, who grabbed him and stopped him in his tracks.

"What happened?" asked Choirosphaktes.

"I don't know. Basil is out to kill me. He wants to blind me."

"Calm down. Give yourself up. I will notify the Patriarch. We know that you broke your house arrest and went to the Zautses home with Zoe. For your own sake, you have no choice, but to take your punishment."

Choirosphaktes handed Prince Leo to the imperial guards, who took him as he was, half naked and cold and threw him in the imperial dungeon.

     STAVROS BOINODIRIS PHD

An hour later, after Choirosphaktes talked to Photius and told him how important his intervention was, Photius was at the Palace, trying to persuade Basil not to blind his only heir to the throne.

"You cannot harm the boy," said Photius. "It is not to your interest, nor the interest of Byzantium. He is the only available heir to the throne and a symbol of continuous stability for Byzantium. He is also a young man and he has his own preference of women, just like you and most of the men in this Palace. He also does not like to be bullied by you."

"He has shown sheer disrespect for me and the promises he made," bellowed Basil. "He did it, to get back on me. I will show him …"

"No!" Photius interrupted. "He did not go and have this affair with his childhood love overtly, to get back at you. He tried to hide it, but he got caught. I believe that you and I can control him, until he matures enough to see the error of his ways."

"What do you have in mind?"

"I propose that he stays on house arrest," said Photius. "Put on him several guards to watch him for every minute of the day, in several shifts. Don't allow him to go on army maneuvers, from where he can escape our monitoring. I will also put one of my people to watch every move that the Zautses family makes."

"What about his training?" Basil asked.

"He already had some training," replied Photius. "The rest of his training can wait. He will have plenty of opportunities to become a good leader when he becomes an Emperor. He will know how to fight, after his first defeat in battle."

Basil scratched his beard thinking.

"I will do it your way, Photius," said Basil. "I hope that your plan works."

"It has to work, Highness."

A few moments later Basil gave the orders to take Leo out of prison and put him under house arrest. Leo could not go anywhere, without having one of Basil's Palace guards next to him.

Photius returned to his office, where Choirosphaktes eagerly was waiting to find out from Photius about the outcome from his meeting with Basil.

"All is well," said Photius. "The Prince will be on house arrest from now on. No more military exercises."

"That is great!" exclaimed Choirosphaktes.

"Meanwhile, I have a side-task for you," said Photius. "I want you to monitor all movements of the members of the Zautses family. That includes Stylianos, Zoe, Zautsina and all their friends and relatives."

"That is not an easy task Eminence," replied Choirosphaktes. "It would take more people and money to do this monitoring."

"I cannot afford too much," said Photius. "Yet, try to do the best you can with the limited budget we have."

"Yes, Eminence," replied Choirosphaktes. He got up and exited. He was relieved that Prince Leo escaped distraction, but he knew that he had a mountain of a task before him. At that moment he decided to head for the Palace kitchen for a drink and to formulate his own plans.

As he was ready to enter, Anna passed him and entered the kitchen.

"Emperor Basil flogged his own son," she said to the people inside with tears in her eyes.

"He flogged his own son?" said Spiro, the cook.

Chariton Psellus, who was inside the kitchen raised his head and interrupted:

"Who flogged whom?"

"I am telling Spiro about how Emperor Basil flogged his own son Leo," said Anna, wailing. "Then he sent him to prison, threatening to blind him. It is awful. This is the young man that I raised him since he was born. How can he do that?"

Choirosphaktes stood inside the door. "Don't worry Anna," he declared. "I just heard that the Emperor decided to parole Prince Leo."

"Is that true?" said Anna.

Choirosphaktes nodded positively.

"I wonder what happened," said Chariton.

Then everyone in the kitchen started theorizing on possible causes for such events. Choirosphaktes decided to get some wine and go and sit in a corner, unobserved, as he was listening to all the gossip of these Palace employees. He listened unobserved until two soldiers walked in. They seemed to be officers that were often used to carry messages. Everyone's eyes turned to the soldiers. The tall one asked:

"Do you have something to eat Spiro?"

"Well if it isn't Andreas. Come and sit down. There are some pickled mackerel and lentils for you. Where did you come from?"

"From the dromond that just landed; we come on official business."

"Will you get upset if I asked you what sort of business?" said the cook. The cook stood, looking at them.

"Don't just stand there," said the shorter officer. "We are hungry. Give us some food and I may tell you."

The cook went and fetched the pickled mackerel from a clay jar. He placed three pieces on each of the two clay plates and added hot lentils next to the fish from a pot on the smoldering fire. He served them to the soldiers with two wooden spoons. The soldiers were busy eating.

"Well?" he asked.

"How about some of that great wine you hide behind the wall?" said the short soldier with his mouth full.

The cook went and fetched them two clay cups with wine. The soldiers grabbed them and washed some of the food in their mouths.

"We come from the Aegean Islands of Andros and Lemnos," said the short officer. The Saracens attacked several islands using their base from Crete.

"Did you say Andros?" asked Chariton.

"Yes; why?"

"My family came from that island," said Chariton. "For some reason they were exiled to Cappadocia and after many years we ended up here."

"Sorry about that," said Andreas. "They did quite some damage there. We captured a few of the Saracens later and found a few things about their operation. We found out that these Saracens were from various parts of the Mediterranean, including Spain, Syria and Africa. They are using small, fast ships in black sails, raiding and taking slaves. They take mostly the youth and killing the rest. We also found out that they sold many of these slaves at Chandax,[14] the capital of Crete."

"Where are you from, Andreas?" asked Chariton.

---

[14] Chandax is today's Iraklion, the largest city and the administrative capital of the island of Crete.

"From Philadelphia,[15]" said the officer raising his cup. "It is a good size city east of Ephesus."

"So, why are you here?" asked Chariton.

"We came to report the events," said the officer "and ask for additional help from the navy against these raiders. Then, we decided to take off a little vacation and go hunting somewhere in the mountains. We have had enough of sea travel. Does anyone know of a good place around here to go hunting?"

---

[15] Philadelphia is today's Alasehir, in Turkey. It was a prosperous Byzantine city, called the "little Athens" in the 6th century AD because of its festivals and temples. The Byzantine walls that once surrounded the city have now all but crumbled away.

# Preparing for a Hunt (Apamea,16 August, 885 AD)

*"This is an excellent place for hunting,"* Zautses thought to himself as he was riding his horse, accompanied by his two Farghanese[17] Turkish servants, also on horses. Stylianos wanted to see again this area, where he had been several times before, while training troops. He also knew how treacherous this place can be, and he wanted to find out if he can use that knowledge.

Suddenly, one of his Turkish riders raised his arm and stopped his horse. The Turk pointed to the trees up front. There Zautses saw a herd of deer. He also heard the clanking of stag antlers. He saw two stags fighting each other for dominance over the herd of females. The three riders stood there in silence watching the show. After several minutes of fighting, one of the stags gave up the fight and took a flight down the ravine.

"I want that stag," said Zautses, as he spurred his horse. The two Turk riders followed. One of them took his bow out of his shoulder, while his horse was trotting behind Zautses. The underbrush was thick, so everyone had to slow down. The stag, tired after the long fight and run, went ahead and down to the ravine where a small brook was carrying water from a spring to the valley below. There it stopped to drink. Zautses saw it and stopped. He signaled to the Turks to dismount and be quiet, as he started to creep upon the animal. One of the Turks aimed his arrow at the animal, while the other Turk was preparing his bow for a second shot. The first arrow hit the animal on the neck; it jolted and started to run downstream, where the other Turk was. The second arrow found the animal on the chest. It buckled down, weak and helpless, until Zautses came and finished it with his hunting spear.

---

[16] This Apamea refers to Apamea Myrlea, an ancient city and bishopric (Apamea in Bithynia) on the Sea of Marmara, in Bithynia, Anatolia; its ruins are a few kilometers south of Mudanya, Bursa Province in the Marmara Region of Asian Turkey.

[17] Farghan is a region in Eastern Uzbekistan.

"I want the skin of this animal to be taken out and preserved as is, together with the head and the antlers," he said with a smile in his face.

All three dismounted, took off their sharp daggers and started skinning the stag. After they finished, Stylianos took the skin and wrapped it with his chlamys, as it was.

"Why aren't you going to wash the fur in the creek?" said one Turk. "It is full of blood."

"No," said Stylianos. "I want it as is. You can take the carcass. We can have it on a skewer tonight at a tavern in the next village, which is some distance from here."

A few hours later the three men were pulling their loaded horses into an inn, outside a village. They secured the animals in the barn and brought the deer carcass into the kitchen.

"Can you cook this for us?" Stylianos asked the cook.

"Sure," he replied, "but I take half of it for my family."

"I agree," replied Stylianos, "provided that you also give us some of the lentils you have cooking and plenty of wine."

"Agreed," said the cook. "Serve yourself on the wine. The cups are on the counter and the barrel is against the wall."

The men went and poured wine out of the barrel into their cups and started drinking.

     STAVROS BOINODIRIS PHD

# Bitter Peace (Great Palace, November, 885 AD)

Prince Leo poured some more wine out of a silver pitcher. He took a sip, looking at his wife, holding a week-old baby. She had just given birth to a girl.

"What name do you think that we should give her at her baptismal?" Theophano asked.

"I don't know," responded Leo. "The first name that came to my mind was Eudokia." He chuckled for a couple of seconds. "That would make my mother, God forgive her, happy."

"Why do you find it funny? Eudokia is a good name," responded Theophano.

Leo shook his head. He looked at Theophano and wondered where that baby came from. It sure was not out of a passion of love. *"It must have been one of those nights, where I was experimenting whether I can get an arousal out of this marble statue,"* he thought and started laughing.

"I am so happy to see you laugh," said Theophano.

Leo looked at his wife, nodded, but slowly his laughter disappeared.

*"This is not what I wanted in my life,"* he thought. *"This is all wrong. But what can I do?"*

He had seen Photius a few weeks ago when he reminded him of his commitment to reverse Basil's misdeeds. Photius was not amused.

"I cannot do much, as long as you are losing your patience and creating problems with your stepfather," said Photius. "After all your escapades with Zoe, you will be under house arrest, until God decides to take your stepfather to his bosom."

"I wish He hurries up," said Leo. "I am not sure I can take this any longer."

"Hush!" said Photius. "Statements like that can be taken as plots against your stepfather and can mean your death. You must be patient and wait your time." Photius had pondered for a few seconds. "I am assigning you a spiritual father to help you in your ordeal. Father Euthymios is a syngelos priest who will help you as an advisor in matters of patience."

"I am patient," replied Leo. "I have avoided any confrontation with Basil for more than a year a half. We are now at peace in the Palace, but for me it is a very bitter peace."

"It may be bitter for you, but Basil is now content," said Photius. "He is content enough to allow you to attend the parades and liturgies, accompanied by your wife and –of course- your omnipresent guards. Choirosphaktes also told me that he even allowed his old enemy, Zautses to come back to the City, to be with his daughter. It shows that he is not afraid so much of any rebellions anymore."

"A lot of good that does me," said Leo.

"Well," said Photius, "having a non-hostile Emperor on your back can make your life a lot more tolerable. From what I understand, he has found various ways of enjoying himself. One of them is going hunting."

"I know," said Leo. "Every time he is away hunting, the Palace has a celebration. No fights with the guards, no yelling in the corridors and no badmouthing of his stepson. Do you know when he is planning to take off?"

"I believe he goes hunting often," said Photius. "Based on what I found out from Choirosphaktes, Basil decided to take with him Zautses on some future hunt."

"Why?"

"We don't know," said Photius. "Maybe you can find out. All we know is that Zautses talked to Basil and told him about an exciting hunting place near his country palace of Apamea. I don't know if, or when those two would become friends again, but things are getting more peaceful for now."

That was a few weeks ago. Photius had left, but neither he, nor Father Euthymios appeared at all.

*"What is going on?"* Leo asked himself. *"Why didn't I hear anything from Photius or his people? I think it is time to find out."*

Since he was on house arrest, Leo had to call someone to come and bring him the news. More than anything, he needed assurances that Photius was doing something to help him psychologically, to bear his predicament with Theophano. He went outside and asked if anyone had seen Leo

Choirosphaktes. When the guard said "no," he asked one of the guards to find him and bring him over, so that he can talk to him.

An hour later, Choirosphaktes was knocking at the prince's door.

"I have not seen the Patriarch," said the prince. "Do you know where he is?"

"He is at Magnaura, My Prince," said Choirosphaktes. "He is extremely busy with the ecclesiastical work of our missionaries. He has been traveling and just came back from a meeting with Bulgarian delegates."

"What happened with the Bulgarians?"

"The Patriarch was meeting with their ruler. Archon Boris wanted to become Christian and to change his people from Tengrism."

"Oh, yes!" said the prince. "I was reading about them in some texts from missionaries. That is quite a weird religion. It is a Central Asian religion characterized by shamanism, animism, totemism, poly- and monotheism and ancestor worship."

"You know more about them than I do," said Choirosphaktes. "Anyway, Boris was baptized as Michael-Boris. He even sent his son Simeon here at Magnaura for ecclesiastical studies."

"Yes," said the Prince, "I met Simeon once."

"So, Boris negotiated with Photius successfully by threatening to join the Pope of Rome and secured an autocephalous Bulgarian Church. In that manner he silenced nobility's concerns about Byzantine interference in Bulgaria's internal affairs. This year, when the disciples of Saints Cyril and Methodius, like Naum were banished from Great Moravia, Michael-Boris gave them refuge and provided assistance to develop the Bulgarian alphabet and literature. So, the Patriarch has his hands full with all that work."

"I see," replied the Prince. "Please let him know that if he needs me, I am willing to give him a helping hand."

"I will pass your message My Prince; if I may say so, you are very gracious."

"Not at all," said Prince Leo. "I hate being cooped up with guards babysitting me every minute of the day."

"I am sorry to leave Prince, but I have another appointment to keep. Don't worry. I will be coming here as often as I can to talk to you."

"Please do," said the Prince with a smile.

Leo Choirosphaktes left the Great Palace entrance and went to the stables, where he had given the keeper his horse. He tipped the keeper for his trouble and mounted his horse. He was heading towards Magnaura, when he saw a group of riders heading out of the City with hunting spears.

"Ah!" he thought. "It is late November. They must be going for a boar hunt."

     STAVROS BOINODIRIS PHD

# The Hunt (Outside Apamea Myrlea, 20th August, 886 AD)

The hunting party carried both, hunting bows and spears. Basil rode in the middle of the column. They had left his country residence of Apamea with several his close friends, some of who also happened to be his advisors. It was a bright, sunny morning. They traveled quite a distance for several hours from Basil's country residence, without seeing any deer to hunt. Soon, Basil and Symbatius were ahead of the main hunting party, except for three scouts that were up front, at some distance.

Symbatius, one of his oldest and closest advisors commented on the scouting trio.

"What does Zautses and the two Turks are doing here Highness?"

"It's alright friend. I allowed them to come as guides. Zautses told me of a superb place where we can hunt deer. He even gave me the fur of one that he bagged last year, which we put on my horse, under my saddle."

"Are you sure that they are safe to have them around you? I suggest that we all go back to your country residence. We have travelled a long distance already. Some of our friends that are lagging behind are complaining that they need to rest."

"Don't worry," Basil said with laughter. "Zautses is up front, scouting with his Turks and not around me. Yes, he was present when my son had his accident and he was a suspect. He may be up to something, by talking to me like an old friend, but I need to find out what is in Zautses' mind and whether he still has any malice against me. Up to now he has been very cooperative and friendly, despite his banishment to the East for a long time. As for our friends, what can I say? If they feel tired, and unwilling to hunt with me, they can go back."

"I doubt that they could find their way back on their own," said Symbatius.

"Don't they know their way back?" asked Basil.

Symbatius could see at a distance Zautses and his two Farghanese Turkish servants up front, scouting and leading Basil's party. These scouts soon started to approach the ravine where the deer were seen frequently. Then, Symbatius saw that Zautses and his servants turned back and approached the Emperor.

"Well, doesn't anyone in that group know their way back?" asked Basil, repeating the question, since Symbatius was too absorbed with the scouts.

"No, Highness. None know the way back, except of me and the scouts."

Zautses caught this last sentence from Symbatius, as he approached Basil.

"The herd is frequently seen in that small forest, Highness" said Zautses pointing with his arm in a low voice, so as not to alert the herd.

"You, Symbatius stay with our friends," said Basil. Then he spurred his horse towards the forest, with Zautses and his Turks behind him. Symbatius stayed behind, following Basil's orders and not wanting to leave the rest of the group stranded. He was all alone, waiting for them to catch up.

As Basil's horse entered the small forest, it faced a large herd of deer with the champion stag leading it. When the stag saw Basil's horse charging it, it raised its nostrils up in the air and smelled something familiar: the challenger stag of the previous year. The smell was coming from the fur that lined Basil's saddle. Zautses sees this and stops at the edge of the forest, observing to see what will happen. The Turks though kept on going.

After a while, the main group of hunters arrived where Symbatius was.

"What is happening there?" one of them asked.

"I don't know," responded Symbatius. "The Emperor is after some deer. He asked me to tell you all that if you are tired, we can go back and rest, but I don't want to leave without him."

Meanwhile, Basil had attacked the herd with his spear, but missed the stag. Instead of the stag, he speared a doe. With Basil's spear stuck on the doe, the stag turned around and with his big antlers attacked Basil's horse with such force that Basil was thrown off the horse and fell right on the antlers of the animal, where his belt got tangled. The animal then trotted down the ravine, dragging the unconscious Basil all the way down to the brook. The Turks were stunned from the scene and kept some distance, until the stag started to drag Basil. Then, they followed the stag carefully, so that the stag does not panic and inflict more damage to Basil.

Zautses saw what happened and immediately followed Basil and the Turks down to the ravine, which was a long distance from the place where the hunt started. There Basil started to recover conscience, but as he was still tangled up in the stag's antlers and started moving, the animal instinctively turned and gored the dazed Basil in his abdomen.

The dazed Basil immediately starts yelling from pain. The Turks rushed to help. One of them, felt sorry for Basil and dismounted. Then he cut off Basil's belt, while the stag had still his antlers inside Basil's abdomen. The stag, freed from Basil's belt gave a last push with its antlers and took off, disappearing in the woods. Zautses, as he was approaching Basil, heard all of Basil's yells of pain.

"Let's make a stretcher," he ordered after he dismounted, holding an axe. "We must carry the Emperor out of here."

"This Turk of yours tried to kill me!" yelled Basil. "I want him dead. I want him dead now!"

Zautses was flabbergasted. If Basil made it alive, he would be in deep trouble if he hesitated. He immediately picked up the hunting spear from his horse and jammed it on the ribs of his Turk servant, who did not expect such an attack. The Turk fell on his knees, dead. The other Turk was so scared that he fell on his knees, pleading for his life.

"Get up," said Zautses. "Help me make a litter, so that we can carry the Emperor out of this awful ravine."

He helped his servant up and the two cut some small, tall trees down. They brought one of the horses and tied it to a tree. Then they harnessed two long poles on the horse. They proceeded to use some horse blankets tied with leather straps between the poles to make a horse drawn litter. Finally, they slowly moved Basil over the litter.

"I want to know: how did I end up here, at the bottom of the ravine?" yelled Basil.

"I don't know Highness," said Zautses. "I presume that the stag dragged you all the way downhill."

"I want you to measure how far that blasted stag dragged me. That is an order."

"Yes Highness. I will do that after we take you back to your home, so that your physician can take care of you."

It took almost an hour for the horse drawn stretcher to reach Symbatius and the rest of the main hunting group. Symbatius immediately ordered several men to make a better stretcher and manually carry the Emperor on their shoulders. With the help of Symbatius and many of Basil's advisors, it took many hours to reach Basil's country place. By the time they arrived it was getting dark.

Immediately, Symbatius brought Basil's physician over and tried to determine all internal damage that the stag had done to him.

News of the event reached Constantinople that same night via light signaling.

*"Emperor Basil was hurt in hunting accident at Apamea."*

A messenger delivered the message to Patriarch Photius that same night. The following morning Photius immediately summoned Leo Choirosphaktes.

"Go to Apamea and find out what is going on," he said sternly to his field intelligence operator. Choirosphaktes hired a ship and sailed across the Sea of Marmara to the port of Cius.[18] There he hired a horse and headed for Apamea.

That morning, Zautses, his Turk servant, Symbatius and a surveyor rode to the site to determine where the attack started and where it ended, gathering evidence for a hearing on the event.

That afternoon, Leo Choirosphaktes arrived at the Apamea residence. He asked and received all the hearsay information from several men in the hunting group. Then, he waited to hear the report from the surveyor's party. The party finally arrived that night. They went straight to Basil's bed.

"We estimated that that stag dragged you around fifty-eight stadia.[19]"

"It is a miracle that you are alive," said Symbatius.

"That is all my good men," said the doctor, coming between Symbatius

---

[18]  The port of Cius was an ancient Greek city bordering the Propontis (now known as the Sea of Marmara), in Bithynia (in modern northwestern Turkey), and had a long history, being mentioned by Aristotle, Strabo and Apollonius Rhodius. It was colonized by the Milesians and became a place of much commercial importance.

[19]  Each stadium is 400 meters. The distance that the stag dragged the body was estimated at 23.2 kilometers, or about 15.5 miles.

and the bed-ridden Basil and by raising his arms. "More than anything, the Emperor needs plenty of rest to recover."

The crowd of well-wishers left the room where Basil was lying in painful agony.

# The Emperor is Dead
# (The Great Palace, August
# 29-September 14, 886 AD)

The painful agony of Basil lasted for nine days, as the resident doctor, as well as specialists that arrived from Constantinople, tried to control the severe hemorrhage of Basil's internal organs. He finally expired on the 29th of August, 886 AD.

During those days, Leo Choirosphaktes remained at Apamea, inspecting the sight and interrogating the two Turks that accompanied Basil.

Meanwhile Basil's body was taken for burial to Constantinople, but before even it arrived, news of his condition and imminent death had spread.

When Photius found out what was about to happen, he immediately travelled to the Great Palace to meet with Prince Leo.

"You better get prepared," he said sternly to Leo. "I am getting ready to declare you as the de facto Emperor, if your stepfather dies."

News of Basil's death came very soon after, through the tower-signaling method. The messenger conveyed it to Photius, who prepared for a funeral and a coronation.

The body of Basil was brought to Constantinople and clothed in full imperial regalia. It was exposed in the Triclinium of Nineteen Beds,[20] where the requiem was chanted. When that ended, the Master of Ceremonies repeated three times:

"Come forth Basileus, the King of Kings and Lord of Lords summons thee. Take thy crown off thy head."

Then the crown was removed from Basil's head and replaced with a simple purple cap.

---

[20] This was a room with nineteen couches on which guests reclined in the ancient manner for ceremonial banquets, typically held between Christmas and Epiphany.

Basil's coffin was carried to the Church of Holy Apostles for burial.

As Photius was making all these arrangements, the Emperor-to-be Leo visits him at the Patriarchal office with his spiritual father Euthymios, the syngelos priest that was assigned to him by Photius.

"I am appalled at all the pomp that you are bestowing on Basil," Leo commented in a stern manner.

"He was our Emperor," said Photius "and our protocol demands such honors."

"So was my real father," said Leo. "I want my father Michael's remains to be brought back from Chrysopolis on the Asian side, where Basil tossed them, so that he will be forgotten. I want him buried the Church of Holy Apostles with honors and place them in the sarcophagus of Emperor Justin."

Photius thought for a second. "I will try to make these arrangements, as soon as we are finished with our current agendas. One item in the agenda has to do with your consecration to become an Emperor. Are you ready for it? You will be consecrated as Emperor Leo VI."

"I am in a bit in a shock," said the twenty-year old Leo, "but I am as ready as I will ever be."

"Being in a shock is understandable," said Photius. "I would be, if I was in your place. You were thirteen when Constantine died. That is when Basil changed his feelings of you from dislike to loathing. Then you had your unwanted marriage to Theophano, the banishment of your mistress and your repeated incarcerations by Basil. You had such a difficult time in your early years that it may have affected your character. I am depending on your education from the teachings at Magnaura that I and the rest of your teachers gave you to keep your sanity and good judgment. They are of absolute necessity to undertake the task of governing this Empire."

Leo looked at Photius.

"I will be fine Eminence," he said bluntly. "I am ready for my consecration as the Emperor."

And so, he was. The consecration of the young Emperor did happen as planned and Photius did make sure that Michael's relics were transferred where his son, now Emperor Leo had ordered.

Immediately after his meeting with Photius, Leo went to the Palace and called a meeting of his trusted friends. None of Basil's advisors were present. Among those invited were Stylianos Zautses, Leo's brother Stephen, general

Nikiphoros Phokas, and syngelos Euthymios, the spiritual father of Leo assigned to him by the Patriarch.

"I want to organize my staff," he said. "I need you to help me on this."

Zautses immediately took over the meeting.

"Up to now, all of us had to bear the blatant insults that Basil has launched upon us," he said. "We need to put a stop on this and bring some civility in the government. We also need to put a stop on the wasteful spending of Basil's on Churches. We know why he did it. He did it to appease his conscience about his decisions and the pain that the loss of his son inflicted on him. Instead of spending money on building churches, we should focus on strengthening our armed forces, so that we can deal with the imminent threats against the Empire."

Leo then spoke:

"For the time being, I am assigning Stylianos Zautses as Logothete, to put down in writing our state policy."

"With all due respect Highness," said Euthymios. "We already have the guidelines of our state policy, outlined in the document of Epanagoge, written by Patriarch Photius and Theodore Sanabarenus on behalf of Emperor Basil. The document was written specifically to balance the judicial powers of Church, Senate Laws and the executive powers of Emperor, so that the powers are distributed. That was found to be the most efficient way to control mismanagement of the Empire."

"I read this document," said Leo. "As far as I am concerned, it has gone too far in favor of the Church. I want no such interference from the Church."

"With your permission Highness," said Zautses. "I smell treason here. Allow me to set up a special committee to investigate the impact of Epanagoge, who influenced its writings and what they gained by such a policy base."

"As a Logothete, you are within your rights to do so," said Leo, "but I warn you to tread carefully. In the end, we all will be evaluating and judging the committee's investigation."

"I am not so sure that the Patriarch will accept this move of forming a special committee to investigate proposals written in Epanagoge," said Zautses. "So, the only way for me to alter Epanagoge in any form, as you suggested is to bypass the Patriarch, who created it."

Leo pondered for a while.

     STAVROS BOINODIRIS PHD

"That means that I have to relieve Photius from his post as a Patriarch," said Leo. "I will prepare the proper document, which you, as my Logothete will take to the Patriarch."

"Who will take Photius's place?" asked Euthymios.

"I want my brother Stephen to go through the paces of being made into a bishop, and by Christmas I want him to be consecrated as Patriarch."

A total silence followed, until Nikiphoros Phokas spoke. Nikiphoros was the son of the founder of the Phokas family, a man called Phokas, a native of Cappadocia.[21]

"Be very careful Highness. You may be moving too fast in altering everything that Emperor Basil has established. Our enemies are watching every move you make, and they will plan to strike us when we are too weak, or too occupied in making these changes."

"I will take your advice under consideration," said Leo. "Meanwhile, I want you to come and stay at Constantinople. Zautses, my Logothete has informed me that the commander in chief of the Byzantine Army, Andrew the Scythian died, and his position is empty. I therefore raise you to the rank of patrikios and name you to the post of Domestic of the Schools, or in effect commander-in-chief of the Byzantine army. You can then decide whom to assign as your replacement in Italy."

Nikiphoros bowed, but his face did not indicate happiness. He preferred

---

[21] During one of the campaigns of Emperor Basil, sometime in 872, Nikiphoros' father caught the emperor's attention and was raised to the rank of tourmarches. At the same time Nikiphoros, still in his youth, was taken into the imperial retinue, and was soon appointed to the guard corps and participated in Basil's 873 campaigns against Samosata. Shortly after, Nikiphoros was promoted to the rank of protostrator and received from the emperor his own palace in the vicinity of the Church of St. Thekla. Eventually he rose to the post of military governor (strategos) of the theme of Charsianon, a post from which he scored numerous successes against the Arabs.

Byzantine troops under Nikephoros Phokas capture the town of in Italy. Miniature from the Nikiphoros remained in command of Charsianon. Just prior to 885 he was sent to Italy from Charsianon at the head of a picked detachment of troops. There he replaced Stephen Maxentios, who was defeated by the Arabs. His command involved the forces of several western themes (Thrace, Macedonia, Cephalonia, Longobardia and Calabria), but Nikiphoros received further reinforcements from the themes of Asia Minor, including a Paulician detachment. When Basil died, Nikiphoros was recalled to Constantinople by the new Emperor Leo.

to be out in the field, rather than deal with the politics and the bureaucracy of Constantinople.

As the meeting was ending, Leo took the arm of his brother Stephen and pulled him to the next room.

"Well brother, how did I do?"

"You did well, except the part that talked about making me, a sixteen-year-old, a Patriarch."

"Why?"

"I don't know anyone that can dream of filling the shoes of Photius," said Stephen, "and I feel that I am the least qualified."

"I disagree with you on that. Don't be so modest and get ready for your consecration. Your brother, the Emperor commands it."

# Patriarch Stephen (The Great Palace, Christmas Day, 886 AD)

The consecration of Stephen as a Patriarch was simple, without much fanfare. That is because the sixteen-year-old Stephen wanted it that way. After the ceremony, the two brothers met privately in the Patriarch's office.

"You don't look so happy to me," asked Leo. "Are you ill?"

Leo always looked after his younger brother, who was since his youth weak and sickly.

"I don't feel well about taking over for Photius, especially under these circumstances. Was it necessary for you to extract the resignation of Photius with such a humiliating way?" asked Stephen. "Photius was our teacher and a recognized influential leader of the Church. How could you do that to him? You know very well that the accusation of treason is unjust, since he and all his aids that wrote Epanagoge acted upon orders of our stepfather Basil."

"He simply had to go," said Leo. "If he stayed, I would be always under his shadow and would not have the self-confidence to rule. Anyway, he is an obstacle on my personal plans. Did anyone from the other bishops or clergymen say anything to you to make you uncomfortable?"

"No! Somehow, they look upon me as an easy person to deal with; and, who can blame them?"

"Good!" said Leo. "Now I may need help from Stylianos Zautses, Symbatius and you regarding the purification of our legal system."

"That is ironic. Are you following on what Basil had started with Photius?"

"Yes, but I am going to make some variations. The purification system is necessary. When the Procheiron is published, the legal documents will have two advantages. One is that they will be in Greek, rather than Latin. For two centuries now, Latin became a dead language in this part of the world. So, why shouldn't people be able to read and understand law in the language that they know? Second, the laws were not arranged in a user-friendly manner. Each book covered a given subject to full extend in a single book, but not referenced anywhere else, leaving blanks as to its relationship with other subjects in complex cases."

"Who will be doing all these revisions?"

"We will direct the work with the staff at the University at Magnaura. They will be doing the actual writing and making copies. For instance, I plan to start a few decrees for revoking older laws because some current political and religious ideas have outdated those that existed five hundred years ago. What the Curia and the Senate thought at that time, does not make any sense now."

"How do these laws impact the Senate or the Church?"

"You, as a Patriarch, represent the Orthodox Church. Of course, for all ecclesiastical matters you require the consent of the clergy. You have a duty to safeguard the Orthodox creed, as defined by the decisions of the Councils. As for the Senate, it must remain active in providing opinions and advice to me, the Emperor, who represents the executive part of our government. I will be the final decision maker on the interpretation of law and justice and the supreme commander of the armed forces. That means that I have to decide on everything that the rest of the government cannot and there is still a dispute."

"How are you coming along with Zautses," asked Stephen. "Is he supporting you with the military?"

"He is very useful in that front," replied Leo. "I am very surprised on how aggressive he was to undertake the tasks that I needed help with."

"I am hearing some rumors about him," said Stephen; "rumors … that implicate him with Basil's death."

"I do not find these rumors credible," said Leo. "Let's find out where they come from and put a stop to them once and for all. All witnesses, including Basil himself say that he was gored by the antlers of a stag. How could Zautses arrange that to happen? I believe it was a freak accident and carelessness on Basil's part."

"I can see how certain people see how we and Zautses benefited from Basil's death," said Stephen. "Just because of that they cannot avoid thinking of a conspiracy in causing Basil's death. I don't care about Zautses, but for my own sake, I want to hear a confession from your own lips brother. This

     STAVROS BOINODIRIS PHD

confession will remain confidential between us and God. Did you have any part in any conspiracy against Basil?"

"I swear to you on the soul of our mother, I did not," replied Leo. "Many times, I may have wished that Basil was dead, but I never took any actions against him."

"Having wishful thoughts does not constitute a sin," said Stephen; "only if someone acts on those thoughts. In fact, I had thoughts of that nature myself, after he castrated me."

"I just hope that nobody else, with less scruples than us, saw our plight and came to our rescue with such a deed," said Leo, as he got up, ready to leave. "But how and why would they do that?"

"I don't know," said Stephen as he got up. He embraced his brother before letting him exit.

Stephen went behind the desk of the Patriarch and sat in the armchair where Photius used to sit. He felt a sense of awe, when he turned and looked at the small bookshelf next to the desk. He picked up one scroll that Photius had used to make notes and got immersed in examining his thought process.

# Photius Trial and Exile
# (The Monastery of Gordon,
# March 15, 887 AD)

Photius was immersed in his writing on his desk, when someone knocked on the door of his cell of the monastery. The Monastery of Gordon was in the middle of nowhere in the region of Armeniakon, with forests all around.

"Please enter," he shouted.

The door opened, and Leo Choirosphaktes appeared. He immediately proceeded to go and kneel at the feet of Photius, kissing his hand.

"Leo!" said Photius. "What a pleasant surprise."

"I happened to be on a diplomatic mission in this area and after I heard what happened to you, I decided to come and see you." Leo paused for a second. "I am sorry Excellency for what Leo has done to you."

"I am fine and finally at peace," said Photius. "The person you and I should feel sorry for is Theodore Santabarenos, who ended up been the scapegoat in Zautses' plan to take over the government. He and Andrew the Scythian had to find someone to blame. Leo trusted these accusations because of Zoe, Leo's love. All the poor man did was to follow instructions, those of the Emperor and mine. For that he was found guilty of conspiracy and exiled."

"So, you think that it was Zautses that set Leo to do what he did."

"Of course, it was." Photius paused for a few seconds. "Listen carefully Leo. We, Greeks are a small piece of the Byzantine structure. Over millennia, we set ourselves a task of taking on and trying to bring some morality, not only among ourselves, but also among other people, by blending with them in collaborative structures, like Byzantium. Some of these people did not develop the same sense of morality as we. We developed it over many generations and occasionally even some of us forget the teachings of the past.

     STAVROS BOINODIRIS PHD

Zautses, Basil, Michael and all these Armenians developed the morality of a wolf, based on primitive survival instincts, without any concern as to whether their actions, sometimes very brutal, bring about results on themselves that they did not wish at all. All we can do is to educate them, the best way we can and hope for the best."

"I would think that the new Emperor, who was a student of yours, would at least have absorbed some Greek morality. He at least should have some respect for his teacher and his protector."

"When you take a child, like Leo, no matter how good his teachers were, and you subject him into the torture of brutal events that he underwent with Basil, the contagion of that brutality will stick on him. He will become just as brutal to others, as Basil was to him. Brutality begets brutality and abuse begets more abuse. As Plutarch said, men who know nothing of decency in their own lives are only too ready to launch foul slanders against their betters and to offer them up as victims to the evil deity of popular envy. What we need is a generation of peaceful and benevolent people, to bring about some degree of peaceful coexistence on this earth."

"Do you think that there is any hope of that?"

"Not in the near future," answered Photius. "But we Greeks have been taught to never give up. The ancients taught us a few things about us humans. They taught us a few things that give us no other option in life than try to improve humanity. And by humanity, we mean every human on earth. We have no other choices. Aristotle told us that knowing about ourselves, as humans is the beginning of all wisdom. We are meeting all sorts of humans, with strengths and weaknesses. The other thing that our ancestors gave us is self-honor, or filotimo, something that is part of our tradition, from parent to offspring. The third is courage. They told us that for the courageous nothing in unattainable. That is what we are. We have no other choice but try to improve humanity until we die. Anyone that feels like being a Greek also feels a sense of pride and a sense of frustrating curse … all bundled together."

"How can I be of help to you Eminence?"

"For me, nothing; I have done what I could Leo. Now I am finishing some unfinished theological and literary work, hoping to contribute some tiny amount to help humanity. You do what you are doing, but make sure that you always use the guidelines that your forefathers set upon you and follow your conscience. Meanwhile, keep an eye on Emperor Leo. Don't hurry up to tell him your findings about Zautses."

"Should we let Zautses continue doing what he does?"

"No! we should never let people like Zautses off the hook. But we should compromise into being patient and observant. The Emperor loves Zoe and he may reject your findings against Zautses by being blind, because he loves his daughter. He is suffering from *willful blindness*. Eventually he will find out what person Zautses is on his own. When he appears to realize his mistake, then it is time for you to disclose to him the truth. Don't forget though, it is not Zoe's fault that her father is what he is. Let's not punish the children for the sins of their parents. I trust that you will be careful in your endeavors and when the time comes, you must help the Emperor get rid of corruption and crime."

"Thank you for your advice Eminence," said Leo, with moist eyes.

Photius looked at Leo Choirosphaktes with a passive smile. Leo kneeled, kissed his hand and departed.

Photius turned back to face his work. Another knock at his door stopped him.

"The lunch that you ordered, Eminence," said a novice monk, as he bowed. Photius had forgotten that he had given instructions to have his lunch brought over to his desk, so that he can work while eating.

The novice came in bringing him a pitcher of wine and a cup and laid it on his desk. Then he went back and brought him a plate of peas with a slice of bread made from oats. Photius thanked the novice and proceeded to pour some wine in his cup.

# Boris of Bulgaria (Monastery of Preslav, Bulgaria, January, 888 AD)

Michael-Boris poured some of the special warm wine in his cup, as he sat in his house at Preslav. His wife, Maria knew how to take care of him during these cold winters, when he felt the chill all the way to his bones. She warmed the wine and added some honey in it to cure the sore throats that he often had these days.

"Aah! That feels good," he said to his wife. "Maybe it will cure my sore throat."

"Your sore throat is because you yell too much," she replied. "Why don't you let your boy take over and stop trying to control him? He is a grown man and can relieve you, so that you can get some rest."

"Vladimir may be a good soldier, but he lacks long term vision," replied Boris. "I will give him lots of credit for his exploits against the Serbs. Yet, until not very long ago, he and his friends were holding forest meetings with their shaman. They refused to be baptized. God knows what debaucheries are still going on in their meetings and what is in that boy's mind. Before I let him become a ruler, I must put some sense into him, to embrace Christianity. He must stop this nonsense with his friend the shaman."

"Vladimir is a good boy," said Maria. "Give him a little time. I understand that Father Naum has been talking to him. Hopefully, he will be persuaded to become Christian and be baptized."

"I am not so sure," said Boris. "The boy was raised in our old religion of Tengrism before we became Christian. Even if he promises to change, I would have a tough time believing it."

"All I am saying is to give him a chance," said Maria. "You are not getting younger and you must take care of your own health. You already sent Simeon to Constantinople. All you have here is Vladimir and Gavril. You must put one of them to rule, so that you can have some peace."

"What it amounts to is that I must choose between two sons, neither of which I like. Vladimir is a good soldier but an idolater. Gavril is a good Christian, but I doubt that he can rule over a flock of sheep. Meanwhile, we have enemies all around us. To the north, we have the Magyars and the Pechenegs. To the west, we have the Serbs. To the south, we have the Byzantines, the only ones that we now are in good relationship, because we struck a treaty by converting to Christianity. They educate us and provide us with help in becoming Christians, but I do not think that they will send troops to help us if one of our enemies invades our territory."

"Then put Vladimir to rule the nation," replied Maria. "I don't think that you have any other choices."

"You are probably right," said Boris. "I believe that I will spend some more time with him, trying to put some sense into him and then I will have to keep an eye on him. If he does not straighten up, I may have to come back from retirement and save our people."

"I foresee more yelling in this house," said Maria.

"I hope you have plenty more hot wine with honey."

"No, but we can prepare some more."

Maria then clapped her hands twice. Two women servants appeared, and Maria gave them instructions to prepare more of Boris' favorite drink.

# Vladimir of Bulgaria (Pliska, Bulgaria, October, 889 AD)

Vladimir sat by the fireplace looking at his two women slaves with pride. He was in his fifties. The slaves were in their forties.

"Did you prepare our lunch?"

"Yes Sir," replied one of them, as she was filling his silver cup with wine.

"Bring in our guest and come and join me on the table," he ordered, as he walked to the dining area.

The second slave went out and led a man in his thirties in to the dining area. The man was clad in a Germanic manner. He wore a large fur coat, which he carefully laid on a chair, away from the fire. They all sat down and started eating venison with leeks and bread. The women also served red wine.

"I understand that you speak our language," Vladimir said to his guest in Bulgarian.

"Yes, I do," the guest replied.

"My soldiers told me that you wanted to talk to me."

"Yes. My name is Otto. I am an emissary of the Frankish King Arnuf. He wishes you well."

"As I do to him," replied Vladimir laughing. "What is in his mind?"

"You are ruler in Bulgaria, yes?"

"That is correct."

"How long have you ruled? I thought that the ruler was much older."

"This year my father ceded me the throne and went to a monastery to rest."

"Are you Christian?"

"No! But I do not care to answer any more of your pesky questions, unless you tell me why you are here."

"King Arnuf thinks that you may have problems against your enemies and that you may want to become allies with him."

Vladimir pondered for a second.

"What enemies?"

"You have enemies in Moravia, the Serbs, the Magyars and the Pechenegs."

"What makes you think that we need your alliance? I fought against the Serbs myself. I invaded Serbia against Mutimir and his brothers."

"Yes, but you did not succeed, did you?"

"Yes, we were defeated, and I was captured, but after the prisoner exchange, we are now in peace."

"It was peace, but at some cost, wasn't it?"

"We exchanged gifts. My father Boris gave them some gifts, and Mutimir gave us these two women slaves, two falcons, two dogs, and eighty furs." Vladimir pointed to the two women. "Stand up!" The women stood up, as they were eating. "These are tokens of peace with Serbia," said Vladimir with pride.

"You are still vulnerable," said Otto. "You may not realize it, but you are being swallowed by Byzantium; they sent you all these missionaries to convert you to their Christianity, so that you can serve them as their slaves. Meanwhile, the Magyars and Pechenegs are waiting for you to weaken, so that they come and take your land."

"We are nobody's servants," said Vladimir. "But you are right. I am a little skeptical about all these missionaries. I think that I can stop all this massive proselytizing. Many of my best boyar friends also don't like this interference in our old ways of life. Some of these monks are telling the serfs that all men are created equal. So, they revolt, and they cause problems for my well-to-do land owners, because their serfs do not work as hard."

"That is exactly my point," said Otto, smiling. "I have a proposal for you." He walked towards his fur coat and picked up a manuscript from one of the pockets. He returned on the table, opening the manuscript. "These are the terms of the alliance proposed by King Arnuf."

Vladimir rose, and the two men started examining the manuscript, as Otto was explaining each item.

# Naum (Pliska Literary School, Bulgaria, April, 890 AD)

Naum was bent over the manuscript and meticulously kept on writing portions of liturgy, translating from Greek to Slavonic language. He was a sixty-year old monk, who was very dedicated to his dream to see Christianity throughout the Balkans.

Naum had worked with Cyril and Methodius and other missionaries in translating the Bible into Old Church Slavonic. He also helped to promote Christianity in Great Moravia and Principality of Lower Pannonia. When Cyril and Methodius were invited to Rome, they took Naum with them. In Rome, Naum became a priest.

Naum returned to Great Moravia, but the missionary work ran into opposition from German clerics who opposed their efforts to create a Slavic liturgy. While in Moravia, Naum and other missionaries devised the Glagolitic alphabet, the first alphabet to match the specific features of the Slavic language. The missionaries also wrote the first Slavic Civil Code, which was used in Great Moravia. The patrons for the missionaries, Rastislav of Great Moravia and Prince Kocel' of Pannonia, as well as Cyril and Methodius had died, and the pressure from the German church became increasingly more hostile. After a brief period of imprisonment due to the ongoing conflict with the German clerics, Naum, together with some of the missionaries headed towards Bulgaria in 886. There, they were welcomed by two main patrons, the governor of Belgrade, then in Bulgaria and the ruler of Bulgaria, Boris.

Bulgaria was ruled then by Boris, who had converted to Christianity in 864. After becoming Christian, the religious ceremonies were conducted in Greek by a Byzantine clergy. Fearing growing Byzantine influence Boris viewed the adoption of the Old Church Slavonic to preserve the political independence of Bulgaria. With such views, Boris decided to establish two literary academies where theology was to be taught in the Slavonic language.

With Boris' help in 885 the first of the schools was founded in the capital, Pliska, and the second in Ohrid, in the region of Kutmichevitsa. The development of Old Church Slavonic literacy had the effect of preventing the assimilation into the neighboring cultures and promoted the formation of a distinct Bulgarian identity. Naum moved initially to the capital Pliska together with Clement and Angelarius. There, Naum founded the Pliska Literary School.

As Naum was working on his desk, thinking of all the work that he and the missionaries had done, his two friends, Clement and Angelarius walked in.

"We have bad news Brother Naum," said Clement.

"What happened?"

"The tsar is at it again," said Angelarius.

"What did he do?"

"He hauled several of our assigned clergy to prison and confiscated their churches," said Clement. "He has even restricted our movements here, by putting guards on the Literary School. We are under house arrest."

"I wonder why he wants to restrict us," said Naum. "I believe that he does not want us to go and inform Boris on the activities of his son."

"We cannot reach Boris in his monastery," said Angelarius.

"I don't accept that," said Naum. "We must find a way. Let us all meet at the Great Hall."

Naum got up and they both walked in a hurry towards the Great Hall, gathering several people of the Literary School on their way.

# Multiple Fronts (The Great Palace, August 15, 891 AD)

The naval officer walked down the streets of Constantinople in a bit of a hurry. He reached the Great Palace and asked the first guard he saw for directions to the office of the commander-in-chief of the Byzantine forces. The guard gave him the information he needed, and the naval officer walked to the entrance of another building. A guard approached him and after seen his credentials, he let him in. The officer rushed in and knocked on the door.

"Enter…" came a voice from inside.

The officer walked in and kneeled in front of Nikiphoros Phokas. There were two more officers inside, all sitting around the big desk of Nikiphoros. One was Leo Choirosphaktes and the other was Nikiphoros Katakalon.

"News from Italy my lord," said the officer and took a scroll, tucked between his tunic and his breastplate. He handed the scroll to Nikiphoros.

The commander-in-chief read the scroll and then laid it on the table.

"This letter is from Sybbaticius," said Nikiphoros, "the Byzantine commander that I had assigned in Italy. He claims that he deposed Ursus of Benevento, captured Benevento and established our forces there. Is that true officer?"

"Yes sir," replied the officer. "I just arrived from there with a dromond."

"Very well; get some rest and something to eat. I want to send a reply to him, congratulating him for his deeds. I also want him to establish all the required governing structure for the theme of Longobardia, with Benevento as the capital. I will have more details for you tomorrow morning."

The officer bowed and exited.

Nikiphoros Phokas turned to Katakalon. Phokas addressed him simply as Katakalon, to avoid confusion.

"Now, let me understand Katakalon. You told me what you heard from some of the monks that have been prosecuted in Bulgaria. How reliable are these sources?"

"They must be reliable sir. These were peasants fleeing Bulgaria. We have various instances, from different locations. The peasants claim that monks and missionaries have been beaten and abused. It seems that the new ruler of Bulgaria, Vladimir does not like us being there. He seems to be an idolater and he wants to keep us Christians out of his country."

"What about his father, Boris?"

"It seems that Vladimir has not touched his father's monastery. He keeps him isolated and ignorant of what is going on."

"Let's see if we can do anything to get him informed," said the commander-in-chief. "He has a son here with us. Let's see if we can use Simeon to help us inform his father, despite all the resistance that his brother Vladimir presents against us."

"I know Simeon reasonably well," said Choirosphaktes. "With your permission, allow me to talk to him on this and see if and how he can help us."

"Meanwhile, let us keep our ears open," said Phokas. "I want you Katakalon to document all occurrences of any Christians fleeing Bulgaria, so that we can build an irrefutable case against Vladimir."

Phokas paused for a second. "Do you have any other suggestions?"

"No sir," the two officers responded.

"That is all then for now."

The two officers got up and left.

Phokas sat and faced Choirosphaktes and Katakalon. "We cannot act hastily with Bulgaria, or we will be seen that we meddle in their affairs. We must be certain of what is happening and be patient with them."

# Abbot Regino (Prum, Bulgaria, 892 AD)

Abbot Regino was out of patience. The news all around him was that Christendom was in a siege by Vladimir's boyars and troops. He felt helpless and isolated. Then, a peasant arrived at the monastery of Prum and said that he wanted to see him. He was in his thirties and dressed in ragged dirty clothes and looked like an every-day beggar.

"What can I do for you my man?" the abbot asked.

"I was told to come and see you and give you a piece of paper. In return, I was told that you would give me food, drink and lodgings."

His language betrayed that the man had some education.

"Let me see the paper," the surprised abbot replied.

The beggar handed him a short note, which the abbot read.

*"Receiving reports that something is wrong with Christian missions in Bulgaria. Please enlighten us of your situation.*

*Signed: … Leo Choirosphaktes and Prince Simeon of Bulgaria…"*

The surprised abbot sat in his chair staring at the window. Then he took a bell, sat on a chair near his desk and rang it.

"What is your name?" he asked the beggar.

"My Christian name is Michael."

Soon a monk appeared. "Take this man and give him food, drink, bed and any facilities we have to make him comfortable."

The monk and the beggar disappeared in a dark corridor. Then the abbot took a clean scroll, made of sheepskin and stretched it on a flat board. He then took quill and ink and started writing his name, the location and the date. He added the title of *Chronicon* (or news of the day). He continued:

> *"Boris, the Prince of our people, as they say, after accepting*
> *the blessing of Baptism, showed such a perfection, that during*

*the day he appeared to his people in kingly garments and during the night, covered in crude clothes entered secretly in the church and lying on the floor of the temple, he spent his time in prayer, putting only sackcloth below. Soon he left the earthly kingdom and after he put into his place as a Prince his eldest son, he tonsured, took the garment of the holy asceticism and became a monk, dedicating his day and night to charity, vigil and prayers. In the meanwhile, his son whom he placed for Prince and who was by far less zealous and active than his father began to plunder and spend his time in drinking, feasts and debauchery and with all means to turn his newly baptized people back to the pagan rituals."*

Then, abbot Regino was ready to sign it, but he hesitated. *"What if it falls in the hands of Vladimir? He can destroy our monastery."* he thought.

*"I should rather send an oral message to Constantinople with this beggar,"* he concluded.

He immediately took the *Chronicon* and went straight to the dining room. He saw the beggar eating on a bench and he sat across from him.

"I want you to memorize what I have written and take it back to the people that gave you the note you brought me," said the abbot in a stern voice. "In order to prove the authenticity of what you are telling them, you must show them this." The abbot took off his ring from his finger and gave it to the beggar. "You must leave as soon as you memorize what I wrote and after you have rested."

A day later the beggar was on his way to Constantinople. Among his rags, he had sown hidden a metallic ring.

# Simeon of Bulgaria (Monastery of Preslav, Bulgaria, June, 893 AD)

Simeon pointed the metallic ring of abbot Regino to his father, staring at him with disbelief.

"I came back here because I thought you needed me to help you with the ecclesiastical affairs. What do you mean by coming to this monastery and declaring me King of Bulgaria? Some time ago you told me that because I had two older brothers, you wanted me to go to Constantinople and get educated in religion to become an archbishop, or a cleric that supports my brothers. Well, I did what you had told me to do. I even interrupted my education and came back. Now, with the help of Naum, an eminent scholar and student of Cyril and Method, I am planning to be engaged in active translation of important religious works from Greek to Old Church Slavonic. I even brought with me several other students from Constantinople to help us out in this work. Now you tell me that all your previous plans were wrong."

"Yes," said King Boris. "I was wrong. I set your oldest brother Vladimir on the throne and thought everything would be fine, as I went to find some peace in a monastery. There, I find out that Vladimir, instead of following the Godly path of Christianity, he attempted to reintroduce paganism. He started the process of destroying Christian churches and persecuting our clergymen, because he regarded them as instruments of Byzantium. He thought of the priests as spies, trying to influence the Bulgarian kingdom. He had very little support, so he signed a pact with Arnuf of Carinthia, the illegitimate son of Carloman of Bavaria to attack Byzantium. After I received a message from you regarding abbot Regino, I discovered numerous complaints from our population, and our regional representatives. At that time, I was forced to act and take him down. I had to put him in prison and blind him, for the security of our throne."

"I know all that," said Simeon. "But why me…? Why not put Gavril to rule, your other son?"

"Because I do not think that he is as capable to do the job, as you," said Boris.

Indeed, in a few days' time, Boris had brought down Vladimir and set Simeon as a ruler of the Bulgarians.

At Prum, abbot Regino attended Simeon's coronation.

After the ceremony, Simeon handed the ring back to abbot Regino.

"I believe this belongs to you," he said. "Our people thank you."

After attending Simeon's coronation, the abbot went back to the monastery of Prum. He picked up his half-finished *Chronicon,* changed the date by erasing it from the sheepskin with a special citrus essence and continued writing from where he had stopped a year earlier:

> *"… In the meanwhile, his son whom he placed for Prince and who was by far less zealous and active than his father began to plunder and spend his time in drinking, feasts and debauchery and with all means to turn his newly baptized people back to the pagan rituals.… When his father learned that, inflamed by great anger took off his monastic clothes, put again the military sash, put on the royal garments, and called to action those who feared God and set against his son. Soon he captured him without much difficulty, pulled out his eyes and sent him to prison. Then he gathered his whole empire and placed for Prince his younger son [Simeon I] and threatened him before everyone with the same punishment if he would betray the true Christianity. After he thus arranged that, he took off the sash, put on the holy monastic clothes and returned to a monastery. There he spends the rest of the time of his present life in holy asceticism …"*

The abbot continued writing until he heard the chime of the monastery. It was time for all the monks to gather in the large dining room for a feast, celebrating their deliverance from idolatry.

# The Zautses Policy (The Great Palace, November 15, 893 AD)

The dignitaries started to sit in a feast in the large dining room next to the palace kitchen. Leo and Zoe were sitting at the center. Leo wore a black ribbon on his sleeve, because he was in mourning. This past year he lost his beloved younger brother and Patriarch Stephen. In his place he chose a moderate and easy-going ex-monk from Phrygia, named Anthony Cauleas.

After Leo and Zoe were seated, Stylianos Zautses came and sat next to Leo and next to him sat Nikiphoros Phokas. Next to them were the new Patriarch Anthony Cauleas and Leo Choirosphaktes. Next to Zoe sat all the ladies-in-waiting of the court. These days Choirosphaktes was reporting directly to Emperor Leo, acting as an intelligence officer and advisor. The Emperor knew the close relationship that Choirosphaktes had with Photius and wanted to tap on his experience to help him on foreign policy and help his brother on legal and ecclesiastical matters.

"I restricted the attendance in this meeting for financial reasons," said Leo. "The defensive deployment against the Arabs in the East and those in Italy are depleting our treasury. We must take care, so that we have the resources to counter these attacks. The Patriarch is also telling me that we may have some added expenses in Bulgaria, where our churches had been threatened by Vladimir."

"We can recover some of those expenses Highness," said Zautses.

"How?" replied Leo.

"By getting some of our money back from our Bulgarian merchants," replied Zautses. "The Bulgarians bring their products here in Constantinople and sell them without minimal custom fees and our own producers find it difficult to compete. If we set rules, where our own merchants buy their products and sell them, then we can tax these merchants based on their business and thus put our own producers on an equal level. The Bulgarians can sell their products directly as before, only in a market like Thessaloniki, because of the transport costs from Thessaloniki to Constantinople, their products will not impact our own. This subject was brought forward to me by two of our own merchants who found that the Bulgarians are taking unfair advantage of us, because we want to be in good terms with them for political and religious reasons."

"I am not certain that this idea is good," said Anthony Cauleas. "We do not want to antagonize the Bulgarians."

"The Bulgarians are in disarray," said Zautses. "Anyway, what can they do now, especially since their ruler is one of our own?"

"Are you telling me that Simeon would not react in a hostile way against us?" said Leo.

"He will not," said Zautses. "He was actually educated by Photius to become a bishop. He is a bookworm, dedicated in establishing our church in Bulgaria. What can he do? Throw away all the time he invested with us and our good friendship and become our enemy? No! I think that he will stick with us, even if his merchants lose some of their profits to us."

The Emperor turned to Choirosphaktes. "You were close to Simeon. What is your opinion on this?"

"Simeon was a brilliant student," said Choirosphaktes. "He may look to you very docile, but if provoked, he could be a formidable enemy."

"Nonsense," said Zautses. "As a priest, he is trained to love his enemies. He is a priest for God's sake."

"Beware my Lord," said Choirosphaktes. "We may gain something in a short period of time by saying Byzantium First, but this does not last. We are a federation, dependent on alliances for our survival. If we lose our fidelity with our allies, we would have to spend tenfold in defending ourselves."

"I need to think on this," said Leo. "We certainly could use the extra income for a short period of time."

"Of course, we could," said Zautses. "An added income could make the difference between a broke Byzantium and a great Byzantium. We should all think: Byzantium first."

# Trade War (Pliska, Bulgaria, March, 894 AD)

"Is that what Zautses said?" asked Simeon, "Byzantium first?"

The young man nodded. Simeon listened to the reports of this Bulgarian youngster that he had enlisted to monitor the events in the Great Palace. The youngster was working there as one of the servants that prepared and served food at the dining room.

"Go back and keep up the good work," said Simeon when both exited his quarters. Simeon then proceeded to the Great Hall. He had a lot of work there with some very angry people. He sat on his throne of the Great Hall of his Palace and started listening to the complaints from all sorts of representatives. Among the complainers were boyars, rich aristocrats and land owners, merchants and farmers. Next to him he had a minister, called George Sursubul. This was a man that volunteered his services with a very difficult task of ruling a nation. He also had Naum, now ordained as bishop of Drembica and Velika, replacing Clement.

"What you are telling me is that Leo decided to move your open marketplace for Bulgarian goods from Constantinople to Thessaloniki. What happens if you try to bring your animals, or grain to Constantinople?"

"The Byzantines will stop us at the border and prohibit our sale," said a merchant. "We are told there that we can only sell to specific Byzantine merchants, but these merchants offer us much less than what our products sell in Constantinople."

"I want to know how much money each one of you is losing by this move," said Simeon. "Give my minister here all the figures, to find out how serious the problem you are presenting is."

George Sursubul led all the plaintiffs to a room next door, which was his office and with the use of a scribe they started cataloguing the plaintiffs, the volume of products they had sold the previous years and the cost of selling these products under this year's conditions.

Meanwhile, Simeon was consulting with Naum.

"What do you think is happening?" Simeon asked Naum.

"I think that someone in the Great Palace in Constantinople is taking us for granted," said Naum. "Just because we are eager to become Christian, it does not mean that we are eager to be enslaved to their whims. My people are farmers and they will be working for nothing. They can barely survive with the prices that the Byzantine middlemen are willing to pay."

"I would like us to compose a letter of complaint to Emperor Leo about his policy," said Simeon. "I want to make two copies. One copy must be sent to Leo and another to Patriarch Anthony Cauleas. We need to make it clear that this practice must stop, or we will be forced to take action."

"I can help you with such a letter," said Naum.

Within a day, the letter was written and sent by a courier to Constantinople, with the orders to ask and wait for any reply.

Meanwhile, George Sursubul gathered as much information as possible from the merchants, the boyars and the farmers. He appeared in front of Simeon with the bad news:

"Unless this situation is corrected, our farmers may be starving in two to three years and our revenue will drop appreciably."

Simeon listened to the report patiently. After George finished, he stated: "Let us wait awhile and see what Constantinople has to say."

The courier presented the letter to Stylianos Zautses, who was Logothete, or secretary of state. He asked for a response and waited for it. Zautses read the letter, written in Greek and smiled. He returned to the courier with the statement: "*No response.*"

The courier then took the copy to the Patriarchate and presented it to Patriarch Anthony Cauleas. He read it and responded: "I will discuss this subject with the Emperor. If any new developments arise, I will send you a messenger with such information."

The courier left for Pliska with these answers, leaving Simeon hanging with indecision. He decided to wait for a while longer, but in order to keep himself informed, he sent some of his close friends from Magnaura, now serving as monks in the Pliska Literary School to Constantinople to gather more information on what is happening.

A day after the courier arrived, Patriarch Anthony Cauleas appeared in front of Emperor Leo with the letter from Simeon, but bypassing Zautses.

"I am worried about this," he said to the Emperor. "Have you seen this letter from Simeon?"

"No!" replied Leo as he was reading the letter. "Yet, I leave all affairs that deal with the neighboring countries in the hands of Logothete, the state department. Zautses must have seen it and thought that it was not worth mentioning it to me. Do you think that Simeon is seriously thinking about harming us after all we did for him?"

"I don't know," replied Anthony Cauleas. "Yet, if he is cornered, as he says that he is, he can be very disruptive. Do you know why?"

"Why?"

"Because he knows us too well; he knows our strengths and weaknesses. After living with us for ten years, he knows how to hurt us."

"I will bring up the subject with Zautses," said Leo, "but I am afraid he will tell me not to worry."

# From Trade War to Hot War (Pliska, Bulgaria, September, 894 AD)

"So, Zautses told the Emperor not to worry," Simeon said out loud.

"Yes Sire," said one of the informer monks. Simeon had to wait for his informer monks to come back and tell him that the Emperor does not take him seriously. They found that out by listening to the Patriarch complaining about the intransigence of Zautses.

It was time for Simeon to start preparing the Bulgarian army. As he was doing that, he sent again back his informers to find out the disposition of the Byzantine army. He asked them to see when the Arabs were getting ready to invade again in Anatolia. This was not very difficult, since the Arabs were doing seasonal raids on Byzantium, like clockwork. They did that every year to loot and weaken the Byzantines, but when the Byzantine army showed up, they retreated. His informers arrived in late August telling him that the Byzantine army was on the move to Anatolia, headed by Nikiphoros Phokas. At that time Simeon ordered his troops to march on a raid to Macedonia.

When news of the Bulgarian raid arrived in Constantinople, a surprised Leo took Zautses aside for conference.

"You told me that Simeon would do nothing," Leo yelled. "What now? Our people are being slaughtered and their property is being stolen, creating losses much greater than the benefits of your trade war. What do you say for yourself?"

"Don't worry Excellency," replied Zautses. "What we have here is a small band of troublemakers that will disband when they see our soldiers."

"What soldiers? I sent Nikiphoros Phokas and our first line troops against the Arabs in Anatolia."

"We still have troops here Excellency," replied Zautses. "They may not be first line, but for the Bulgarians, they will be more than enough. We have

     STAVROS BOINODIRIS PHD

a contingent of mercenary Khazar city guards and a smaller Byzantine army detachment, now on leave that we can send to crush Simeon's troublemakers."

"Do it and do it fast, before we have a disaster in our hands."

"Yes Excellency."

"There is something else we can do," said Leo. "We can send word to the Magyars to start raiding Bulgarian lands, so that Simeon withdraws. I know also who can do this job."

"Leo Choirosphaktes?"

"Of course," replied Leo.

Zautses immediately gave the order for the Khazar guard contingent and the small army detachment of tired soldiers to begin marching, with the Byzantine army officer in command. News of their departure arrived in Pliska, before the Byzantines were half way in meeting the elusive Bulgarian raiders. Simeon then took his reserve forces and immediately moved against them. He found them near Adrianople.

The Bulgarians took most of the Khazar mercenary guardsmen prisoners and killed many leaders of the Byzantine detachment, including the Byzantine army's commander.

As the Bulgarian army was occupied with the Byzantines, one Byzantine was on his way to the North by sea. Leo Choirosphaktes was on a mission of counterinsurgency. He had with him another man, a Khazar monk, who was studying at Magnaura, used as a translator to help him in his negotiations.

As Choirosphaktes was ready to leave the port of Constantinople, he handed an imperial order to the local naval commander, ordering him to muster a handful of river transports for a secret operation.

"This is where you must be at the time designated here," he explained to the commander. Then he boarded his ship and headed north.

# Bringing in the Magyars (North of Danube River Delta, February, 895 AD)

Leo Choirosphaktes disembarked from the Byzantine merchant ship on the banks of a small town to the North of the Danube River Delta. The Byzantines came there often to trade, bringing in cloth, copper utensils, tools and other products in exchange of livestock, hides, and grain.

The Khazar translator, who knew the local language talked to a man and waved to Leo to follow him. Leo got some help from two sailors, to help him carry a basket ashore. He paid them to carry the basket and come with him. Soon they approached a large house, built in wood, with tiled roof. In the front of the house there were several guards.

"This is the house of their leader, said the Khazar. His name is Arpad."

Leo proceeded to one of the guards and produced from his tunic a scroll with the Byzantine Emperor's seal. The guard took it, went inside and after a few minutes he was out waving them to come in.

"I guess, we have an audience with Arpad," he said to his Khazar translator. "Let us bring some of the gifts we brought for him from the ship." He then asked the sailors to come with them, carrying the basket.

The Magyars were in good terms with the Byzantines, but not so with the Bulgarians. The Magyar tribes of Arpad lived along the banks of the Dnieper River and were in continuous friction with the Bulgarian tribes to the southwest.

The Magyars were initially farther to the East, around the Don River and were subordinates of the Khazar khanate. Their neighbors were the predecessors of the Bulgarians called Onogurs and the Alans, a Germanic tribe from which they learned gardening, cattle breeding and agriculture. Around 830 AD a rebellion broke among the Khazars. Three tribes of the

Khazars split off and became the Hungarian tribes. One of them was the Magyars, who moved to a territory west of the Dnieper River, between the river and the Carpathian Mountains. The rest of the Khazars and the Oghuz Turks made an alliance against the Pechenegs. The Pechenegs lived in the step corridor between the rivers Ural and Volga. Outnumbered by the enemy, the Pechenegs started a new migration. They invaded the dwelling places of the Hungarians, forcing them to leave and go farther west. As they did migrate, they forced their way into the Carpathian Basin against the German tribes of Moravia to the west and the Bulgarians to the south of the Danube River. All these movements of population were monitored closely by the Byzantines and occasionally they sent missionaries there, formed alliances and very often traded with these tribes.

Arpad was sitting on a wooden chair, with several men around, discussing some subject of importance to them. Choirosphaktes asked the sailors to lay the basket down and to go back to the ship. Then he and the Khazar translator waited patiently for Arpad to finish his business.

After a few minutes Arpad noticed them. He immediately stopped his discussion and waved the men he was talking to, to leave. All, except three, left the room. He waved to Leo and the Khazar to come forward.

The Khazar said something to the effect of a greeting to the "mighty Magyar ruler," and Arpad asked Leo to state his business. The conversation back and forth went through the translator.

"I am here on behalf of your friend, the mighty Byzantine Emperor," Leo said. "He is at war with the Bulgarians, who are also your enemies and would like to see if we can work together in deterring threats made by them against us. We would like to see if we can plan a coordinated attack against them."

"What are we to gain by doing this?" replied Arpad.

"Your people would gain access to the rich lands to the south of the Danube River," replied Choirosphaktes. "Your people have been chased out of your lands by the Pechenegs and you and your people could use some relief. Instead of being scared and always on the move, you will find it easy to occupy the land south of the Danube, because Simeon will be occupied with us."

"I don't know how we can do this," replied Arpad. "I still need to move many soldiers for a strong attack against Simeon. I only have a few river craft on our disposal. When a few of us cross the river, Simeon will be warned and send enough troops to butcher us."

"Don't worry," said Choirosphaktes. "Behind my merchant ship, we planned for a small flotilla of ships to arrive and anchor at the mouth of the Danube, just for this operation. Your guard took a scroll from me, which is in front of you. All you have to do is to put your seal of accepting the terms outlined in the document and I will be out of here and take the boat out to bring you enough transports for a massive attack."

"I need to consult such a plan with my chieftains," replied Arpad. "Meanwhile, you can stay in this house. I will notify you."

"Very well," replied Choirosphaktes pointing to the basket. "As a token of our good faith, my Emperor sent you these gifts, for you and your chieftains."

Arpad stood up, went to the basket, opened it and looked inside. In the basket he saw silk material for making elegant tunics, excellent swords and daggers with gold-plated sheaths decorated with jewels, gold coins, gold plated belt buckles and pins for tunics. Arpad smiled and asked two of his men to take the basket to a room close by.

Choirosphaktes and his Khazar cohort were led to a room, where food and drink was brought to them. A few hours later, Arpad was visiting him with the Imperial scroll in his hand, bearing a seal. He had with him the youngest man that was in the audience room earlier.

"I will make my preparation, waiting for the transports," he said. "I have one condition though. After the initial landings, you must leave enough ships here for resupply and for a possible retreat, if something goes wrong." Then he pointed to the young man. "This is going to be the commander of the landings. He is my son Liuntika. Leave your interpreter here, as a token of good faith."

Soon, Leo was on the ship that brought him over and on their way to the anchorage at the mouth of the Danube River. As he was leaving, he turned to the Khazar, who was plenty scared about his future.

"Don't worry. Everything will be fine. I will send the naval commander to you. You must work for him now. Help him in his communication with the Magyars."

When his ship arrived at the mouth of Danube River, he spotted a handful of anchored ships. His counterinsurgency operation was in effect. He met with the naval commander, that he talked with in Constantinople and showed him the scroll with Arpad's seal. He also told him about the added condition that Arpad had added to the terms, about the contingency fleet required for retreat. The naval commander had been ordered by the Emperor to support the landings, but there was no mention of subsequent support. The naval commander agreed to Arpad's terms and then, when the wind was favorable, ordered for the fleet to move to Arpad's location in order to load the Magyar landing forces.

Choirosphaktes took off, leaving for Constantinople. He knew that the Khazar translator will work fine with the naval commander in the Danube River and achieve the planned landings.

It took a little more than two weeks, for the first wave of Magyar forces with Liuntika as a commander to land on the southern side of the Danube. They immediately started attacking, pillaging and occupying the Bulgarian homesteads south of Danube.

As all this was happening, Nikiphoros Phokas and some sections of the Byzantine army were recalled from the East. They hurriedly prepared and Nikiphoros prepared to march against Simeon. During those preparations, Choirosphaktes arrived at the port of Constantinople and immediately went to the Great Palace to report what transpired to Emperor Leo.

"Great job, my man," said Emperor Leo, smiling. "Now, I have another job for you, much trickier than the previous one. I want you to be the ambassador to the Bulgarian court."

"Why me?" asked Choirosphaktes.

"Because you are the most qualified," said the Emperor. "You know what is going on with the Magyars and you know Simeon better than anyone else. I need for you to assess the situation and see how we can have peaceful coexistence with the Bulgarians. I want you to carry a message from me, offering peace to our old friend Simeon."

"When am I to leave for his court?"

"You should leave as soon as you pick up my letter of your assignment and my personal letter to Simeon. They should be ready soon."

The Emperor summoned his staff and they started working on the letters. Both letters had the gold insignia of the Byzantine Empire, with the double-headed eagle. The next day, Choirosphaktes, accompanied by a Bulgarian monk from Magnaura was heading for Pliska, carrying these letters. Their coach had a small military escort up to a certain village. From that village on, they had to travel unescorted, until they met with a Bulgarian garrison. They apprehended them and took them to their officer, who knew Greek. Choirosphaktes immediately showed him the scroll which indicated his status as an ambassador. From that point on, they had a Bulgarian escort until they reached Pliska.

Meanwhile, Simeon, unaware of the threat that Choirosphaktes had prepared from the north, was not in Pliska. He had rushed to meet Phokas' forces, but the two armies had not engaged in a fight yet. A messenger was sent to Simeon, telling him that a new ambassador had arrived.

When Simeon heard the messenger, he rushed back to Pliska, asking his commanders to avoid any engagements.

"Well, look! Who is here?" said Simeon as he saw Leo Choirosphaktes. Leo bowed and presented his letter of assignment as an ambassador.

"Well, mister ambassador, I hope you have something worthwhile for me, to have come all this way to see me."

"Yes Highness," replied Leo, as he handed him the second scroll. "I have here a letter from Emperor Leo, offering terms of peaceful coexistence with your people."

Simeon took the scroll, opened it and examined it carefully.

"Guards!" yelled Simeon. Two huge Bulgarian guards appeared, fully armed. "Take this ambassador here from Constantinople and put him in the prison cell of this building."

"What…" exclaimed the surprised Leo. He struggled when the guards lifted him up. "Why…?"

"Don't hurt him," said Simeon. "Just lock him up."

Simeon's spies had told him about the Byzantine army and about the departure of their navy in the Black Sea right after Leo Choirosphaktes had left with another ship, but he did not know any more. He had no idea that the ambassador that was in front of him was the planner of a pending Magyar attack. He knew though enough about Choirosphaktes not to trust him.

The next day, Simeon went to see Leo in his cell.

"I want you to tell me, old friend, why were you traveling up in the Black Sea several weeks ago?"

"Who, me?" replied Leo. "Who told you that I was?"

"I also want you to tell me, old friend, why a whole armada of dromonds left from that same port a few days later?"

"I wouldn't know," replied Leo. "I am not a navy man."

"When you feel like talking to me, old friend, send for me," said Simeon, as he left the prison cell.

It took a few days for Simeon to figure out what counter-insurgency plans Choirosphaktes had concocted up in the Danube. When he figured it out, he ordered the Byzantine navy's route into the Danube to be closed off with ropes and chains, intending to hold it until he had dealt with Phokas. By the time the Bulgarian army was mobilized to block the Danube, the fleet had taken the Magyars across and most of the Byzantine navy was out in the Black Sea. When the Byzantine navy commander heard of the Bulgarian attempt to close the Danube, he managed to take out the rest of the fleet.

# Bulgarian Prison Negotiations (Pliska, Bulgaria, March, 895 AD)

The Magyars, under the command of Liuntika were initially very successful in their raids. They had taken many prisoners and many of them were handed over to the Byzantines, before the Danube River was totally blocked by Simeon.

Simeon, when he finally saw the damage of the Magyar attacks, he went straight to see Choirosphaktes at his prison cell.

"I know that you had a hand on this, old friend," said Simeon sarcastically. "I am not going to respond to your peace offer, until I find out from you all I need to know before I negotiate."

"I don't know what you mean, old friend," replied Choirosphaktes. "I am only an envoy from Emperor Leo. Is that what they do to envoys now in Bulgaria? Is that what Photius taught you to do to envoys? Here we are, me imprisoned in this miserable dungeon by one of our boys that we took, educated and were hospitable to for ten years. I was personally responsible for your upbringing and your happiness. Is that how you treat your benefactors… by stabbing them in the back?"

Simeon smiled. "That is an excellent act you are putting on. It is you that betrayed us by slowly stealing us blind. I sent repeated letters asking for Leo to repeal his order of restricting the markets to our products. It seems that Leo's brains are below his waist. He is listening more to the father of his dear Zoe than common sense."

"So, what are you going to do with me? Kill me?"

"No, old friend," replied Simeon smiling. "Sorry for the inconvenience, but you are very useful to me here. Even if I don't get a straight story out of you, I have plenty to gain by keeping you away from doing me further damage." Simeon smiled and then, after a small pause continued. "You are going to earn your salary here as an ambassador. Since you are an ambassador, I will make your stay here more pleasant. You will be out of prison during the day, and sleep in a more comfortable prison cell at night. During the day, you will be free to roam around this house under guard, but you will not be allowed to leave it. Other than that, you will be my guest. You can have anything you need or want. You will eat what I eat and drink what I drink."

"Thank you, old friend," said Choirosphaktes.

Simeon gave orders for the release of Choirosphaktes and ordered them to treat him with respect as his guest.

Choirosphaktes was always invited at the dinner table to dine with Simeon.

One evening Simeon looked at Choirosphaktes smiling.

"I don't think that you will like this," he said. "But your plan will not work as well as you planned."

"What do you mean?" asked Choirosphaktes.

"You always thought that the Magyar counterinsurgency would be a success. Well, someone in Constantinople thought in the same manner and ordered Nikiphoros Phokas to withdraw his forces."

"Weren't the Magyars successful?"

"Only for a while," replied Simeon. "As we speak, my forces are heading north to stop the Magyars."

"Yes, but now that you have no forces to the south, Phokas can return and capture you and this palace," said Choirosphaktes.

"I thought of that," said Simeon. "That is why I left some of my troops at the southern border to prevent a possible attack by Phokas." Simeon took a silver pitcher full of wine and filled his cup and that of Choirosphaktes. He handed one cup to Leo and raised his to a toast.

"To the successful negotiations for peace," he said smiling, "with my old friend Leo."

Leo smiled and they both drank.

# The Pecheneg Counter-Insurgency (Pliska, Bulgaria, June, 895 AD)

What Choirosphaktes did not know was that Simeon did exactly to the Byzantines, what the Byzantines did to him. He was a fast learner.

After he found out that the Magyars were on the attack and the Byzantines were behind this, he set up his own envoys to go over the Carpathian Mountains and contact the Pecheneg leaders with gifts, telling them to get rid of the pesky Magyars from their lands once and for all. After all, they had now the opportunity to do it, since a major part of the Magyar army was below the Danube River, unable to retreat fast, because he was getting ready to block the Danube River against the Byzantine Navy.

As all this diplomatic activity was going on, Simeon's army tried to stop the Magyars. During the first two encounters, the Magyars defeated his army, forcing the Bulgarians to retreat to Drastar. But soon, the Pechenegs attacked the Magyars from the north, forcing Arpad to ask help from his son in the south.

The Magyars were caught in a vice. Arpad on one side of the Danube and his son on the other, without the Byzantine ship transport capability to unite their armies. The result was that Simeon defeated the Magyars as they tried to fight on both sides. Soon after his victory, Simeon sent a messenger to the Magyars with an ultimatum demanding the release of all Bulgarian prisoners as a precondition of peace.

The Magyars agreed and slowly they returned to their lands.

As all this was happening, Leo Choirosphaktes was spending his nights in the Bulgarian prison and his days talking to Simeon, trying to make him accept a peace treaty with Byzantium. Simeon did not budge, until the Magyar threat was gone. When that was concluded, he again invited Leo to his dinner table gave him a cup of wine and after he raised his cup, he made a toast:

     STAVROS BOINODIRIS PHD

"To peace, my old friend," said Simeon smiling.

A surprised Leo responded: "What do you mean?"

Simeon reached in his tunic and took out a scroll. "I have signed the peace treaty you brought me. You are now free to go." He pointed to a man next to him, slapping him on the shoulder. "You may return to Constantinople with my envoy here. His name is Theodore. You two can negotiate the details of the peace treaty in Constantinople. This can include prisoner exchanges and how these are to be handled. Theodore will provide you everything you need for your trip."

Leo was pleasantly surprised. He drank his wine, got up, shook hands with Theodore and walked out of the dining room on to the garden, smelling the fresh air. He then noticed something that went unnoticed before. The garden was full of blooming roses, which now emanated a wonderful aroma.

Two days later he was traveling with Theodore to Constantinople.

# The Battle of Buh (Pliska, March, 896 AD)

Leo Choirosphaktes arrived a little less than a year ago in Constantinople with the Bulgarian envoy Theodore with Simeon's peace treaty agreement in his hands. He immediately went to the Great Palace and deposited the peace treaty document, as it was produced and signed by Simeon. He found that Emperor Leo was at that time quite occupied with the Arab threat to the East.

"I accept the terms in principle," said Emperor Leo. "I want you to take this to Stylianos Zautses. He and the Bulgarian envoy Theodore can work the details of the treaty, so that I can sign the detailed document. One of these details has to do with Byzantine and Bulgarian prisoners. I will give the order for the exchange of all these prisoners."

As Choirosphaktes was ready to depart with Theodore, the Emperor added:

"After you set Theodore up with Zautses, I want you back. I have a lot of work for you in the East."

"Yes, Highness," said Choirosphaktes and bowed before leaving.

Leo Choirosphaktes introduced Theodore to Stylianos Zautses. When Zautses saw the document, he threw up his hands.

"This document is incomplete," he yelled at Theodore. "It states that the prisoners to be released must be either Bulgarian, or Byzantine citizens. Instead of that, it should state Bulgarian, or Byzantine captives. Your army has captured a great many Khazar mercenaries, who were not Byzantine citizens. In fact, you captured them and rehired them as your own mercenaries and now they are fighting in your army. Many of their officers were accused for being traitors and were sentenced to death in absentia. We want them back."

Theodore looked at Zautses with a surprised look.

"This is a touchy point with our ruler Simeon," said Theodore. "I am not authorized to agree to this change. That means that for this change to occur, the document must be rewritten and be taken back to Pliska. If he does not, then you must escalate the issue to Emperor Leo, so that the two can decide for a resolution. All this will take time, the hostilities may resume, and people will die."

"I am Logothete of this Empire and assigned to deal with the foreign policy," said Zautses. "I cannot accept the terms, as they are. I will generate a detailed treaty document. You can then take it to your ruler."

Theodore left the office of the Logothete and sent a messenger back to Simeon, explaining what happened. Then, he waited in the quarters assigned to foreign envoys for Zautses to prepare his version of the treaty document. While he was there, he did not waste much time. He started inquiring all about Zautses, his daughter Zoe and how Zautses was involved in the "trade war" with the Bulgarians. He also probed on Emperor Leo and his relationship with Zautses. He went into taverns, where Zautses went to relax, listened to conversations and occasionally asked certain questions about all of them.

Meanwhile, Simeon kept the pressure on the Magyars, with help from the Pechenegs. He wanted them out of his northern borders. When Simeon heard what happened in Constantinople, he redoubled that pressure. Simeon went to his father Boris to ask for help. His father, the former *tsar*, left his monastery retreat to assist his heir in this occasion. As the Pechenegs began to combat the Magyars on their eastern frontier, Simeon and his father gathered an enormous army and marched to the north to defend their empire. He crossed the Danube River and chased the Magyars all the way to the River Buh, where the Magyars made their stand.

Simeon had ordered three days of fasting, saying that the soldiers should repent for their sins and seek help in God. When this was done, the battle began. It was a long and unusually fierce battle but in the end the Bulgarians were victorious over the Magyars.

The result of this great Bulgarian victory forced the Magyars to abandon forever the steppes of southern Ukraine, as well as their aspirations of subduing Danube Bulgaria, retreating to the newly occupied lands beyond the Carpathian Mountains, centering on Pannonia.

As the Magyars fled west, they fought their way against the Moravians this time, defeating them and establishing the state of new Hungary.

The victory at the River Buh against the Magyars allowed Simeon to turn his attention to the south. At that time, Zautses, after great delays, had finally handed to Theodore his proposed detailed treaty document.

Theodore traveled with the document to Pliska and explained to Simeon the objections of Zautses.

"That is not acceptable," said Simeon. "But at least we have gained some time. Tell me about this Logothete Zautses. What kind of a person is he? How does he fit in?"

Theodore had done his homework. He gave plenty of information on Zautses and his relationship to Emperor Leo.

"Since Emperor Leo had not signed the treaty, "said Simeon, "insisting that all the Khazar mercenaries of Zautses are freed, we have to teach Zautses a lesson. If we manage to do that, maybe the Emperor Leo will know what kind of a man he placed in the office of Logothete."

# Bulgarophygon (Pliska, Bulgaria, June, 896 AD)

The office of Logothete was surprised to hear that a large Bulgarian army was heading south. They heard of a large battle that occurred around the River Buh, but details of the battle were sketchy. Leo immediately called Zautses to a private meeting room in the Great Palace.

"What is going on?" asked Leo. "I signed a treaty with Simeon, and I gave it to you to fill in the details. Why are the Bulgarians ready to attack us?"

"We had a disagreement on the wording, because it impacted the details of prisoner exchange," said Zautses. "We had to rewrite it."

"Why didn't you consult me before you decided to take such drastic steps?"

"First, because I thought that you assigned me the job to work out the details," said Zautses. "Also, I did not involve you because you were occupied with the Arab incursions in the East."

"What now?" he asked angrily. "How do you suppose that we stop him? Our army with most of our select officers is in the East."

"We must raise another army, Highness," responded Zautses.

Emperor Leo left the meeting room, slamming the door behind him. He immediately asked for a recall of his armed resources from the East.

Leo Choirosphaktes was operating as a diplomat at that time with the army in the East. He received an urgent message to return to Constantinople.

Emperor Leo tried to assemble some elements of fighting men, including his Palace guards in a hurry and he sent them to stop Simeon.

As Simeon led his troops south, he was met in Thrace by a hastily assembled Byzantine army.

Simeon annihilated these Byzantine forces in a battle outside Bulgarophygon. Soon, elements of the Bulgarian army were seen in the outskirts of Constantinople.

In desperation, after the Bulgarians besieged Constantinople, Leo armed Arab captives and used them as mercenaries to fight the Bulgarians. He repelled their advance in front of the city walls.

By then, Choirosphaktes and some of the army units from the East arrived in Constantinople.

When Leo Choirosphaktes appeared in front of Emperor Leo at the Great Palace, the Emperor was relieved.

"What took you so long to come back," he said to him. But before Choirosphaktes could open his mouth to explain, the Emperor continued:

"Never mind any of your excuses. I want you to go to Pliska."

"Why? What happened?"

The Emperor explained in a few sentences how Zautses scrapped the peace treaty that Choirosphaktes brought to him, enraging Simeon, who now had an army parked in front of Constantinople.

"That is why you must go back to Simeon and ask for terms of peace," concluded the Emperor.

A few days later, Choirosphaktes, with another Bulgarian monk was back to Pliska. This place now was very familiar to him. He went and presented himself to the guards, but before they could check on him, news of his arrival had already made their way to Simeon and his staff, who came to greet him.

"Greetings," my old friend, said Simeon, with open arms. "How is your master treating you?"

"He is not very happy with you," replied Choirosphaktes. "He sent me over to see if we can strike a peace treaty between us, without Zautses in the middle, so that we stop the slaughter among our people."

"Under those terms, I will be very happy to work with you," replied Simeon.

Finally, the war ended with a peace treaty, whose conditions were much worse for Byzantium than that originally drafted, signed by Emperor Leo, but rejected by Logothete Zautses. The Khazar mercenaries were to stay with Simeon.

To compensate for the losses of the Trade War, Byzantium was obliged to pay Bulgaria an annual tribute in exchange for the return of allegedly 120,000 captured Byzantine soldiers and civilians.

Under the treaty, the Byzantines also ceded an area between the Black

Sea and Strandzha to the Bulgarian Empire, while the Bulgarians also promised not to invade Byzantine territory.

"You strike a hard deal my friend," said Choirosphaktes, after reading the new treaty in Simeon's office. "Now that you humiliated Leo, what do you plan to do next?"

"I had no intention to humiliate Leo, my friend," replied Simeon. "But I love to see the face of Zautses when he sees the conditions of this peace treaty. He is a bad man with a mean streak. My spies told me that it was all his idea to save money by going through this trade war."

"Your spies may be right," said Leo.

"On the other hand, I also found out that in secret he donated a hefty amount of money to some monastery in Armenia," replied Simeon.

"I would very much like to know the name of this monastery," replied Leo. "He may be preparing for himself a nest egg, so that in case things get hot around him, he can retire there."

"I will find out for you, what you need to know," said Simeon. "I will give you all that information before you leave. When you see Leo, please tell him my suggestion to him about Zautses. He should get rid of him as soon as possible."

"I will convey your message, my old friend," said Choirosphaktes. "Yet, something tells me that the days of Zautses' influence on Leo are over. By now, I believe that even the Emperor started to know him better."

"As for what I plan to do my old friend," said Simeon laughing, "come and see me occasionally, to see how I deal with my other bad neighbors. I have to straighten out my neighbors in Serbia."

Simeon got up from his office desk, took Choirosphaktes by his shoulder and the two men went outside in the rose gardens.

# Zautses Conspiracy (The Great Palace, Constantinople, October 897 AD)

Emperor Leo came through the rose gardens of the Great Palace and entered a large conference room, filled with all his advisors. They were all forced to stand up too.

"I want everyone out!" he yelled. "The only ones I want to stay with me here are the Patriarch and Leo Choirosphaktes."

Everyone in the room started exiting the room. Stylianos Zautses paused for a second, ready to utter something, but the Emperor pointed him to the door with a wild look. Zautses stopped, and exited, shaking his head in disbelief. Choirosphaktes showed his surprise on what the Emperor did.

"Why are you surprised Leo?" asked the Emperor. "I want you to give us details of what transpired in Pliska with Simeon, but I don't want the rest of them involved in this."

Leo went through all that transpired during his negotiations with Simeon.

"So, Simeon told you that I should get rid of Zautses," said the Emperor, looking at Choirosphaktes.

"Yes, Highness," replied Choirosphaktes. After a small pause, he continued. "Maybe it is now time for me to tell you my conversation with Patriarch Photius about him. Yet, I cannot tell you anything in this palace. Here, the walls have ears."

"Fine," said the Emperor. "Come with me." He signaled the Patriarch to stay behind.

Choirosphaktes followed the Emperor into the palace chapel. There, the Emperor handed Choirosphaktes a hooded robe of a monk, as he was putting on one on himself, leaving his imperial garments with his sword under them. The two robed men walked to the palace stalls, mounted on two horses and rode to the gate of the palace. Choirosphaktes took off the hood and ordered the guard to open the gate, while the Emperor hid his face.

The two men drove to a forest, outside the city and sat on a fallen log, making sure that none followed them.

"Well…?" asked the Emperor.

"In short, Highness, I discovered that Zautses was responsible for the assassination of Prince Constantine and Emperor Basil. Patriarch Photius knew all this, but for your protection he forbade me to disclose any of this. If Basil knew that about Prince Constantine, you would certainly have been killed, because of your relationship with Zoe. Basil would consider you as a member of the conspiracy. If I told you about Basil, you may have ordered my death, because of your blind love with Zoe and because you wanted so much to protect her. At that time, you would consider me as a conspirator to take down Zautses. By the way, Zoe had nothing to do with her father's deeds."

"What makes you tell me now?" asked the Emperor. To Choirosphaktes' amazement, the Emperor was not surprised.

"Now, I see in front of me an Emperor, who is trying to put behind him what happened in the past and focuses on sorting out good from evil, as it relates to all things, from thoughts to people. In addition, I am very concerned about your own safety. You know that last year, Zautses' son Tzantzes was brewing a conspiracy to assassinate you, using help from inside the palace."

"I had no proof of that allegation," said the Emperor. "I dismissed his son, but I could not accuse Zautses of anything."

"Zautses is very cautious and extremely dangerous my Lord. He keeps his hands clean, as he puts many of his relatives in key positions, while taking bribes. He does not play a primary role in the conspiracy, but he is certainly behind it. He has infiltrated so much of the palace with his people that you are certain to be next in his assassination list. He probably wants one of his own on the throne, while he goes on a retreat to the Tatev monastery in Armenia."

"What do you know about this monastery?"

"Well, I did not know about this until Simeon told me. I verified it though. Zautses has been sending money to this monastery, for his retirement."

"Blast!" yelled the Emperor. "He takes money from us, probably in bribes, to finance his retirement."

"Yes, my Lord."

"What do you suggest that I do?"

"Keep your guard, my Lord, but do not confront Zautses openly and suddenly. If he realizes that you know of his plans and try to take him down, he may act suddenly and kill you. What I suggest is that you slowly dismiss all his relatives and associates from the Great Palace."

"Can you help me on this?"

"I am at your service, Highness."

"From now on, I want you to be my personal security advisor. Bring as many people as you see fit. I will give you a written document, authorizing you to hire and fire any or all personnel in the palace."

"Yes, Lord. May I suggest, that after our meeting, try to act as if nothing has happened. Let's do this gradually. If Zautses' numerous relatives, who had benefited from his patronage, were fearful of losing their positions they would conspire to overthrow you."

"I understand friend. Thank you."

The two monks started returning to the Great Palace on horseback.

"I understand that besides your uncanny abilities as an envoy, you are also a literary man," said the Emperor. "I bumped into some of your hymns. When do you find time to do all that?"

"Ever since my wife died, I spent my spare time at Magnaura, Highness. I find peace in reading books and occasionally in writing."[22]

"It is amazing!" said the Emperor. "That is how I find peace, since I was a child."

After a while, the two men in monk's outfits rode back and entered the palace with Choirosphaktes ordering again the guards to open the gate, while the Emperor had his hood covering his face. They went back to the chapel and took off their robes. Then, they returned to the conference room where Patriarch Anthony Cauleas had around him all the advisors that were dismissed earlier.

---

[22] Leo Choirosphaktes did compose some theological works in the form of hymns and epigrams. He also wrote celebratory poems on the marriages of Emperor Leo VI, one on a new palace bath built by the same emperor, and later on the marriage of Emperor Constantine VII with Helena Lekapene in 920. He also wrote poems on the deaths of prominent figures of his time, such as Leo the Mathematician and the patriarchs Photius and Stephen I.

*"They are probably trying to find out from the Patriarch what is going on,"* thought the Emperor.

"I want to talk to the Patriarch in private," he exclaimed. "Please, everyone out."

Zautses and the advisors joined Leo Choirosphaktes as he walked out.

"What did you two discuss?" asked Zautses.

"My hymns and poems," replied Choirosphaktes.

While Zautses was trying to figure out what Choirosphaktes was talking about, the Emperor, inside the conference room looked at the Patriarch:

"Theophano is very ill. She is not expected to live long. When she passes away, I want you to marry me to Zoe."

# Empress Zoe (Constantinople, the Great Palace, November 17, 897 AD)

Patriarch Anthony Cauleas looked at the Emperor.

"Do you really want to do this, this soon?" he said staring him in the eyes.

"Of course, he does," said Zautses. "He always loved my daughter, as you very well know. He was never happy with Theophano, a wife that Basil forced on him."

"I am talking to the Emperor, if you don't mind," replied the Patriarch turning to Zautses with a loud voice. "We just buried Theophano a few days ago. Her death is still fresh in the people's mind. What you are asking me to do is to give you a special dispensation to marry a widow, namely Zoe. I want the Emperor's answer, not yours."

"My answer is yes," replied Leo. "This arrangement serves us well. In fact, most of the people in the Palace know that lately she sleeps with me and that she gives me moral support. Now that we are not bound by any promises made at our unwanted weddings, I believe that we can make ourselves happy, content, and moral in the eyes of the people and of the Church. We talked about this before Anthony and you agreed with me; some animals, after their mate is dead, retire into perpetual widowhood. Human beings, on the contrary, unconscious of the shameful nature of their weakness, are not satisfied with one marriage, but proceed immodestly to contract a second and, not content with that, go from the second to the third. Let this marriage be blessed by God, not imposed by a high authority. Do you see any problem with that?"

"No problem," replied the Patriarch, "as long as you are not been forced into this wedding by others." As he finished his sentence, he looked at Zautses.

"Then, that is it," said Leo. "We will have the wedding in Aghia Sophia next Sunday."

"Then, when is Zoe going to be declared as an Empress?" asked Zautses. "I am asking this as an interested father."

"At the same ceremony," replied Leo.

After the meeting with the Patriarch and Zautses, Leo went to his chamber where Zoe was waiting for him. She started helping him to get undressed.

"How was your day my love?" Zoe asked.

"I just had a meeting with the Patriarch and your father. We are getting officially married next Sunday."

Zoe hugged Leo and kissed him in the mouth.

"I am happy for us," she whispered.

"Well, this time next Sunday you will be officially my wife and you will be coroneted as Empress Zoe."

"Whatever you wish my love," replied Zoe.

"This is not what I wished," said Leo. "I wish that what happened to us never occurred. I wish that I had a father when I was growing up that cared for me. My father was slaughtered by my stepfather and my stepfather treated me like an animal."

"Next Sunday you will have a father that cares for you," said Zoe. "My father is a good man and thinks highly of you. I will talk to him about your feelings. Don't worry; he cares for both of us."

Leo looked at Zoe, as she pulled his night tunic over his head and went under the covers. He said nothing to the praises of Zoe about her father. He joined her and the two embraced and made love.

The following Sunday Aghia Sophia was full of pomp in the ceremony of Leo's marriage to Zoe. Patriarch Anthony Cauleas, with the help of other priests conducted the wedding ceremony and that of the coronation of Zoe as Empress. Leo was dressed in his imperial regalia, but everyone's eyes fell on Stylianos Zautses, who ordered an extravagant outfit and proudly paraded up front, leading his daughter to become an Empress.

As Stylianos delivered his daughter, he kissed her.

"Thank you, father," Leo said to Zautses. Then he turned to the audience and with a loud voice he proclaimed. "I call Stylianos Zautses my father, not because he is, but because I give him the title of *basileopator*, a title that makes him equivalent to my father, since I was deprived of one for most of my life."

The people in Aghia Sophia went completely silent for a few seconds and then the whispers of comments and gossip were heard throughout the cathedral. At that time, Patriarch Anthony Cauleas ordered the bells of the cathedral to chime and the chanters to start the liturgy of the Imperial wedding. After the wedding, the trumpeters sounded for the procession of the coronation to commence. After Zoe was declared legally an Empress, the royal coach took the couple to the Great Palace. The festivities were held to a minimum, with only the closest advisors and staff present.

After the ceremonies the Emperor and Zoe retreated to their bed chambers and soon, they were naked in bed. Zoe snuffed her candle on her bed stand table. Leo let his candle lit and was staring at the ceiling, when Zoe turned and hugged him.

"What are you thinking about?"

Leo did not say anything for several seconds. Then, he turned his head towards Zoe.

"How well do you know your father?"

Zoe frowned. "As I told you many times before, I really don't know him that well. You see, most of the time he was out in the field being a soldier. We rarely saw each other, but when we did, he was kind to me. He never beat me. So, my mother raised me and disciplined me until I met you. After you were jailed, I never saw him, because he was practically exiled to the East. Then, Basil married me off to Theodore Gutzuniates."

"I thought so," said Leo. "We are both exhausted Zoe. Let's call it a night and go to sleep."

"As you wish," said Zoe and she turned to her side. Leo snuffed off his candle, turned towards her, hugged her and the two went to sleep.

# Reunion (Palace Kitchen, Constantinople, August 2, 897AD)

Spiro Psellus went to sleep two nights ago and never woke up. Chariton went to his room and realized that the cook was dead after trying to revive him in vain. He had seen him the night before and the two had prayed together, since Spiro was not feeling well. In the morning, after examining his dead body, the doctor told Chariton that Spiro had a massive heart failure. The family prepared for the funeral.

There were many people at his funeral. After the body was laid down in the cemetery outside the City walls, the people dispersed throughout the City. Chariton and Anna returned to the Great Palace kitchen with several close friends and relatives, all dressed in black. Spiro was seventy-five when he died. Everyone was silent. Maria, a new hire, who was left behind to monitor the kitchen rushed to greet them.

They walked slowly to an auxiliary kitchen, equipped for imperial cooks and tasters. The auxiliary kitchen was also used to feed the palace staff. They saw a young man behind the counter, his back turned towards them and preparing several pots of delicacies over wood-fired grills, built with brick. He was Maria's husband John Psellus, the new replacement for Spiro in his cooking duties.

John Psellus was also Chariton's nephew. He was the son of Sarantis Psellus from Kalivarion of Cappadocia. John, now twenty-eight, hated farming. Instead, he had served as a cook in the army of Emperor Leo. The Emperor now had a new name, being "Leo the Wise," because of all the work that he was doing on the judicial front for Byzantium. After that, John ended up at Constantinople, helping Spiro. There, he met Maria.

Some young men meet a girl that they like, and start using their logic or consult with friends and relatives. Others just plunge into marriage. John Psellus just plunged, without consulting anyone, especially his uncle.

Anna and Maria proceeded to the great table while John Psellus fetched them all some wine from the kitchen. He laid the cups on the great table. Chariton Psellus got up and raised his cup to a toast with his left hand. The others watched him with surprise.

"When every one of us was born, and with God's help," said Chariton, "our spirit constructed a body out of borrowed material. This was nature's stuff that our mother ate, drunk and breathed during her pregnancy. It is nature's stuff because it is all around us, forming God's Universe. We keep our body throughout our lives and to the best of our ability. We use more borrowed stuff from nature, which we call food. When we die, we are obliged to return all the remaining material of our body back to nature, just like the many living spirits before us as they appeared and disappeared in this Universe."

He looked around him, at the confused faces of his audience before continuing.

"I may want to add that it is at that time that a 'thank you' would be appropriate. At that deathbed, it is proper to thank God for letting our spirit materialize into a form, even for a short, painful and imperfect life span. Without that form, we would not experience our best and worst moments; such moments are needed in showing future generations how to improve on our short life spans. For the first time in my life I heard a man, namely Spiro, to give his thanks to God at his deathbed. I drink to Spiro; may he rest in peace."

He crossed himself with his right hand and then lifted his wine to his lips with his left. The rest followed suit. A pregnant pause with silence from everyone followed. Anna broke the silence.

"How are you doing with the kitchen duties John?" Anna asked.

"I am doing fine," John Psellus replied. "Maria is helping me when I need to go and do my shopping from the market, but we could use some additional help these days."

"How are your children Maria? How old are they now?" asked Chariton.

"They are doing well. George is now fourteen and Evanthia is seven," responded Maria. It was her turn to ask. "What do you hear from your son and his family?"

"Gabriel joined the monastic life," said Anna, cutting in for her husband.

"My daughter Styliane married a man from Chrysopolis and has two daughters. I am hoping to have a grandchild."

"Congratulations," said Maria smiling.

At that instant a man walked into the kitchen. He looked like a professional. The man proceeded to sit on the near-by table.

Chariton looked at the man. He got up and approached him. The man was about the same age as he.

"I have seen you somewhere around," he said. "Have we met?"

The man looked at Chariton.

"I am not sure," he responded. "I spent most of my time at the University at Magnaura."

"I do too," said Chariton. "My name is Chariton Psellus."

"Psellus?" said the man with surprise and stood up. "My name is Constantine Psellus."

"The two men stared at each other. Anna stood motionless. John also turned around and stared motionless. He uttered:

"My name is John Psellus, and I am his nephew."

"What do you do at Magnaura?" asked Chariton.

"I teach Greek and Latin literature, history and philosophy. I was just assigned as a tutor here."

"I also teach those things," said Chariton. "I also give private lessons here for quite a while now. Where were you before?"

"I spent several years in Philadelphia.[23] I started at Magnaura, but Patriarch Photius sent me to Philadelphia after the assassinations started. I told Leo the Philosopher how disgusted I was with what was going on here and he asked Photius to send me away from here to a more civilized city, like Philadelphia. With his letter of recommendation, I managed to teach there, giving private lessons to wealthy families and had a good time. I even was married there to my wife Eudokia. I just came back by order of Patriarch Anthony Cauleas, because he heard of me and of my work." Constantine paused for a while. "It is interesting that we have the same surname. Where do you come from?"

---

[23] See 3.

"I was born here, but our family came from Kalivarion, a place in Cappadocia, about a day's ride from Tyana,[24]" said Chariton.

He pointed to Maria, who smiled. "Maria is John's wife." Then he pointed to Anna. "Anna is my wife."

The two women came closer to Constantine.

"Where do you come from Constantine?" asked Anna.

"My family is from the island of Andros," said Constantine. "We fled Andros because of the Saracens."

"We are also told that we come from Andros," said Chariton. "It seems that our ancestors were taken for some reason from Andros by Leo the Isaurian and moved to Cappadocia. One of these days we must sit down and figure out if and how we are related."

"We must be relatives," replied Constantine. "I vaguely remember that my grandfather was telling me that some of our relatives were taken by Leo the Isaurian East somewhere. So, you must be a cousin, several times removed."

The two men stared at each other and hugged laughing.

"Now I understand what that strange fellow meant, when he asked me if I had any relatives from the islands at Magnaura," said Chariton.

"Which strange fellow…?" Constantine asked.

"He is now a big shot, but at that time he was a mystikos. His name is Leo Choirosphaktes."

"I knew Leo," said Constantine. "I met him at Magnaura before I left for Philadelphia. What a character? I wonder how he fared with everything that happened these last thirty years."

"He survived all the storms," said Chariton. "Ever since the assassination of Theoctistus, our Christian moral standing started to deteriorate. People within Byzantium lost their confidence in our government and people outside of our borders thought of us as barbarians. We lost so much moral credibility abroad, that even the Bulgarians, that were just coming into Christendom give us lessons in morality. All this because our imperial families are so self-centered that they cannot see how much harm they do by focusing on their personal ambition in ruling, by ignoring their children, who will soon be expected to become the new rulers. Sons that are ignored

---

[24] Tyana was a prominent ancient city in Cappadocia, Asia Minor. Today the town of Kemerhisar, south of Nigde lies over it.

and abused can easily kill or be killed, because they lack Christian morality of their own. The moral standing of a person cannot be ignored when he is to be chosen to become a ruler. An immoral ruler will sooner or later fall flat on his face. He will not be able to have friends that support him. All the good people will abandon him. He will then be destroyed either by his own inability, or by the hand of those immoral friends that he was left with."

"It is amazing," said Constantine, "how much an Empire's health is dependent on the health of individual families. It is also amazing how much influence women have in the running of this Empire. Women like Theodora, with her self-centered behavior, caused so many deaths and suffering."

"That is because they were abused by their men," intercepted Anna. "I lived through it. Theodora was selected to marry Theophilos because his stepmother set up a bride show, like the show where animals are paraded for buyers to choose. She was only fifteen. After that humiliation, she had to endure her husband's insults because he was an iconoclast, while Theodora held fast to the veneration of icons. She always kept hidden icons in her chambers. A servant witnessed her venerating her icons and reported her to the emperor. When her husband confronted her about the incident, she stated that she had merely been "playing with dolls." She simply was afraid of being tortured, or worse by her own husband. What do you expect from women like her, or of Ingerina after what they went through?"

"I agree with Anna," said Constantine. "When people are forced to compromise their own honor and dignity for their own survival, they become as unpredictable as animals with rabies. They cannot forget easily the humiliation that they went through. Unfortunately, the higher someone climbs in government, the higher the probability that one day he or she would someday be faced with the option of compromising their honor and beliefs, for the expediency required by their position in government. Whether they admit it or not, it hurts. They cannot forget it easily and sometimes they lash back without reason. What I hope for is some sort of civility, morality and understanding within our government that alleviates that hurt."

"We are the richest and most advanced place in the world," said Chariton, "but we seem to be standing still in our progress in civility, morality and understanding. God help us." He paused for a few seconds. "I wonder Constantine if a thousand years from now, we could have people in the government that put their honor over their self-indulgent, arrogant selves."

"I hope so," said Constantine. "I hope that we as humans realize that no matter how high rank we are bestowed, we lose our self-respect and the respect of others when we lie, cheat, or arrogantly declare that we know everything, and we are the best. It may take us a few centuries to improve ourselves, but I think that eventually human logic will be able to prevail over such weaknesses in our character."

The group sat and chatted more about current events, families, children, ancestors and all they could think of, drinking wine. Then Maria served everyone stew in clay bowls and placed wooden spoons, wrapped in cloth napkins next to each bowl. Everyone started eating.

"John, your stew is wonderful," said Constantine.

John bowed smiling and said nothing, leaving them to enjoy his dish.

Constantine put a spoonful of stew in his mouth and started chewing as he raised his head. From where he was sitting, he had a good view out of an open window. He could see the rooftops of houses and hear the bustle of the city. At a distance he could see Bosporus, where a merchant ship was sailing from the Black Sea to the Sea of Marmara.

*"What a superb view,"* he thought.

   

# Retribution (Armenia, Tatev Monastery, September 5, 899 AD)

Figure 6 Tatev Monastery, Armenia [25]

The superb view of the forested Armenian mountains failed to compete with the more important thoughts in the head of Leo Choirosphaktes. He was riding for days to reach his destination in Armenia and he felt that what he was about to do was very risky.

He had with him two troop groups of select cavalry. He also had direct orders from Emperor Leo, signed and sealed. With the document he had in his saddle, the Emperor authorized him to order any local Byzantine force to be attached to his small force, as he saw fit. These were his assets.

---

[25]  Licensed from Alamy Inc. Invoice number: IY01109051.

He knew that if his target found out what he was after, he would muster his own force to oppose him. So, he depended on a surprise move. On top of that, he had to make sure that the accused target was guilty beyond any reasonable doubt. These were his liabilities.

"Do you trust your soldiers?" he had asked the Armenian officer that he had contacted at the outpost near his destination.

"I do, because I pay them in gold from the Emperor's money," the leading officer responded. "The Emperor's seal and your signature lets me get the gold I need to pay my troops; a fifth at the start from the gold you gave me and the rest when we are finished."

Leo shook his head. The answer was not the best he was hoping for, but he had no other choice.

As he was approaching the monastery of Tatev that morning, he turned to the leading officer of his troop.

"My plan is to bring to justice a criminal that is inside the monastery. We do not want him to get alerted, because if he is, he can bring a much larger force against us. He is well respected in this part of Armenia and has many friends."

"Who is he?"

"I would prefer not to tell you his name," said Leo. "but I think I must, as long as you promise to keep it to yourself."

"I promise."

Leo leaned from his horse to the ear of the officer and whispered his name in a way that the rest of the riders did not hear.

"I heard of him," said the officer. "Don't worry. I have no ties to him."

"Good. I alone will go in to do some scouting, while you and your soldiers hide outside the monastery. I will do some probing inside on my own. You must wait outside and watch the monastery. You must also detain anyone exiting from the monastery. If someone does exit, you must arrest him and then you must enter the monastery fast, storming it if necessary. If not, wait until noon and then enter the monastery anyway."

"Then what?"

"It all depends on what happens inside. If I am killed, you must complete the task of taking him as a prisoner to the Emperor. That is how you and your men will get paid the rest of the gold, when I cannot place my signature on your final payment."

The officer halted his horse suddenly. "I hope you don't plan to get killed," he stated as he stared at Leo.

"I hope I don't get killed either," said Leo. "As long as you are alert and move fast, we can come out of this fine."

A short distance from the monastery Leo Choirosphaktes stopped his horse. He reached into his satchel and exchanged his heavy robe with a monk's robe. Then, he took a deep breath and rode alone towards the monastery.

The Tatev was a new monastery, built partly with funds from Armenian aristocracy, like Zautses. It was located on a large basalt plateau in southeastern Armenia. The term "Tatev" usually refers to the word "monastery." The monastic ensemble stands on the edge of a deep gorge of the Vorodan River. The monastery was like a fort, with walls and a main gate.

Leo approached the main gate, where two monks were chatting. He bowed to them as he passed the main gate of the monastery, and after proceeding a short distance he dismounted and secured his horse on a post in front of what looked like a barn. Then, he calmly walked towards some monks and asked them for the whereabouts of Stylianos Zautses. They pointed him towards a structure with cells for monks. He was told that Zautses had the biggest cell. He walked and knocked on the door of the cell. A monk opened the door. Leo bowed and asked to see Zautses. The monk led him in and then he saw Zautses near the fireplace, sipping from a mug, something that seemed and smelled like warm wine. A clay jug of wine was kept warm next to the fireplace.

"Well, well…" said Zautses with surprise. "What brings you in this part of the world Leo?"

"I wanted to find out if Simeon was right," said Leo. "After you disappeared from Constantinople, people said that you were dead. Now I see that they were all mistaken."

"Simeon? What did he say about me?"

"Never mind about Simeon. Now that I found you, I must bring you messages from back home, brother," said Leo. "I am though very tired. Can you make me room by your fireplace?"

"Sure," replied Stylianos. He waved to his monk aide, who brought a chair for Leo. As Leo sat, he looked at Stylianos, while rubbing his hands in front of the fire. Stylianos went with the monk aide outside and after talking with him for a while, he came back alone. Leo smiled. He was hoping that Stylianos would ask for help. He just hoped that the monk went for an outside help.

"I had a tough time finding you," said Leo, as Zautses sat back near the fireplace. "Nobody knew your whereabouts. Finally, I verified your location from one of Empress Zoe's servants and decided to bring you the news personally."

Zautses looked at Leo with suspicion. Then he waved over to his aide to come closer. His aide bent over and Zautses whispered something to his ear. The monk looked at Leo and then went out the door.

"How is my dear daughter, Augusta Zoe?" asked Zautses. "I am a bit surprised to see you here Leo, on an errand to bring me news, since you and several others were responsible for accusing my son and grandson to the Emperor, bringing their demise. We are talking about friends stabbing their friends in the back."

"They were found guilty by the Emperor himself to be responsible for a coup, my friend."

"You are no friend of mine," said Zautses staring at Leo with enmity.

"I came to tell you that Augusta Zoe died. She died after you disappeared. You have my sincere condolences."

"That is a lie," replied Zautses, as he gulped the cup of hot wine and refilled it. "It can't be."

"I am sorry for your loss."

"Don't tell me that you came all this way to give me such horrible news."

"Emperor Leo asked me to convey the news to you personally."

"Why?"

"Because, with the death of his dear Zoe, he wants to close completely any dealings he had with your family."

"What do you mean by that?"

"The Emperor does not want anyone from you or your family anywhere around the palace. In fact, he is getting ready to marry yet again, choosing Eudokia Baiana as his wife."

"Really?" replied Stylianos.

Leo thought for a moment. Now that he established the preliminary, it was time to get to the hard part. Emperor Leo had asked Choirosphaktes to go, and if possible, to verify directly from Zautses if and how he had perpetrated the murders that he was suspect of.

"I liked Zoe," Leo blurted. "She was an innocent bystander. She grew up an innocent girl into a mess of a situation. She loved Leo and she loved you, her father, even though she did not know you very well. Did she?"

"What business is that of yours?"

"You lost your daughter," said Leo, staring at Zautses. "Don't you have any feelings? I, through the Emperor was just her servant and my heart aches for her. I want to drink, remembering this sweet woman. You, on the other hand, her own father, did not care enough to serve me some of his wine, so that we can drink for her soul."

Zautses got up and Leo saw that he was stumbling. With an unsteady pace he went to a shelf and got another clay mug, which he handed to Leo. Then he plopped down in his chair. Leo knew that he was on the right path. He reached and filled his cup from the wine jug. Then he filled the cup of his host.

"Yes, she was an innocent bystander," said Leo as he raised his cup. "To her peaceful rest…"

Stylianos raised his cup and drank.

"It is not fair," said Stylianos. "Not fair. No. I did not know my daughter very well. Yet, I tried to give her everything. I did everything I could for her and my own kin. After all I went through to see my daughter crowned…, now you tell me that she is dead before I am gone."

"Oh, come off it. You did nothing more than a normal father does, to see them grow up and happy. What else did you do?"

"I did plenty," said Zautses smiling wryly. "But … if I told you, I would have … to kill you."

"So, tell me and kill me," said Leo jokingly.

"I am not … joking Leo," said Zautses with a somewhat slurred speech. "Thinking that you came here to kill me, I have asked for two armed monks outside to stand guard. I also sent for additional support from men of the nearby village. Soon, there will be a mob of armed men here, ready to lynch you when I tell them that you came to kill me. You see, I am very popular man in these parts. You do not get out of this monastery alive."

Leo paused and drank from his cup. "Why would anyone want to kill you? What have you done?" Leo drank some more wine. "Yet, if you want to kill me, do it. But before you do, I am entitled to know what you did that was bad enough, or important enough for me to die for."

"I know that you know … that I killed them. I heard about your investigations on me after their deaths."

"I don't know what you are talking about. Whose deaths…?"

"Both son and father…"

"Constantine?"

"Yes."

"How…?"

"Hmmm…. I set a trap for him. I cut off his saddle strap, wounded the rump of the horse and I provoked him a bit to make him careless. So … his horse ran wild after the first spur, causing his strap to snap and he fell. I remember thinking, how lucky I was to bump onto the wounded Constantine, as I was doing my reconnaissance … in front of my troops at Amasea. I ordered the trumpeter to sound … "enemy sighted." The, I saw him there, half dazed on the ground. I had to finish him off … with the butt of my spear. I can still see his face as he was dying."

"Oh God…! Why did you have to kill the poor boy?"

"Isn't it obvious? That brat was in the way. I had to see Leo and my Zoe on the throne."

"But Basil also was your friend," interrupted Leo. "How could you kill his son?"

"Because… his son was in the way of my dreams for my family," replied Zautses.

"Yet, that did not work, did it?" said Leo

"No. Basil intervened and married Zoe to Gouzouniates."

"So, Basil had to go," said Leo with his head facing the floor.

"Yes. But killing Basil was very hard. He was no friend of mine. I had to repay him for the exile and the humiliation. He, whom I helped get the throne. I knew him well. I knew that I could not reason with him. So, I had to kill him. All I wanted is one chance to be alone with Basil. But… tell me, how can I do that without anyone finding out?"

"I don't know; how?" said Leo while he refilled the cups with wine.

"Hmm;" pondered Zautses, as he laid his cup down. "You are trying to get me drunk, aren't you? It won't work. I got so used to this wine, that I can outdrink anyone."

"I am certain that you can," said Leo. "I am already getting dizzy." He paused. "You were telling me how you were planning to kill Basil."

"Hmmm;" continued Zautses. "The chance appeared when he talked about his love of hunting. But making the plan work with an expert hunter, like Basil, is another story. It was then that I started to go hunting with one question in my mind: How can I make it look like an accident? It was sheer luck to bump onto the stag-fighting in one of my hunting trips at Apamea. Then, I learned that these stags don't forget the smell of enemy stags, just like we, humans don't forget old friends that stab us in the back. So, I took the skin of the opponent stag and laid it under Basil's saddle. I had to plan his death for more than a year. Finding the male stag, putting the scent of it on Basil's horse and making sure that he went hunting there were very difficult to plan and execute. Even I was surprised to see how well that worked."

"Did it really?" asked Leo.

"I believe it did, to some … extent…" Suddenly the noise of horses, galloping into the monastery was heard.

Before he had finished his sentence, Zautses got up and even stepped on his cup on the floor. "Now my friend, it is time for you to join them all in the afterlife."

The door opened and a huge monk with a sword walked in. Another one also appeared on the doorway.

"Take him in the back," said Zautses. "You know what to do with him, but not in here."

"Yes sir," said the monk. He walked and grabbed Leo by the arm. Leo's cup dropped on the floor and crashed. The monk dragged Leo outside, on the stone porch, but as they stepped outside the door, the second monk crashed on the floor, hit by an arrow. The monk that held Leo was surprised enough to turn and face the attack. That is when Leo escaped his grasp and reached for his dagger under his own monk's robe. He swung with it and found a soft spot in the monk's abdomen. The wounded monk yelled in pain and turned raising his sword to strike Leo, when another arrow found its mark on the shoulder of the sword-arm, under his armpit. He immediately let his sword fall. Leo took it and looked around. His men were approaching on the stone floors of the monastery. One of them finished the huge monk off.

"Good marksmanship," he yelled at his officer. "You are late."

"We had a tough time locating you," said the officer.

"Come with me," said Leo.

The two men walked in Zautses' cell, where they saw Zautses drinking after he retrieved another cup and filled it with wine. As he saw Leo with the Byzantine officer, he dropped the cup and fell back in his chair. He suddenly seemed to be sober, watching the embers of the fireplace.

"Stylianos Zautses," said Leo. "You are under arrest by Imperial orders." He paused, looking at Zautses. "Emperor Leo gives you two choices. One choice is that you are taken back, and after being judged for your own admitted crimes, you will be executed, and all members of your family will be blacklisted in history and all property confiscated, including that of Empress Zoe."

The surprised Zautses gulped, and in a dry, hoarse voice uttered: "What is my other choice?"

"The other choice is for you to end your life, here and now," said Leo calmly.

"Leo, my old friend," said Zautses. "Can you help me get out of this situation? I promise to give you anything you want."

"There is nothing that I can do, or you can offer me that can get you out of this ... old friend."

"Can you at least help me up?"

"You can get up on your own, old friend," replied Leo, as he reached from behind him, grabbed his arm and took out a dagger that Zautses had hidden under his robe.

Zautses got up and walked slowly to the door. He walked past the bodies of his monks and was surrounded by Leo's Byzantine troopers.

"Let him pass," said Leo to his troops, "but keep him under guard."

Zautses walked towards the walls of the monastery. Two troopers held the captive messenger monk that they caught as he was riding out for help.

"Let them free!" yelled several monks at the troopers. "Why are you treating us like that? What did we do to you?"

"What do you want us to do with the captured monk that rode for help?" the second in command to Leo asked. "He says that he is Zautses' nephew."

Leo turned and faced the captive.

"Bring him along. Bring all these misled vermin along," he said it loudly while pointing to the rest of the shouting monks. "Let them see what happens when one of their relatives becomes - with his own admission - an imperial assassin."

The monks stopped talking and looked at each other in disbelief. The Byzantine troopers dragged the captive, following Leo, who followed Zautses under guard.

When Zautses reached the walls of the monastery, he climbed on the parapet, turned around and faced Leo, among the gathered crowd.

"Nobody should blame a man for trying to do all he can for his family," he yelled, as he let himself fall backwards. His body crashed down the deep gorge of the Vorodan River onto the cliff rocks. All the monks kneeled and crossed themselves praying.

Leo turned and faced them. "What a waste," he said disgustingly to them. "Your relative and benefactor had no honor as a human being. He was always looking after himself first and then his own family, ignoring that he was part of a society that requires and demands moral strength from every member to exist. We and you must never compromise with people like him, no matter what gifts he gave you, or promises he made. He was found guilty for killing two members of the imperial family for his own benefit alone, leaving us to pick up the pieces of a government in ruins."

Leo paused and then, with a loud, menacing voice shouted: "Hell is too good for him."

The monks started praying and they crossed themselves as Leo turned to his troops. He looked at his second in command and pointed at the captive monk.

"Let him go," he said in a dry tone. "Our task has ended here. It is time to go back and see if we can bring some sanity in this world. I don't want to stay here in this monastery any longer. We will camp somewhere on the way back."

A trooper brought him his horse, as the two troopers released the captive monk. They all mounted up and rode out of the monastery, towards the roads that led to Constantinople.

As they did, Leo sensed that his troops were somewhat depressed, having to come all this way to storm into a monastery to kill a single monk. He turned to his second in command:

"Let's sing!" he ordered, while passing the gate of the monastery. "Let's sing TI IPERMACHO, loud enough, so that the rest of these monks know that we are not assassins, but we follow the law of the land, based on the morality set upon us by the Church."

Every Christian in the Byzantine State knew this famous hymn that became popular since the 7th century. It was repeatedly sung in honor of Virgin Mary, commemorating the saving of Constantinople from the Avars at 626 AD.[26] The second in command turned to a soldier from Paphlagonia, known as a good tenor and pointed to him with a smile. The man smiled back and started singing this famous hymn, as the whole troop was clearing the gate:

Ti ipermákho stratigó ta nikitíria,
os litrothísa ton dinón efkharistíria,
anagráfosi i Pólis sou, Theotóke.
All' os ékhousa to krátos aprosmákhiton,
ek pandíon me kindínon eleuthéroson,
ina krázo si - Khére, Nímfi anímfefte.[27]

---

[26] The hymn was the equivalent of the national anthem, a practice that started much later. If Byzantium remained as a state, the lyrics of this hymn would have been adopted as their national anthem. Spain adopted the Marcha Real in 1740, the first adopted national anthem. The Netherlands has an anthem dating back to 1518 but it was adopted after Spain's.

[27] The hymn lyrics can be translated as follows:
*Unto You, O Theotokos, invincible Champion,*
*Your City, in thanksgiving ascribes the victory*
*for the deliverance from sufferings.*
*And having your might unassailable,*
*free me from all dangers,*
*so that I may cry unto you: "Hail! O Bride Ever-Virgin."*

# Epilogue

Leo VI, or Leo the Wise ruled until the year 912 AD. In his lifetime the people genuinely loved and respected him. After Zoe's death a third marriage was technically illegal, but he married again, only to have his third wife Eudokia Baiana die in 901. Instead of marrying a fourth time, which would have been an even greater sin than a third marriage, Leo took as mistress Zoe Karbonopsina. She was the niece of admiral Himerius and relative of Chronicler Theophanes. He married her only after she had given birth to a son in 905, but incurred the opposition of the patriarch Nicholas Mystikos, who had replaced Anthony Cauleas in 901. Replacing the Patriarch, Leo got his marriage recognized by the church (albeit with a long penance attached, and with an assurance that Leo would outlaw all future fourth marriages).

The future Constantine VII (Porphyrogenitus, or purple born) was the illegitimate son born before Leo's uncanonical fourth marriage to Zoe Karbonopsina. To strengthen his son's position as heir, Leo had him crowned as co-emperor on May 15, 908, when he was only two years old. When Leo VI died on May 11, 912, he was succeeded by his younger brother Alexander, who had reigned as Emperor alongside his father and brother since 879.

After Leo's death, his younger brother reigned for only 13 months. He died as a result of a stroke. After that, another mess of intrigue plagues the Empire, but that is another story.

Leo VI was an intellectual and a scholar and did not build monuments to his memory like his stepfather, other than his writings. The mosaic over the Imperial Door of Aghia Sophia,[28] showing him prostrating before Christ dates from several years after his death.

In the subject matter of legal works, he established a legal commission that carried out his father's original intent of codifying all existing Byzantine law. The result was a six-volume work consisting of 60 books, entitled

---

[28] Part of this mosaic with Leo VI is shown in the front cover of this book.

the Basilika. Written in Greek, the basilica, translated and systematically arranged practically all of the laws preserved in the Corpus Juris Civilis, thereby providing a foundation upon which all later Byzantine laws could be built.

Leo then began integrating new laws issued during his reign into the *Basilika*. These books were concerned with ecclesiastical law (canon law) as well as secular law. Most importantly, they finally did away with much of the remaining legal and constitutional architecture that the Byzantine Empire had inherited from the Roman Empire.

Leo also issued the *Book of the Eparch* and the *Kletorologion of Philotheos*, testifying his government's interest in organization and the maintenance of public order. The *Book of the Eparch* described the rules and regulations for trade and trade organizations in Constantinople, while the *Kletorologion* was an attempt to standardize officials and ranks at the Byzantine court. Leo is also the author, or at least sponsor, of the *Tactica*, a notable treatise on military operations.

All we can say about Leo VI's reign was that he ruled wisely and conscientiously over his subjects for 26 years. Although he was not a good military leader and his forces suffered many defeats, he left the Empire, at least internally, in a far better shape than when he inherited it.